NOTHING TO DEVOUR

BOOKS BY GLEN HIRSHBERG

The Book of Bunk

The Snowman's Children

American Morons

The Two Sams

Motherless Child *

The Janus Tree

Good Girls *

Nothing to Devour *

The Ones Who Are Waving

*A Tor Book

NOTHING TO DEVOUR

GLEN HIRSHBERG

TOR

A TOM DOHERTY ASSOCIATES BOOK

NEW YORK

This is a work of fiction. All of the characters, organizations, and events portrayed in this novel are either products of the author's imagination or are used fictitiously.

NOTHING TO DEVOUR

A Tor Book
Published by Tom Doherty Associates
175 Fifth Avenue
New York, NY 10010

www.tor-forge.com

Tor® is a registered trademark of Macmillan Publishing Group, LLC.

Library of Congress Cataloging in Publication Data

Names: Hirshberg, Glen, 1966– author.
Title: Nothing to devour / Glen Hirshberg.
Description: First edition. | New York : Tor, 2018. | "A Tom Doherty
   Associates Book."
Identifiers: LCCN 2018038931| ISBN 9780765337474 (hardcover) |
   ISBN 9781466834439 (ebook)
Subjects: | GSAFD: Occult fiction.
Classification: LCC PS3608.I77 N68 2018 | DDC 813/.6—dc23
LC record available at https://lccn.loc.gov/2018038931

Our books may be purchased in bulk for promotional, educational, or
business use. Please contact your local bookseller or the Macmillan
Corporate and Premium Sales Department at 1-800-221-7945, extension
5442, or by email at MacmillanSpecialMarkets@macmillan.com.

First Edition: November 2018

Printed in the United States of America

0 9 8 7 6 5 4 3 2 1

For Kim, a trip back to the beginning

For Kate and Sid, one more secret place to play. But take us with you when you go, okay?

And for Jonas, Mark, and Rex, for thirty-plus years in the butterfly pavilion, wishing good night to no one

NOTHING TO DEVOUR

1

Five years later . . .

One night, an otter got in the house. Eddie heard the commotion all the way upstairs. He'd been nestling in the mound of blankets on his top bunk. He had the pinecone men Joel had carved arrayed across his pillow, standing up fat on their pinecone bottoms. *Like little soldiers,* Uncle Benny had said the first time he'd seen them set out this way, and he'd smiled wide through his white cat whiskers. Misunderstanding, as usual.

Like guards, Trudi had said, the one time Eddie could ever remember her coming up here. That was closer, though also wrong.

Like meerkats, Rebecca had said, not too long ago. *Like you. Little meerkat, with your head always sticking up to see.* And of course, that was right. Rebecca always got it right. Even Eddie hadn't thought of it that way before.

Lifting his favorite pinecone meerkat—the red one, with the stickpin-eyes that reflected the orange from the sunset outside—Eddie held it toward the open door, the hallway, the commotion downstairs. He cocked it to the right, the left, and let it listen.

"Are they *laughing*?" he whispered.

Red-cone meerkat nodded. Eddie returned him to the pillow and lay where he was a few seconds longer. It wasn't as though he'd never heard this sound in the house before. As a matter of fact, he'd heard it a lot, and more and more, lately, now that he thought about it. Even from Dedo, sometimes.

But not this loud. Not from all of them together, all at the same time. Never once, in his memory, had Eddie heard his whole family shouting and laughing.

The sensations it caused in him—banging heart, prickling skin, sympathy grin sprouting on his face even though he had no idea what they were all laughing about—made him nervous even as they made him happy. He flipped the sea-star duvet Dedo had made him over his head and pressed himself into the wall, making himself flat as a sea-star. Then he willed himself silent, imagined his inside-fist grabbing his heart, squeezing it still so it wouldn't flutter the duvet, and he lay quiet, and he listened.

After a few seconds, he felt ridiculous, and he was still grinning. Even so, he didn't come out right away, or let his heart loose. Kaylene would have said he was being a Dug, if she were up here instead of down there in the racket. Until a month or so ago, when she'd finally showed him her favorite game on her phone, Eddie had just thought *dug* was her crazy-Kaylene way of saying *bug*.

Sitting up as a new burst of laughter erupted, he nestled deeper into the corner, right where the steepled ceiling met the cedar walls, and touched his fingertips to the glass of his porthole window. Across the grass out back, over the roof of the old windmill-shed where Dedo and Trudi slept, Eddie could see the sun sinking into the firs toward the Strait. He should be downstairs, he knew. He wanted to see what everyone was laughing about. And yet he waited, as he did whenever he was alone in his room at right about this time. When the first wisps of every-night mist crawled up onto the horizon and began their long float across the water toward land, Eddie sucked in a breath and held it as long as he could. Out there, over the water, more wisps pulled themselves onto the surface of the Strait and began gliding across it.

With a single, explosive sigh, he unleashed all the air he had in him. The glass fogged and his reflected face vanished in the mist he'd made himself. Wiping fast with his fingers, he cleared the glass, and there were the wisps, seemingly knocked off course by his exhalation, already cohering into plain old clouds. He watched the clouds fold together as he sucked in another breath, held it. Held it. Let fly.

Blowing up a storm. One of his favorite in-bed games. He hadn't needed Joel's or Kaylene's or Rebecca's or Dedo's help for this one. He'd come up with it all by himself.

The clouds collided and swelled, and the orange in the sky faded to gray. Nothing out there lit up, today. No thunder boomed. Sometimes, it didn't.

Still, even float-clouds were good for blowing, and in the breaks between bursts of laughter from downstairs, through the whistling crack between the window glass and the warping pane, Eddie heard or thought he heard the okras (which is what he'd first called them, and so now everyone in this house called them that). Maybe they were back, down in their cove at the foot of the cliffs, spouting and snuffling, maybe even singing. Calling him out.

"Oh, yeah?" Joel said, downstairs. "It's dancing you want?" Then came more shuffling sounds—Joel-dancing sounds—and more laughter.

Quiet as a Dug, Eddie slipped from his bunk, stepped into his no-tie sneakers, and made his way across the loft so he could peer over the edge of the landing. He saw the otter immediately, up on hind legs in the center of the circle his housemates had formed around him, chirring like a little grandfather telling them all off. Or like one of the munchkins in that movie they'd showed him last summer, with the flying monkeys and the mean, green witch. Or like one of Joel's pinecone-meerkats, come to life.

As Eddie watched, Uncle Benny edged closer to the otter from behind, a giant soup pot in his white-whisker hand-paws. The pot still dripped whatever he'd just washed out of it. No, it was still full, Eddie realized.

"Oh my God, it's not a fish!" Kaylene howled at him, and burst out laughing again, grabbing Joel's arm as she doubled over. Joel had a broom in both hands; he was using it mostly to swat Kaylene.

The animal dropped, whirled, darted in Benny's direction, and Benny startled and lost the pot, which flipped in midair, launching water all over Dedo, who barely even flinched, just closed her eyes. Eddie grabbed the stairway banister, almost screamed. He hated when Dedo stood like that, absolutely still with that Dedo-look on her face that said—where had Eddie gotten this? How did he know it? What did it even mean?—*I love you. It's okay. It's all over, now.*

She's melting, he thought, clutching the banister but making no sound.

Instead of melting, Dedo opened her eyes. She glanced toward Benny, who was gaping at her, then down at her dripping self. Then she laughed, too.

"Sorry, Jess," Uncle Benny murmured.

"Shit, where is it?" Joel said, and they all craned their heads around. Rebecca dropped low to look under the table. Kaylene edged up to the window, gave the half-drawn curtains a smack, and leapt back. Eddie was sure they'd see him, call him down or tell him to stay put. Instead, they all turned, seemingly as one, toward Rebecca. She was crouching by the couch, now, with that Rebecca look on *her* face. The one that just said, *Shhh.*

"Under here," she said, and they all went quiet, though they kept smiling. Every one of them. The only one missing, Eddie realized, was Trudi. She was probably holed up in her room in the windmill-shed, as usual. If she'd been here, and if *she'd* smiled, too, then Eddie would have suspected that this really was a magical night. Or a dangerous one.

The sudden warmth at his crotch surprised him so much, he almost cried out.

He calmed himself by chanting, inside his head, the things Dedo would inevitably say when she found out he'd wet himself again. *Happens to everyone.* He imagined her balling up his sopping pants, bundling them away and giving his hair a pat. *We'll throw them in the wash, and it'll be like it never happened.*

So comforting, those things Dedo said. Her movements and reassuring touches. Everything but her face, which sometimes looked like all the gears inside it had caught, locked. Snapped . . .

Pushing her hair behind her ear, Rebecca settled lower on her bramble-scratched knees. They were scratched, Eddie knew, because she walked the woods the way he did: off-path, wandering everywhere. Sometimes, whenever he asked, she did that *with* Eddie. Now, he watched her edge back from the couch, her head sinking still further, until she was eye-level with whatever was under there.

Rebecca could talk to otters. Eddie had no doubt of this. Rebecca could talk to anything. He glanced around at everyone else: Dedo, drenched, was leaning into Uncle Benny, the way she occasionally let herself; Benny had shifted on his bad ankles and draped one arm carefully around her, as if Dedo were the otter and might dart away; Joel held his broom in front of his chest, sword-like, and his shiny green rain pants—which he wore because they were shiny, not because it was raining—winked in the window-light like the pin-eyes on his pinecone meerkats; Kaylene hunched over Rebecca, the streak in her long, black hair blazing orange tonight like new lava. That meant she'd recolored it, which meant she and Rebecca were headed out performing, later.

Family was a word no one in this house used, at least not to or about each other. Eddie wasn't even sure where he'd learned it, or why he thought of it at that moment.

But he did. The thought scared him. He glanced down at the wet pants clinging to his legs. He wanted to fly down the stairs like one of the Wicked Witch's monkeys and spirit everyone off before they could get away. It was all too much. Confusing. And he didn't have the words.

So when the otter exploded out the side of the couch and screamed over its shoulder at Rebecca, tried to hurl itself up a wall, slid down, banged off Joel as Joel attempted to sweep it through the open patio door, and hurtled off again toward the kitchen, Eddie didn't laugh or shout. He clutched the banister, watching his *family* collide, bounce off one another, scramble after the animal. When they were all turned toward the counter behind which the otter had scurried, he edged downstairs, tiptoed along the far wall, and slipped out through the open patio door. Then he darted down the little steps, across the lawn, and away into the woods.

The second he hit the tree line, smells engulfed him. They were his favorite smells: resin, fallen apples, wet pine, dead leaves, and underneath it all, binding it together, that tang, so sharp it stung, especially in October, between rains. It wasn't just sea-spray or ocean air, but air *they* had breathed. His okras. He was breathing air that had been *inside okras,* and had therefore been where they had: out to sea, or all the way down at the bottom of the ocean with the shadow-fish that glowed and flickered. Air that tasted like whale-dreams.

He knew he should have signaled at least one of his family that he was going. He didn't mean to worry anyone in the house, and he knew they did worry, though less than they used to, when he slipped out. But they were busy, and somehow, after watching them all together, *laughing* together, he really needed to see his cove, catch a single glimpse of black and white skin-shine surfacing in the black-green water. Just one glimpse of just one whale sounding, surfacing, blowing okra-air in his direction. Then he'd go straight home. With luck, he'd be back in his own pod before they even noticed he was gone.

Overhead, and also straight ahead, through the haze of hanging leaves, Eddie saw stars in their millions. Glowing, winking, shadow sky-fish. He wondered what the air up *there* tasted like, and how long it would take a sky-okra to get down—or up—to them. Nothing moved around him, and yet he could hear movement up in the madrone trees and in the centers of the pines. Night whistles, and little skitters so light and quick that they didn't even stir the needles on the ground.

Where had all his clouds gone? He wasn't sure he'd ever been out on such a clear night. Certainly, he'd never been out alone after dark on a night like this, without Rebecca or Dedo or Joel. A few wisps still floated offshore, and none at all overhead, though around him—between the pines, and amongst them—the fog-foxes had come out, prowling silent, as always, in their fog-fox pods. They melted away whenever he turned to look.

He really could hear okras, now. At least, he was pretty sure he could hear one, making the unmistakable huff and burble that was Eddie's favorite sound in the world. He was almost running when he emerged from the pines right at the top of the cliffs at the edge of the island and stopped. Across the Strait, he saw the Mummyrocks, even whiter by moonlight than they were in the day. Hurrying along the cliff, he went right past the twisty tree, and only stopped and turned around when he'd gone several steps farther down the path. That's when he saw her for the first time.

She was perched in the crook of two twisty branches, neither of which looked thick enough to hold her on its own. He'd been up in that tree, too, lots of times, usually with Rebecca. But he'd never been that high, and Rebecca never let him go anywhere near the branches that swung out past the edge of the cliff, seemingly suspended in the empty air like the arms of construction cranes.

She'd seen him, too, watched him stop. Now that he was looking, she turned her gaze out to sea, down toward the okras in their cove. His okras, in his cove. Eddie didn't like that, started to say something, and her gaze swung back and pinned him in place.

She didn't say anything, just gazed down, looking remote as a nightjar up there. Her blond hair sparkled almost white in the starlight and the moonlight. Her legs swung out into the emptiness, swung back, swung out, in odd, mechanical jerks. Stop-start. Out-in. In-out.

Slowly, she grinned. It was a huge grin. "Hi, Eddie."

Everything about her—movements, voice, gaze— fascinated him. He watched her up there, dangling her feet over the emptiness. The sight reminded Eddie of something. So many somethings, really, all from stories he'd been read or shown on the TV, or heard from one or the other of the people he lived with. Mostly, he just stared at her smile. A smile in a tree.

"Are you a cat?" he whispered.

The woman exploded into laughter, rocking back against

the trunk. She kicked out her legs, watched them collapse back toward her. Somehow, her grin got wider. It really did seem just to hang amid the leaves, lit up with moonlight, in air twinkling with whale-dreams.

"You *are,*" said Eddie.

The woman stopped laughing, stared down. She straightened her stained and ripped jean-skirt over her leggings. Then she patted the branch beside her and smiled even wider.

"Why don't you come up here and find out?"

2

*Lately, despite the bone shudders it triggered every
time she stepped outside, Aunt Sally had come to
appreciate wind. Down in the Delta where she'd
spent the entirety of her life—lives—before the Great Unmaking, what breeze there was had curled up in hollows,
in the lee and leaves of cypress trees. It had stirred only
when the whole Delta stirred like some great, ancient animal shaking off flies. Most often, it had simply lain still.
So that was what Aunt Sally assumed air did, most nights.*

*Then poor, doomed Caribou had brought her Ju. For
reward, Aunt Sally had Unmade him. She'd Unmade all
her monsters. And then, free and together, she and Ju had
fled the piney-green forests and the drying swamps, escaping into the country she'd heard about all her life—lives—
and never known.*

*Now, five years later, here they were in yet another new
town, emerging from daysleep into a world positively*

wild with wind that rattled any anchored thing and flung everything loose into motion.

What town was this, anyway? Aunt Sally had never valued individual places enough to learn their names.

Was this Ames? Bozeman? Hadn't there been an Ames, at some point?

Laramie, according to the wooden sign nailed over the entrance to the post office across the tumbleweed-strewn street.

So that's where they were. Yet another stretch of miles farther from the Mississippi than Aunt Sally had ever been. Tonight, for some reason, she could feel the river's absence like a weight in her blood. A stilling. More accurately, the river's absence increased her awareness of the stillness that was always inside her.

The place around her whirled and sang. Sometimes, it seemed her world had been doing those things ever since the moment of Ju's arrival.

In the sidewalk shadows just outside the cone of light from the juddering lamppost overhead, which leaned like the trunk of some cliff-side tree in the torrent of air, Aunt Sally watched. Paper pumpkins and pillowcase ghosts danced and dangled in ribbon-nooses from awnings and overhangs. The wood and red-bricked buildings whistled, stood their ground but did so loudly, expelling sounds as the wind worked into cracks in century-old mortar, through warped windowpanes and slowly buckling doorframes. Newspapers tumbled by, and a hat. Even the press-on Halloween decals on the windows of the coffee shop—mostly leering, black-and-white skeleton-cattle in pirate scarves—seemed to bubble in place, shiver with the glass.

Inside the coffee shop, on the other side of the glass, Ju strolled among the natives. On every shabby couch, at each stained and grooved wooden table, the denizens swiveled to watch, flinching when she unleashed that smile of hers, each hair on their faux-cowboy beards straining toward her like long grass with a wind in them. It was the same each night, each time Ju convinced Aunt Sally to stop. Ju preferred college towns, which amused Aunt Sally and also confused her a little. Ju was only fourteen and, due to her circumstances both before and after the Great Unmaking, she wasn't the most likely university candidate.

Yet she always seemed so poised in these places. Downright comfortable instead of careful-cagey like she usually was. Always, she gravitated to the local all-ages music hangouts, where beardy boys and the inexplicable girls (and less beardy boys) who groomed and petted those beards clustered around sludgy espressos and whisper-sang miserable tunes about miseries Aunt Sally supposed they imagined they felt. Sometimes, they'd sing old ballads or blues they'd inhaled, somewhere. Those typically made Aunt Sally laugh, which was why Ju wouldn't let her come inside anymore, made her go off to find her own amusements or lurk on the streets with only the wind and whoever had the misfortune of happening across her path for company.

Through the shuddering glass, she watched Ju make her slow, head-down way to the microphone on the little bear rug near the order counter. Once on the little stage, she lifted her head high enough to speak into the mic. Aunt Sally couldn't hear, but she knew Ju was using that rustling-leaves murmur that the beardy boys read as shyness.

But it wasn't shyness. Aunt Sally had spent the most

pleasurable parts of the past five years figuring Ju out. She had come to suspect that what the girl really signaled, most nights, was a reluctance to unleash. *What Aunt Sally hadn't figured out was exactly what Ju was holding back.*

A mystery! A bottomless, glinting cave of a person to explore! Not even Mother had brought such fascination to Aunt Sally's nights, such renewed reason to bother to wake. Not even close.

Out here, far from the Delta, in this windy world full of creatures whose nights ended in sleeps that melted into days they got up for, she supposed they'd *call whatever Ju radiated* charisma or presence, *maybe even* talent; *all Aunt Sally knew was that it was there, winking in the girl's deceptively placid green eyes, in the lava curls of her hair where it escaped from her braids. Some nights, Aunt Sally could literally feel it rising off her like heat when she slept.*

Another gust roared down the street, pouring into Aunt Sally's nostrils but carrying no smells, filling her ears but telling no tales because it came from nowhere, from the empty plains, meeting no one on its way. She huddled deeper into the checked wool coat Ju had picked out for her somewhere, its greens and blues and oranges ridiculous, like the coloring on an old-time picnic blanket. Like the picnic blanket in Aunt Sally's father's plantation house—the house she'd burned to the ground, more than a hundred years ago, during her very first Unmaking—which he'd spread in grassy places along the perimeters of his tobacco fields on sunny afternoons so he could hear the work songs of his picaninnies. The one he'd most enjoyed raping her on. Come to think of it, he'd probably made *Aunt Sally on that blanket, one of those times he'd raped her mother on it.*

Not that Ju knew any of that, of course. How could she have known? Except that every now and then, when Ju lifted those firefly eyes to her, Aunt Sally thought that maybe . . . somehow . . .

At the microphone inside the coffee shop, Ju was singing. When she sang, Ju's eyes narrowed but stayed open so she could watch the effect she was having. She swayed just enough to set her lava hair swirling. When the door opened to admit another beardy boy, Aunt Sally heard her voice briefly, husky-quiet. The context was completely wrong, so it took Aunt Sally a moment to recognize the tune. When she did, she shook her head. What a strange, marvelous girl she had chosen to Make, instead of Unmake.

"Grace Holler." One of those ballads that had seemed to swell from the very earth in the Delta, to float, already whole, on the sweet summer breeze, streaming out of some half-imagined shadow-past no one could quite remember. Of course, that song recounted a very real incident, or two incidents, really: the nights Aunt Sally's monsters—acting on Policy, doing exactly as Caribou had said the numbers decreed—swept down on that tiny hamlet at the edge of the piney-green woods, and left it empty and silent as the lost Roanoke Colony.

From the trees, poor boys
From the trees, poor girls
They came, and they went,
As if heaven sent . . .

Heaven sent, Aunt Sally thought, half humming, missing the Delta if not her monsters. She missed Mother, too,

23

of course. She even missed Caribou, briefly, in a particular, between-her-legs sort of way. Both of them gone these five years, now.

Way down in the humming, Grace Holler–emptiness of Aunt Sally's heart, something stirred, wakened. Turning away from the window, she caught sight of her own reflection and stopped.

Ju's song dropped away. So did the street. The wind, the line-dance racket from the bars next door and the more-than-occasional wolf whistles from passing manboys in their pickups, it all winked out, as though she'd switched them off. Or her reflection had.

Was that really her face?

That sharp? That thin?

With her fingers, she traced the edges of the cheekbones, twin points of a single blade. An Aunt Sally ice pick buried in there. How long had it been? she wondered. She reached out toward the window, but whether to cup her reflection or try to smear it away, she had no idea.

Months, she realized. It had been months. A year? Was that even possible?

In the beginning, the not eating—the eating less—had been a sort of game, like the Parties she'd once thrown her monsters just to give their nights variety, give them all something to look forward to. Or like Policy. It had provided structure and, better still, intensity to the endless, traveling nights with Ju. It had also been a challenge, the sort of sacrifice she'd been told mothers made for the good of their children. Aunt Sally had decided to make this one for Ju, so that Ju never had to see, or even know, until and unless Aunt Sally decided she should.

But eating nothing? *No one? Was that even possible? Shouldn't the Hunger have come for her, by now? Or rather, shouldn't it have overwhelmed her, left her no choice? Because the truth was, it never left. It never had, not even in the old days, not even right after she'd eaten. Certainly, it was with her now. It was practically screaming inside her.*

"From the trees, poor boys."

From the trees, poor Sally . . .

The hand she'd raised trembled on its thin wrist like the last leaf on a dead branch. Aunt Sally cocked her head and watched it.

Hunger, *she hummed, in an almost-tune she was inventing on the spot.* Why have you forsaken me?

The man appeared over her left shoulder, out of nowhere, as though she'd summoned him out of the glass. She mistook him, at first, for another beardy boy; he had the beard, all right, and wore the same sort of heavy, crabapple-red checked overshirt. But he held his head too high, and his hands floated comfortably at his side, didn't fold over each other or disappear mournfully into pockets. Also, he stood too still.

A beardy man, *then. Beardy grown-up. Assuming that's what beardy boys eventually did, if they got the chance.*

Then it hit her. Startled and even scared her.

How was it possible for this guy to stand this close to her—barely five feet away, right over her shoulder—and stay that still? Even if all he could see was her reflection, and even if she'd barely noticed him?

Had her own charisma dissipated, along with her Hunger? Just how much of herself had she traded away or cast off for Ju's sake?

"They grow up so fast," said the man through his beard, and even before he'd finished, Aunt Sally started to laugh. She was relieved, she truly was. The issue wasn't whether she'd looked at him, wasn't her at all, in fact. The issue was that he hadn't looked at her, yet. Not all the way.

She eyed his reflection in the glass. He was staring right through their reflected selves into the coffee shop, toward whichever beardy boy was his. Aunt Sally saw him smile.

"I shouldn't be out here watching, I know. He'd kill me if he saw me. I just . . . I kinda love seeing him . . . I don't know . . . claim his world, you know? Does that make any sense? Am I a terrible father?"

Laughter exploded out of her and shut him up. This was astounding, she thought. Amazing. Even better than mesmerizing or unmanning or—God knew—fucking them. It was better even than Hunger.

Or rather, this was a better kind of hunger. Tonight, it had come to her heightened, seasoned with something brand-new: the sensation of standing in the evening chill with another parent—caretaker, guardian, whatever—and keeping an eye on the kids, together. Watching them do their kid things. Claim their world.

Aunt Sally, Scourge of the Delta. Soccer mom.

The guy still hadn't noticed her, yet. Not consciously or properly, though the process had begun. Aunt Sally could see it in the slow swivel of his hips as the pull she exerted trickled into him, through all the usual, vulnerable places. He kept on chattering away, though.

"Sometimes, you almost forget there are other people going through the same stuff, you know? You get so

locked up in your own shit, or your kid's shit, which, let's face it, is pretty much your shit by this point, at least all the shit you have time for, right?"

"So right," Aunt Sally said. She put a hand over her mouth, but laughter spilled out through her fingers. That made her laugh even harder.

"What?" said the beardy man, starting to turn his head. Aunt Sally quickly lowered her own, prolonged the moment just a little, because this was so much fun. Because it really was new . . .

The guy laughed, too, but not like he knew why. "Okay. Why are we laugh—"

"It's just like you said," Aunt Sally purred. "Here we are, without even trying. Without even planning to be here. Just staring through a window, standing together in the cold."

"This isn't cold. Not for Laramie. You're not from here, are you?"

"Standing together where our kids can't see us, but we can see them. Sharing a little . . ."—she could barely get out the words through her giggles—"adult conversation."

And with that—she couldn't hold on any longer—she lifted her face and let him see. He really was lonely, poor guy. A single dad, perhaps, and nearly as starving as she was, in his way. Because even that first, sloe-eyed, shadowy glimpse completely blew him out, shut him down, like an old speaker with too much music cranked through it.

There he stood, all locked up. Even his beard erect.

"Sorry," Aunt Sally said, and laughed even louder. She touched his face carefully. She thought he might explode like a firecracker she'd lit.

The thing that made it all so marvelous was that she really did feel sorry, at least for a second. She thought she did, anyway. This was some poor beardy boy's dad, after all.

Positively snorting her delight, she put a hand to the man's chest, slipped her thin—so thin!—fingers between the buttons of his heavy shirt and felt the beating under there. The sensation restored her, some. Reawakened her. Resexed her, she thought, laughing still more. Lady Macbeth in reverse.

"Come on, partner," she said.

More gently than she could ever remember—not that she bothered remembering these moments often—she led the beardy dad around the corner, into the alley between the coffee shop and the line-dance bar. The guy's arms wriggled pitifully. His substantial, faux-cowboy body seemed to curl in on itself: an ant in the midst of giving up wriggling, succumbing to her flood.

She had continued talking out of habit. Teasing, the way she used to tease Caribou on the nights she let him fuck her. Or, to be fair to his memory, make love to her. That's what he would have called it, surely. Almost certainly what he'd imagined he was doing. It had been fun, in its way, and for a surprisingly long time. Decades.

Then she'd burned him alive. Twice! That had also been a type of fun, Aunt Sally thought, though cruel. She didn't especially want to be cruel, tonight.

So she jammed the beardy dad up against the cold bricks, slid her hand behind him, and pulled his head back to expose that magical, bristled, beating, soft place, complete with little Adam's apple to bob for. So delicious.

"About the kids," she murmured, leaning in slow, holding his eyes. Letting him like it. She'd forgotten how much fun it was sometimes to let them like it. How sexy that could be. Mother used to go on and on about that in the days when she ran around with the whistling fool she'd somehow Made. Before she'd up and ran off with him. And look where that had gotten her. "The thing is, kids just get so reckless. I have to admit, I find that kind of . . . inspirational. You know?"

At the mouth of the alley, the wind whimpered like a wolf. One of her man-wolves from back in the camp, waiting for her scraps.

Poor beardy dad's every muscle was twanging now, stretching toward and recoiling from her at the same time. This was how guys like this reacted sometimes. The ones that fought her, that actually wanted to stay. Again, she felt a flicker of something like regret as she lifted on tiptoes, covered his mouth with her own, and sucked him in.

Then, and only then, did real Hunger sweep down on her. Oh, she'd forgotten. How had she forgotten this? Already, so fast, her lips slid to his throat. Against her breasts and hips, the man bucked, swelled, sighed, shuddered. She opened her mouth wide, wider, welcoming the whole world back in. She was literally at the instant of releasing her jaws when Ju laughed.

Jerking as though she'd been Tased, Aunt Sally froze, her teeth imbedded in the beardy man's skin but not clamped together, his Adam's apple against her top teeth like a pit and his juices oozing warm around it. In horror—in something approaching actual fear—she glanced toward the mouth of the alley.

Ju laughed again, a light and silvery sound, like rain down sheet metal. Aunt Sally wasn't even sure if it was the sound or the sight of Ju there, the look on her face, that terrified her so. But the effect proved so strong that for a second, she couldn't even get her teeth free of the beardy man's skin.

There was nothing new about Ju's expression, she realized. It was the one Ju almost always wore, the one that had bewitched Aunt Sally from the moment they'd met. That smile just seemed so unconstructed somehow, unpracticed, equal parts amazed and joyful and mocking. Or maybe none of those things. Aunt Sally had never been able to sort it out. It was just . . . a pure smile. Smile in its elemental form, with neither judgment nor doubt nor pleasure nor malice clouding it, which made it almost inhuman. Fairy-like.

That thought was silly enough to rattle Aunt Sally out of her stupor. Keeping the beardy dad pinned with her palm, she eased back, scraping bits of beard off her teeth with her tongue and the insides of her lips. "Hi, hon," she called. "I was just—."

Ju's next laugh silenced her, unsexed her all over again. That was the laugh that went with that smile, for sure. Pure laugh. Fairy laugh.

"You think I don't know?" Ju said.

Aunt Sally gaped. Stared. The sensations that flooded her now were new, all right. Delicious. Horrible.

What did Ju know? And how did she know it? In five years of traveling together, the girl had never asked about anything, really. Not where they were going—except when Ju suggested another college town—or why Aunt

Sally had chosen and taken her. Not whether they could have some home other than Aunt Sally's Le Sabre or a hotel, or if they could travel by daylight, see some sun. She'd never asked to go back to the orphanage where Caribou had found her and say good-bye to the survivors, assuming he'd left any. She'd never even asked what had happened to the little boy and girl she'd come to the camp with on the night of the Unmaking, when Aunt Sally had erased the monsters she'd created from the face of the earth—interred them in the ballads disappearing along with her beloved Delta—and vanished into myth. Started over, with Ju by her side.

"Know wh . . . ?" Aunt Sally started, but she couldn't make herself finish the question. She was afraid of the answer.

Actually afraid.

So thrilling. What an adventure! Her first adventure in decades, maybe the first real one of her entire endless, merciless life.

Aunt Sally, Scourge of the Delta. Laid low by motherhood.

"What do you know, little witch-girl?" she finally managed.

But by then, Ju had vanished from the mouth of the alley, her laughter trailing behind her.

3

An hour after the end of Storybooktime, with less than twenty minutes to go before the new, budget-mandated electronic timers shut down the lights and the air-conditioning, Emilia Restrepo stood alone behind the circulation desk, watching the boy, Dixon, scratch relentlessly at the cheap sketching pad she'd given him. There was something so sad about this kid, way beyond the fact that he was always the last child here on Storybooktime day, and usually the last patron in the building, period. His mother had to work, Emilia understood that. She suspected Dixon did, too. The sadness was in the way he attacked the sketchpad, driving the point of the pencil into and sometimes through the paper, as though instead of drawing he were performing surgery or disemboweling something.

Right on cue, fifteen minutes before shutdown, the lights dimmed, shrinking the usable space into the little square of illumination around Dixon's table and the cone of yellow over the circulation desk. In truth, Emilia thought, the city could probably save a few more pennies and eliminate the circulation desk light, too, given that there was almost nothing left on the shelves of her library to circulate.

For a long moment, she let herself sag against the clutterless desk and stare around at the empty rusted metal bookcases that ringed the room. Her father, Emilia knew, would have been appalled, would have flung a hand into his still-black hair and declared that the whole place looked more like a nursing-home bingo room than a library. He wouldn't have been wrong. All that was left, now, with six weeks to go before the Jackson, Mississippi, municipal system closed its Butterfly Weed branch for good, were the cracked and coffee-stained computer terminals where migrant workers and the homeless checked their email, some scattered and misshapen beanbag chairs from a failed, long-ago county redesign initiative, and some spinning wire racks stuffed with twenty-five-cent VHS tapes for sale, incomplete book-on-tape sets, and scratched rental DVDs that no one rented.

Not for the first time, and for reasons Emilia never let herself examine too closely, she imagined wandering over to Dixon's table, luring him to his feet with another Fun-size Milky Way from the candy bag she kept under the counter, and asking if he wanted to get out of here with her. Hop the bus, take it all the way into downtown Jackson, and do something really dramatic. Something insanely stupid and luxurious and unaffordable. Like maybe see a movie.

After that, she'd bring him back, probably. Depending on the day, they might even make it before his mother showed up.

Reina del Drama, her mother would have snorted, if Emilia had told her any of these things. Then she would have suggested—again—that perhaps Emilia could get dramatic and reckless about something *truly* exciting, like finding another job. One that let her use her knowledge of books instead of how to catalogue them, or allowed her to live out any reasonable version of the daughter-of-immigrant success stories with which both her parents had filled her childhood.

Briefly, and to her own surprise, Emilia had to stifle an urge to call her parents. Her dad, anyway. Her mom would demand to know why she was calling during work hours, then tell her how much she loved her, then order her to get a new job. Whereas if she caught her dad in his little community college office, and if he'd had a decent day with at least one or two of his nineteen classes (or whatever obscene number they had him teaching these days), and if her mother had packed him a container of leftover *sancocho* and he'd actually remembered a fork, she might get him talking about flea-marketing. About his latest fifty-cent vinyl discoveries. If he'd had a *really* good day—if the twenty-year-old microwave in the Comp and Lit Department office was actually working, say—he might even sing to her.

But that would probably make her cry. Though she wasn't unhappy, most days, and she didn't feel like crying today.

So she shoved herself away from the desk, grabbed the

paper towels and 99-Cent Warehouse Mr. PineyClean from the supply shelf, and wiped the circulation counters even more spotless than they already were. As she worked, she sang to herself. Not one of her dad's beloved *cumbias* but a Kacey Musgraves song that she'd been loving lately. The merry-go-round one.

Every now and then, as Emilia cleaned and hummed, she glanced through the metal detectors and the bug-smeared front doors into the parking lot. Out there, she knew, the Mississippi heat lingered. It seemed to do that deeper into October every year, now. But here, inside the Butterfly Weed branch, even with the air already shutting down, the room still *looked* cool—because it was windowless, because the lights had dimmed—and so it felt cool, at least to her. Comforting, like her parents' tiny Mississippi house five hundred miles away, where her parents both still came home from teaching, every single day, dropped their books and bags, and played Scrabble to *cumbias* or Carter Family records deep into the night.

And now here she was slipping from Kacey into the Carter Family. Keeping on the sunny side.

She looked up from her wiping and polishing just in time to see Dixon hurrying for the doors, head down. Presumably, he'd seen his mother or she'd texted him to wait out front. He'd left his sketchpad on the table, of course, and the pencils Emilia had lent him scattered on the floor under his chair like peanut shells.

"*Adiós,* Dixon," she called, watched him vanish, and turned toward the office to shut down her own computer terminal.

When the front doors *shushed* open once more, she

didn't turn back or glance over her shoulder. She knew who it was, and he didn't like her to look. But she felt her smile creep over her face again. *"Hola,* Invisible Man," she whispered to herself. Then—because she was feeling bold today, even a little sassy—she called out, "There's microwave popcorn left, from Storybooktime. We could share a bag . . ."

Of course, by then, the Invisible Man had already vanished into the Records and Reference Room in the back, where he always went to rustle around in the file cabinets and microfiche cartons Emilia had never seen anyone else touch during her six years at Butterfly Weed. Not even the librarians.

Right on cue, the last fluorescents winked out, leaving only the tongue of sunlight lolling through the front door, plus the emergency lights over Emilia's desk. There would be one more dot of brightness left, she knew, though she'd have to creep to the Records and Reference Room door to see it: the little North Star of the Invisible Man's penlight glowing faintly over whatever papers or files he'd pulled this time. Plus maybe the dim, green glow of the microfiche screen.

Just like that, without any warning, her eyes really did tear up. Apparently, she was indeed *Reina del Drama* today. Because as much as she liked to joke about it, and as much as she'd always assured her parents she loved her work—and the occasional and surprising conversations with the migrants, and her reading time and riverbank walks, her Delta Cooking classes at the Y down the block— she was still as alone as her namesake *(and why,* she wondered, for the thousandth time, *had her father chosen that particular Faulkner story to pay homage to with his only daughter's name?).*

Soon, possibly even sooner than the date the city had set, Butterfly Weed would close for good. And apparently, she wasn't finished inhabiting it yet. And neither were the migrant workers, or furious little Dixon, or any of the other Butterfly Weed denizens she barely knew but saw and nodded to every week or every day.

She would never even get to see the Invisible Man's actual face, on the day those bandages finally came off. Ever since he'd first started slipping in here—Butterfly Weed's most solitary denizen of all—she'd found herself wondering what was under there, imagining the day he came in without them. As if that day would have anything whatsoever to do with her. As if he even knew who she was.

Still. Solitary they all might be, her fellow Butterfly Weeds. But this place had been their home. At the very least, it had been her home, the first she'd had since leaving her parents to their Scrabble over a decade ago.

How and when had she wandered so far out into the main room?

Right. She'd meant to collect Dixon's sketchpad and pencils. But the sounds from Records and Reference had distracted her, and now they lured her like a butterfly to color.

Or a moth to light, she thought, glancing down at her beige work blouse threading at the wrists, her dark brown skirt that had lightened in patches with too much washing.

37

She was fluttering toward the back of the library, humming still more Carter Family. *"Will they missmemissme . . . when we're gone . . ."*

She could just see him in there, hunched in his long, gray coat that seemed way too warm for the weather, leaning forward over one of the tables, a file fanned open to his left, his bandages less lit than tinted by the penlight in his mouth and the faint green glow of the microfiche machine.

Like a diver underwater, Emilia thought, approaching the doorway.

Like—

The bellow ripped through the room, smacking into Emilia like a wave and actually lifting her off her feet. Staggering back, she felt a cry fill her mouth but somehow snapped her lips shut just in time. Even as she did that, grabbing the nearest empty bookcase to steady herself, she wondered why she was bothering. And why she was more concerned about the sound she *hadn't* made than the one the Invisible Man actually had, because that bellow had definitely been him.

Instinct, she thought, getting control of her breath, her heartbeat. *Self-preservation.*

But that made no sense, either.

Preservation from what?

In the Records Room, the Invisible Man was pawing through papers, scattering them across the table and onto the floor like a cat shredding a newspaper. Or hunting a cricket. The mess annoyed Emilia, and her annoyance steadied her. Dixon strewing pencils for her to collect in the dark was one thing. But a grown man, invisible or not . . .

At least he wasn't bellowing anymore. He was grunting,

and possibly muttering. She could see the bandages around his mouth moving, but she couldn't quite catch the words.

Reina, she thought, edging forward, humming under her steadying breath. *Relax . . .*

The Invisible Man never stopped muttering and pawing, never looked up except once or twice at the microfiche screen. He leaned even farther forward, as though he might climb onto the table and *into* the machine, imprint himself on whatever he'd found there and vanish into history.

As she reached the doorway, Emilia stopped humming. Just to listen, surely, not to keep the Invisible Man from hearing or noticing her. Why should she?

Even this close—less than ten feet away—his words were barely intelligible. Possibly, she realized, his lips still hadn't healed. She suspected they might never heal, given how long he'd been showing up at Butterfly Weed—months, at least—and how many times his bandages must have been changed and rewrapped in that time.

Maybe that was why he always came so late in the day, when the sunlight had weakened. Maybe, in his horrifically vulnerable condition, sunlight could burn him even through bandages.

Crouching, as the remaining light in the library rose like smoke, leaving more darkness closer to the ground, Emilia tilted her head into the room. She couldn't help herself.

"Be here," he muttered through the bandages, again, and again, as if saying grace or casting a spell. After a while, the words changed, or else Emilia heard them better. Not *be here.* "Be her." Over and over, interspersed with very occasional interjections of "Come on. Come *on.*"

All at once, he went still. He stood and stared at the screen, holding a single piece of paper in one gloved hand. He glanced back and forth, back and forth from paper to screen, the movements robotic, completely mechanical. *Like a table fan,* Emilia thought, imagining she could actually feel a breeze blowing off him, ghosting over her.

His mantra changed again, too. Not *be here* anymore. Not *be her.* But "Be you. Be you."

Had she really meant to slip all the way into the room? And why was she no longer crouching but standing straight, leaning toward him, all but touching his shoulder as she strained forward?

To help, surely. That's what she was here for, after all. Also, yes, sure, she wanted to see. Because like most people who sensed that their own lives had never quite started—which Emilia suspected was most people, most of the time—she was drawn by desperation, or any unchecked eruption of emotion, really. Lives with color, with stories already imbedded in them.

"Ohhhh," said the Invisible Man. Dropping his head, he slumped over the back of the chair in front of him without lowering the paper he held or dimming the microfiche screen. And so, finally, Emilia got a glimpse at both.

On the screen was a registry, a list, something official and civil. Marriage licenses or birth certificates. Maybe he was tracing a daughter given up for adoption. Or an ex-lover.

The paper in the Invisible Man's bandaged hand was a blurry, blown-up copy of a photograph. The photograph might have been a Polaroid, originally, judging by its square, white border, its flat yet garish colors. A Polaroid of a bearded man dancing alone in a grassy place in the Delta somewhere. At least, it looked like the Delta, had that Delta light, that specific shade of green, somehow sloshy and dusty at the same time. In one of the dancing man's hands was a parasol or something. A bent broomstick or broken baseball bat.

Unless that was an arm?

This time, the gasp escaped Emilia's mouth before she could stifle it. Before she could duck from the room, raise an apologetic hand—before she could so much as blink—the Invisible Man was on her, the flung photo floating in the air behind him as he grabbed her by the neck and slammed the back of her head against the metal door frame. Sparks exploded in her eyes and breath massed in the suddenly shut tunnel of her throat.

And yet, even then, she found herself more fascinated than frightened. Instead of panicking, she was peering through pain-sparks, shaking her head to clear her vision rather than escape the crushing hand, so that she could finally get a look at the Invisible Man's eyes. She glimpsed ridges of skin under the bandages that hinted at more ridges, mountains, and canyons, as though she were staring at the surface of Venus through its cloud cover.

But the eyes themselves. They were the loveliest, loneliest eyes . . .

All at once, to her surprise as much as relief, the pressure at her windpipe lessened. As it did, the bandages ringing the Invisible Man's mouth seemed to split, pull apart, as though he were a pumpkin carving itself from the inside. Emilia flushed with feeling so intense, so strangely uncomplicated, she thought it verged on love.

Yes, she thought, awhirl in this poor man's eyes. *I could love you. I could love anyone who smiled like that.*

Reaching with his free hand back toward the table, the Invisible Man grabbed the Polaroid where it had floated to rest, along with the top papers from his scattered stack.

"I've got it," he said, waving the picture and papers. "I *know.*"

"You've finally found what you're looking for?"

"It's him. It's her. I know!" Abruptly, like a snake striking, his head shot toward hers. She ducked back, banging her head again as loose bandage ends brushed her throat and cheek. His breath swept over her. "I know," he whispered, and leapt away into the main room like a deer darting into the shadows, taking those tragic, hungry eyes with him.

The words flew so fast from Emilia's mouth that they didn't even feel like hers. More like words he'd breathed into and through her.

"Why don't we celebrate, then?"

He was almost to the front doors already, at the edge of the shrinking spill of sunlight. He'd forgotten, she realized, with a thrill that rippled over her flesh and raised gooseflesh all the way down her skin, that she'd have to unlock those doors for him. And she wasn't going to do that. Not just yet. Not until she got at least one more of those smiles.

He'd stopped when she spoke, and now he turned. For a long moment, he just stood there, his posture positively regal despite everything he'd suffered, and his eyes, even from across the library in the shadowy near-dark, so lonely. So much lonelier than she suspected her own looked. Once more, he glanced down at the bundle of papers in his hand, the Polaroid, then back up. For the second time, Emilia watched that shy, slow smile carve itself into his face. She fought down a surprising flutter of panic, and at the same instant realized she was tearing up again. Flat-out crying, now. And for what?

For nothing at all. For Dixon and Dixon's mama. For her own parents, Scrabbling and dancing away their solitary evenings in their tiny living room with the empty turtle tank, because the turtle they'd bought when they first came to this country had died years ago. For herself and her unstarted life. For her parents and theirs. She felt herself moving across the room, now, noted her fingers gripping the empty bookcase to her right as though clinging to it, and commanded them to let go.

"You're right," said the Invisible Man, watching her come. "We *should* celebrate." His grin got wider still, chiseling through bandages across his cheeks. "We'll have a party."

4

*E*ven now, five years after she'd gotten sweet, curly-
haired young Dr. James to sew her back together,
Sophie couldn't get walking quite right. She could
walk, okay, but weirdly: lurch, shuffle, lurch-tilt, drag. As
though her lower half were a balky remote-control car she
was driving instead of part of her, and subject to whims.
Frustrating as that could be, it had also become its own
sort of fun, adding unpredictability even to the most pe-
destrian activities, keeping them fresh, because she never
knew when those neurons wouldn't quite make it through
their kinked pathways to muscles and tendons. And that
meant that every now and then, at the most unexpected
and amusing moments, she found herself sitting down, or
turning into a wall.

That was yet another reason she'd come to love the
night ferries. On open water, even when it was calm, she
could lurch, tip, catch herself, and when she looked up

there'd be someone else recovering from doing the same thing, some sauced-looking grandpa splashing coffee drink all over his Seattle Seahawks sweatshirt or a windy-haired twelve-year-old who'd lost her balance, then her cell phone as she came unmoored from the deck. They'd grin at one another, then, grandpas and kids and Sophies. As though they were all in the same boat.

See what I did there? *she'd think, imagining actually saying it aloud to herself or Natalie.* Same boat? *Occasionally, on the weirdest, loneliest nights, she even imagined saying things like that to Jess, of all people. Then she'd imagine Jess's scowl and give herself a little wriggle of pleasure.*

Eventually, she'd find her way to a rail, especially if it was raining, which was most of the time. She'd watch islands materialize out of the mist, dissipate into it. On clear trips, she saw container ships and fishing boats clustered on the horizon, sprawling across the expanse between oil derricks, creating what looked like the skyline of some seaborne ghost city. A magical, mist-wreathed place where she might settle someday, if she could ever actually reach it.

But for now, whenever she needed to get off the island, or needed people, for one reason or another, the ferries more than served. She loved the little casual interactions: smiling at random fellow passengers, some late-night business mom or kissing college couple or track-marked street kid; tugging them along behind her for a while like cans on strings as she lurched into the dining cabin, up to the view deck, back toward the stern to watch the white wake in the black, black water; cutting them loose, eventually, leaving them unharmed, shivering and stranded in the misty starlight, a little hungrier and lustier and lonelier than they'd already been, because now they'd seen their deep dreams walking. Lurching, anyway. Because they'd glimpsed possibilities they'd maybe imagined but never imagined possible. Because she'd let them glimpse their deaths and then let them live.

Mostly, almost always, she let them live.

She'd come to love the ferry so much that she even enjoyed the cold, in a way. Not that she had a choice, because she was always cold, even before the boats shrugged free of their lines and docks and harbors, got out from under the lee of the land and leaned into the wind to run. Even indoors, on wet nights, the cold circled and swarmed at the windows, erupted through the cabins and up and down stairwells like a pack of screaming six-year-olds every time some idiot opened a door. Sometimes, the chill got so ferocious that it pinned her to the walls. Sometimes, it seemed so elemental and gleeful that she wanted to throw open her arms and embrace it.

Inevitably, dealing with the cold became another of Sophie's ferry-games, a constantly changing challenge. Some nights, she tried lurking indoors without collecting onlookers or unwanted attention. Some nights, she prowled the decks outside for warm spots, steamy places where the engines vented, or bench seats a couple or family had just vacated, leaving their heat in handprints on the railings and their scent in the air. She'd sit or stand in their absence and watch seabirds skim the wake, which is what those birds mostly did. Only rarely did they dive, snag whatever it was in the water that had caught their eye at just that *wrong moment, and rise with their prey dripping and flapping in their long mouths.*

They were her, she realized. She was them. Sophie Seabird, skimming the Strait or the Sound.

Was that why she'd stayed in the Northwest so long? Because she'd at least found other living things to identify with? Why had she even come? There were whole stretches of time she genuinely couldn't remember, now, when her mind really did go blank as a seabird's and she just rode the rumbling engines through waves and wind. They scared her, those times, when she stirred from them. Though while they were happening, and she was just gliding . . .

Later, eventually, when she did stir and remember, she'd sometimes laugh at the flukiness of it all. The serendipity. Unless it was fate, or God's hand, or even Natalie's. Maybe sweet, stony Natalie was guiding her still. Sophie's mother would have called that idea flat-out blasphemy. At least, she would have during one of her dried-out times, when she could talk sensibly at all. And even back then—at age eight, say, in their rusting trailer with dead flies and Cheez-It crumbs for carpet—Sophie would have challenged her to explain the difference.

Because it really had seemed so strange. Almost miraculous.

There she'd been, not twenty-four hours removed from finally giving in and giving Dr. James—poor, curly-haired Dr. James—the reward he'd craved, had begged so pathetically for, had certainly earned, and hadn't deserved. Regretful in a way she rarely let herself feel, unsteady on her twitchy legs, fully expecting to topple off them with every step, Sophie had caught a midnight bus back to East Dunham, New Hampshire, to collect what remained of her things from the locker where she'd stored them. She'd particularly wanted the bag of cassettes Jess had made of Natalie speaking. Not only were those cassettes the closest Sophie would ever get to the one true friend she'd had, she suspected they were the closest she'd get to anyone, ever again. Ever, in this case, meaning a very long time indeed.

When she'd emerged from the bus station, weaving and wobbling her way toward Campus Avenue with the taste of Dr. James still slicking her tongue and strands of his hair coiling on her palate and around her tonsils and making her gag, she'd paused for a single moment by the side of the road in the drizzly, late-September dawn. The very first car to pass her was a police cruiser, with the big, reedy black guy from Rebecca's orphanage—Joe, she thought his name was, or Joel—riding in the back.

That had stunned Sophie, at first. She'd assumed they'd all fled months ago, right after that night in those woods. And indeed they had, it turned out. Joel had been brought back as a witness, and also a potential suspect. A Person of Interest. Pretty amusing, that. Sophie could have told them he just didn't have the teeth for it, if anyone had asked her.

Eventually, of course, the police had let Joel go. And for lack of anything better to do—or maybe because that guiding hand was propelling her yet again—she'd trailed behind him as he left the station, followed him right onto the bus to Boston, and hopped his plane to the wet and windy west. She'd tracked him north from Sea-Tac under a mercifully overcast sky, through Seattle and up the coast, onto a boat and out to the island Jess had somehow already found, where her surviving clan and the new strays she'd collected could hole up together.

That very night, without really considering why, Sophie had set up camp all by her lonesome on the other side of the island. And so she'd gotten to see orcas, and stars whose reflections glinted way down in the depths of the Strait, as though everyone and everything that had ever lived was floating around in those waters. And because that sight had transfixed her for so long, and because she had nowhere else to be or go, she'd decided to stay. And because she'd stayed all this time, she'd finally met Eddie. Re-met Eddie.

Natalie's child. Whose weight had once felt as familiar in her arms as her own baby's. Whose heavy-lidded, brooding eyes were his mother's, but whose smile was very nearly Sophie's. Wide as the world.

That was interesting. Getting more interesting every time they met.

Meanwhile, she had ferries.

Because she really did have all those things to occupy her, now, she only hit nights like this occasionally. They always seemed to be lurking, though, anytime she let herself become undistracted. Every time she fully surfaced behind her own eyes, in her own skin. Sophie Seabird, returned once more to her nest. Even then, the worst thoughts only seized her at particular instances: when she was alone on deck, with rain banging on the windows of the passenger cabin or sweeping in and around her, the cold so cold she no longer felt it, really, more dissolved into and became it, the way water became icicle. Or Sophies became seabirds.

These were the times—the only ones—when the Emerald City and its star-strewn, whale-haunted surrounding isles didn't glow, when the mist stopped sparkling and instead just closed off her view of mountains, moon, sky. Sometime in the midst of her four or five or fifteen crossings on nights like tonight, she'd look down into the spray, over the water, and there the wake would be. The only bright and winking thing left in her world, flung wide on the black surface of the Sound like open arms.

Those were the only times Sophie actually considered just letting herself topple over.

What stopped her, every single time—at least, it had stopped her so far—was the sight of just one of her fellow passengers, in the midst of one of those things they always seemed to be doing to pass time or acknowledge it or avoid acknowledging it. She'd catch a glimpse of a pilot or crewwoman up in the window of the bridge house, staring right out over the prow of the boat into the misty blackness with her chin in her hand, a Silver Surfer comic book clutched against her chest like a bible. Or some sad homeless woman muttering or singing to herself inside the cabin, just on the other side of the window from Sophie, as she tried somehow to tuck her sopping newspaper-blanket more tightly around herself without shredding it. Or a kid and his dad, out way too late, on their journey home from some secret adventure, playing iPad checkers. Sometimes, the kid or the dad would even look up and smile at her. Sometimes they did that so fast that Sophie realized she wasn't even making it happen.

Other times, of course—rare, and getting rarer, which made them that much more satisfying when they did come—she just got hungry. She'd cut down so much, these past years. It amazed her how much she'd found she could. Her hunting evenings occurred quarterly, now, maybe less.

When the Hunger did come, her main challenge, just as Natalie had predicted, had turned out to be choosing. So far, Sophie hadn't so much solved that problem or developed a system for dealing with it as rejected its problemness.

How did she choose? The only way she could. The only way that seemed fair. Meaning, the same way people chose packs of chicken at the market, or seabirds selected fish: she simply picked the one who presented an opportunity at the moment the need became acute and the circumstances appropriate. She'd tried to take looks or smiles or any sort of attraction out of it, poor Dr. James being the notable exception. She still preferred indulging people she was drawn to, or who were drawn to her, rather than devouring them. She'd toyed with the superhero thing, seeking out shitheads in the midst of trashing other people's lives, but that had proven too much work when the need got on her, and involved too much frantic prowling around. And in the end, picking meals that way had felt just as random and prone to unintended consequences— for herself, her victims, her victim's victims—as any other.

She also tried not to be vicious about it. She never sought to enjoy or prolong it. She had in fact taken to thinking of herself as a sort of kosher predator. Humane. If, when the need finally swamped her, she could find

someone lost ... someone sleeping ... someone too focused on being a shit or a psycho to someone else on a cell
phone ... and if those people were alone, out in the fog
or by themselves in their cars down on the auto deck ...

Sometimes, it was that easy.

Regardless of circumstances, she always tried to imagine herself appearing in a shimmer of sea mist, lurching,
moving wrong, her arms spread wide and her smile wider.
She'd hover in their presence, lure them rather than dive
down on them. She'd give them what she could, whatever
they seemed to want, time and surroundings permitting.
That was only right, and also fun, in assorted ways, for all
concerned.

Then she'd take what she needed. Afterward, she'd wrap
whatever was left in whatever was nearby and handy and
heavy, and nudge it all gently over the side into the sea.

She'd vanish, too, along with her victim, and make sure
that her next victim came from one of the hundreds of
other ferries cruising the waterways between Tacoma and
Vancouver.

It was a good system, or not-system. The best thing
about it, for Sophie, was that it had a sort of rhythm, a
narrative. It had become a story she was living rather than
an endless, circular skein of nights. When the time came
for her to leave the Northwest, as it inevitably would—
when there was no longer a reason to stay—she'd already
decided she would send a sort of accounting to The Stranger,
her favorite regional alternative paper, since this whole
area seemed to love its monsters even more than most
places. Everyone here still talked about the Lady Killer,
and the Green River Killer.

Ha.

In her accounting, when she wrote it, she'd include whatever details she remembered for as many specific victims as she could, hopefully providing an extra bit of closure for any still-mourning survivors.

And she'd give them her new name, which she'd come up with herself. Maybe she'd even sign it across a selfie. An appropriately blurred one, haloed in sea shimmer.

With Love, she'd write, because she had loved them all in her way, and still did. From the Ferry Godmother.

5

Kneeling with her phone to her ear, Kaylene snapped open her guitar case. She checked for spare strings and brushed the black and orange Halloween pom-pom she'd affixed to the top of the tuning pegs. She'd first started clipping baubles there right after she got the instrument, long before she and Rebecca started playing live: ribbons; a shell bracelet Eddie had made her on her last birthday; a cutout cardboard square from a strawberry Twinkie box she'd dangled there in honor of her murdered friend Marlene. When Rebecca saw that one, she'd cried, but she hadn't made Kaylene strip it off.

Once upon a time, not so long ago—before the whistling freak first stepped out of Halfmoon Lake woods—the decorations would have been instantaneous, automatic, the kind of thing she had always done without even thinking. The practice necessary to get *good* on guitar, on the other hand, never mind write songs on it, would have taken more time than she was willing to give any one activity, and demanded far too much single-minded attention.

But these days, practicing music distracted her. Playing it live, in lights, onstage, with Rebecca blasting away on her drums from the shadows, positively *dissolved* her. Decorating her instrument, meanwhile, and tricking it out, had become ritual. Sometimes, Kaylene was convinced she had accidentally transformed her instrument into a fetish, or, as Rebecca preferred to say, *spirit animal*. It had even given them their band name, the night Trudi grudgingly donated one of her threadbare, obsidian-eyed creations from her dresser drawer.

From that moment on, she and Rebecca were officially Sock Puppet. The screaming, slamming strawberry Twinkie-accented scourge of the isles. The scourge you screamed along with. Or to.

Who would have believed it of either of them?

"I know, Mom," Kaylene said into the phone now, because somehow her mom was *still* talking. Standing, she checked her elbow-length black pigtails, yellow-striped shirtdress, and violet knee socks in the closet mirror. She looked like a Heffalump in the midst of a *Winnie-the-Pooh* honeypot dream, without the insta-grow trunk and with harder eyes. "I wish I could explain."

Tonight, though, her mom wouldn't let up, couldn't stop herself. She kept right on talking, talking, blaring her loneliness into Kaylene's life like a searchlight and thereby lighting up Kaylene's own. This was why she hated talking to her mother, these days. If she was being honest with herself, she'd hated talking to her mother ever since Half-moon Lake woods. Just one more good thing the freak in the hat had ripped from her.

"I know you're my family," she heard herself say, automatically, same as she always did. "I know Jess and Joel and Benny and Rebecca and Trudi and Eddie are just . . ."

Fellow survivors, she thought, while her mother pleaded, begged, sighed, and missed her. *Just the people she'd wound up marooned with on an island off the other edge of the country, three thousand miles from her childhood home, which was already six thousand miles from her parents' childhood home.*

"Want to know what I'm eating? *Kaylene,* are you still there?"

Even now, Kaylene instinctively stiffened when her mother cracked that voice. She held her breath, waited, realized her mother wasn't going to let her off that easy. Tonight, she was going to make her ask for it.

"What are you eating?"

"Bao," said her mother. And then she actually did it. Crafty Fox-demon. She took an audible bite, right there on the phone, and made her bao-eating moan.

"Pork and shrimp?" Kaylene whispered.

"Red bean," said her mother through her chewing.

"Bitch," Kaylene said, and she got the tone just right, for once. She knew she had even before her mother laughed.

"I miss you so much, Little Dug."

"I miss you, too, Mom. I really do." She really did, she realized. So much.

"Come home, Kaylene. Soon."

Come see me, she almost said, turning to the window and drawing back the curtain. The problem was that the second she said that, her parents would be on a plane. Both of them. And somehow, the thought of them here, in this secluded compound that only *felt* like a fortress, and only because everyone who lived here needed it so much to feel that way, was ridiculous. Disturbing, even. Just the idea of Laughing Dad on Skis and Mom of Warm Bao and Sunday Crosswords appearing in the rain at the pinewood front door, introducing themselves to Jess, trying to make sense of their daughter's relationship to Eddie and Trudi, coming to a Sock Puppet concert and getting an earful of the racket she and Rebecca had taken to unleashing . . .

Across the grass, in the shadow of the firs and western hemlocks that ringed the compound, Kaylene saw a girl-shaped silhouette glide behind the drawn curtains of the single, upstairs window in the stumpy windmill shed out back where Jess, Benny, and Trudi slept. Since Jess was downstairs helping Benny with dinner, Trudi had to be alone out there again, brooding over her books or her knockoff not-nearly-iPhone, texting whoever the hell she texted. Beyond the windmill shed and the trees, above the cliffs and the Strait, the red in the sky intensified as the sun sank. The glow permeated the trees, turned even the evergreens orange.

"*Kaylene,*" her mother snapped again, startling her. She'd forgotten, again, that she was still in the middle of a call.

"Sorry, Mom. Listen—"

"Dinner," said Rebecca, appearing at the door in her stage blacks, brown hair bound up tight at her neck, her drummer's arms positively ropy in her sleeveless sweater. No trace of gooseflesh, despite the cold. She looked ready, Kaylene thought. Rebecca always looked ready, these days. Like an astronaut prepped to climb into the big suit, head out into the void, and just *fix* something.

Or else she looked like a cage fighter. A larger-than-life (but smaller-than-life-size) gladiator. "A drummer you run from or duck under as much as dance to," as that wanky critic-kid from *The Stranger* had put it in his first review of one of their shows. He kept coming back, though.

He also hadn't been wrong.

Because, really. Who'd have thought the Rebecca Kaylene had known in East Dunham, New Hampshire, could ever hit anything that hard?

"Be right there," Kaylene said, touching the pom-pom at the top of the guitar's tuning pegs. She almost asked Rebecca to come touch it, too.

For luck. As ritual. Wondersurvivor powers . . . activate . . .

Right then, she almost blurted out her little surprise, the one she'd finally decided to spring tonight. Her Halloween addition, which she was almost sure constituted the next great leap in their mutual, ongoing life-reclamation project. She was only slightly less sure that Rebecca would think so, too. And yet, Kaylene knew she should probably say something. Give her friend a trigger warning.

She would have if her mother hadn't squealed, "You will? You mean it? You're coming?"

Flinching, Kaylene scrolled back through the last few seconds of conversation. "Wha . . . No, Mom. Hang on. I was talking to Rebecca."

"Joel claims Benny made squirrel," Rebecca said.

Kaylene rolled her eyes. One corner of Rebecca's mouth curled. The frayed edge of her old smile, the one only Joel, and then—very briefly—Jack had ever dragged all the way out of her, back in their Jack-and-the-'Lenes days. Especially toward the end of those days.

Sweet, grinning Jack.

"A squirrel Joel killed himself. With his fists, and some pine needles."

"So we're having barbecued chicken? Again?"

"I'm going to get Trudi," said Rebecca, and left.

Rebecca always went to get Trudi. She was the only one who could. Kaylene wished that the critic-brat from *The Stranger* could see this little drummer woman, who'd frightened him so badly, do *that*.

"Mom," she said into the phone, glancing once more out the window at the fog forming in midair as the dark deepened. The chill made visible. That was another major difference between the San Juans and New Hampshire, and a major part of what she loved here: when the cold came—and it always came—you could see it. She rushed the words past her lips before her brain could stop her. "How about you and Dad come here for Thanksgiving?"

This time, there was no squeal. Kaylene gave her mom credit for that, for recognizing the moment. They'd both progressed. One more life-reclamation checkpoint passed.

"We might just do that," her mom murmured, so carefully that Kaylene burst out laughing. Her mom laughed, too. Carefully. For the thousandth time, Kaylene opened her mouth to explain, to try to find words for why it was good, better, to live here, for at least a little longer.

All that came out, though, was, "Good. Bye, Mom."

"See you soon, hon," her mother said, still holding in her sob. She didn't even yell for Kaylene's father to get on the line so he could hear the news; she just hung up.

Placing the phone on the windowsill, Kaylene leaned into the glass and was surprised yet again by the damp that seemed to surface in anything she touched here, indoors or out—trees, tabletops, telephone poles, pens—at the second she touched it. As though everything on this island were alert, curled up inside itself, rising to each moment of contact like a cat rubbing its scent on you. Reassuring itself, and you, *We're alive. We're alive, we're alive, we're alive.*

To her parents, Kaylene knew, what had happened in the Halfmoon Lake woods had driven their daughter to the other side of an impenetrable wall, behind an iron curtain of grief and horror and sorrow. They still thought that was why she couldn't talk to them about it.

What they'd missed—what Kaylene couldn't articulate aloud, even now—was that to her, *they* were the ones behind the curtain, cut off from critical information about the world as it actually was.

Either that, or Kaylene had somehow strayed from the path her parents had so carefully laid out for her from the moment she was born. She'd found a magic wardrobe and teleported into fairyland, where whistling monsters in sombreros shredded people like string cheese, and bald eagles and barred owls rode arctic winds into the firs and twisting madrone trees, and killer-whale pods huffed in coves and sea caves, and fog came cold and open-armed. A place where Kaylenes and Rebeccas become regional rock stars. Where survivors and refugees holed up in a hundred-year-old A-frame on a grassy hillside with a windmill in the backyard and became . . . not a family, exactly. Not even a pod.

But a colony, maybe, founded less on love, whether felt or expressed, than shared solitude. Shared meals. A teenager and a toddler to protect and raise. And, yes, a grief and horror so deep and black that it seemed, constantly, to be streaming off one or another of them, or all of them at once, as though they were all brand-new creatures. A freshly evolved species that had just crawled up from the abyss—or out of the woods—onto land, into life.

Which, now that Kaylene thought about it, probably made them more like every other household in the world than she'd thought.

Maybe they were a family after all.

With a last, lingering glance through the glass at the oncoming evening, Kaylene knelt, rummaging behind her shoes and the box of college textbooks she hadn't so much as glanced at since arriving here, and came up, finally, with the rumpled canvas bag she'd shoved back there five years ago, and never once touched since.

What had even made her take this? When and why had she hidden it?

For a few seconds, she stayed on her knees, holding the bag, feeling its barely there weight. The thought of opening it—of actually enacting this particular bit of stagecraft—curled around her windpipe, wormed between her ribs and seized her heart.

Her boldest act of life-reclamation yet. Maybe the last one she or Rebecca would ever need.

It really could be. If she could actually bring herself to do it.

She wanted to call Rebecca up here, try it out with her or at least warn her. She knew she should.

But she couldn't risk her bandmate's reaction. What if Rebecca decided she wasn't ready, or got furious? She'd become so much less predictable behind that gentle, remote Rebecca-face these days.

No. Already, Kaylene felt she'd waited too long. She'd let the monster of Halfmoon Lake steal far too much, from all of them, for far too long.

"Asshole," she whispered.

Carefully, as though unpicking stiches, she curled a finger through the drawstring at the mouth of the bag, tugged it open, and pulled out the Whistler's hat.

6

Halfway across the yard, right at the lip of the advancing shadows of the hemlock trees, Rebecca stopped as she always did and stared past Jess's windmill shed into the forest. She wasn't looking for anything, or at least, she wasn't expecting to see anything. This was simply something she did, now, and would for the rest of her life when confronted with clusters of trees: watch to see if anything stepped from them; listen for whistling.

She heard none and saw no one. But the feeling had her now. It had come almost nightly these past weeks. There was comfort in that feeling, or familiarity, anyway. Automatically, Rebecca attached words to it, the ones she'd somehow learned way back before she'd even come to Halfmoon House and met Amanda. Back in her foster-care days, or more specifically the weeks, usually months, between foster-care days. Between new homes. Days when she was nowhere, or nowhere she was staying. She chanted the words silently now, not even moving her mouth. The orphan's catechism.

Something is starting. Something is ending.

Hands in her pockets, bare arms bristling in the misting damp, she flicked her eyes back and forth from the windmill shed to the house. Jess's windmill. Jess's house. Jess's home, which apparently just unfolded off her back and locked into place around her, no matter where she went or what she lost. Or whom she lost. It was simply part of her. Or, it *was* her. Like a carapace, with room for anyone she'd collected along the way, for as long as they could make themselves stay.

Something is starting. Something is ending.

Upstairs in the shed, drapes twitched. As usual, Trudi—the most orphaned of them all—was still in her room. That seemed only right, or at least as expected. Trudi was a hermit crab, same as Rebecca, rattling around in a shell she'd borrowed. Except Trudi had made herself a second shell out of her room, and she rarely came out by choice except to take the ferry to the mainland for school, or else when it was time for someone to lure or coax or drag her out for dinner.

Someone meaning Rebecca.

Shivering in the grass after a last scan of the trees, Rebecca glanced back toward the house. There, upstairs at *her* window, Kaylene stood in her stripy dress, staring over the forest toward the Strait as she fended off her mother for yet another phone call. For so many reasons—because bandmates, because they'd lived across a hall from each other for five years and shared orcas and otters and Jess's moods and Benny's not-squirrel dinners, most of all because they were the last ones standing—Kaylene had come to mean even more to Rebecca than she had back in East Dunham. She was no longer just Rebecca's friend or even her best friend, but her only peer. Sister. Co-composer. Onstage shrieking partner.

The last 'Lene.

Returning her attention to the windmill, Rebecca caught a glimpse of Trudi, who'd possibly been eyeing Rebecca but was more likely hunched over some new windowsill diorama she'd crafted out of the junk she gathered like a squirrel stocking up for winter.

For the first time in days—briefly, tonight, with its claws retracted—that *other* feeling brushed over Rebecca. The one that had been with her ever since the night of the massacre. She still didn't have words for it, no catechism to direct or dispel it. Suddenly, for whole breaths at a time, she simply *wasn't her.*

Mostly, when this happened, she was Oscar, the UNH-D groundskeeper she'd befriended. He'd been the first of her friends to meet the whistling man and the first to die, before Jack, Marlene, Amanda, and Danni. She'd find herself breathing Oscar's cigarette smoke and missing his daughter, whom she'd never met, never known, and hardly even known about until the last night of his life. The trees around her were no longer Pacific Northwest hemlocks but the black gums that lined Campus Walk at UNH-D. The windows she peered through were no longer Trudi's but those of the basement Crisis Center. Through them she saw herself, that long-ago Rebecca, answering phones. Helping people. Back in the days when she did such things, when she was just an orphan, already a survivor but not so unlike everybody else.

Back before she'd killed anybody.

Memories engulfed her, the way they always did. This tsunami just kept coming, pouring in, driving her back five years to the night that had started with her friends dying and ended with her repeatedly smashing a shovel into another woman's face. *Through* it, probably.

Say her name, Rebecca snapped inside her own head. Then she did say it. Mouthed it, anyway.

Sophie.

The person she'd obliterated.

In fairness, Sophie's face had been inside another face at the time. Inside the face of the asshole in the sombrero who'd murdered her friends. Sophie had, in fact, been eating the monster from underneath, from the back of his skull forward. Also, by her own admission—assertion, actually—Sophie hadn't much qualified as a *person* anymore, anyway, by that point. Not a human one, anyway.

But she'd helped kill the monster, and she'd been a living thing. Someone's daughter. Blond-haired, doe-eyed, with a smile stunning mostly for the way it bloomed on her face and just kept spreading, as though her mouth couldn't get wide enough to let all that laughter out or joy in.

It took several minutes—less than it once had, but not much—for Sophie's smile to subside back into its permanent place on the mantel atop Rebecca's memories. Rebecca would keep it there for the rest of her life. She owed Sophie that much. Whoever and whatever the hell Sophie had been.

"Rebecca!" Benny called out the kitchen window, waving a spatula in one of his white-gristled yeti paws. "Dinner. Get that kid and come on!"

Waving, Rebecca started forward again. She lifted a fist to knock on the windmill door, but only as a courtesy. Even if Trudi heard, and even though she'd know full well who was knocking and why, she wouldn't answer. She'd make Rebecca come get her. It was part of their ritual: Trudi refusing to come; Rebecca acknowledging her right to refuse, then cajoling and teasing her out of her cave, across their little inland sea of grass and into the main house to join the rest of the survivors for dinner.

On impulse, Rebecca stepped back from the door and gazed up again at Trudi's window. Trudi was no longer visible, but Rebecca knew she was in there. From the woods she really did hear whistling, chattering, and shrieking. Just birds. Owls and eagles. Swallows and wrens. A thousand creatures living their lives, while Rebecca moved beneath and beside them.

Same as always. Same as before the Sombrero Man came, even. What had she really lost, anyway?

A could-have-been boyfriend; a not-quite-mom; a not-at-all little sister-orphan she'd never come close to reaching except right at the end; a lonely groundskeeper she'd considered a friend yet barely known and said maybe five hundred words to, total, over the course of three years. A 'Lene.

Stooping, she felt around in the wet grass and came up with two pinecone chips, an acorn, and a single pink pebble or splinter of shell. Plenty.

Stepping back, Rebecca held up one of the acorns, took

aim, and couldn't help noting her own arm. It looked so solid, all of a sudden. A branch to perch on. A club for beating the shit out of unsuspecting drums. She could practically feel her sticks in her fists already, see the skin of her snare dimpling and denting as Kaylene shimmered purple and red at the edge of the spotlight at the front of the stage, strummed hard to make herself heard over Rebecca's clamor, and wailed. Not a single one of those sensations would have been imaginable to East Dunham–Rebecca. Sometimes, playing drums made her feel as though she were stoking a steam engine, propelling the rocketing, shuddering thing that was Sock Puppet. Which was a thing you could hop as it hurtled by, if you dared, but you couldn't stop it. Nothing could stop it.

Trudi should come to the show, Rebecca thought, and not for the first time. Trudi should *join the band*. She could do her sock puppet dance. Pummel a tambourine.

Right as she threw the acorn, whacking it off the windowsill overhead, the door to the main house opened behind her. Rebecca glanced that way just long enough to see Jess looking around the yard, moving slowly in Rebecca's direction. Through the sliding glass door behind her, Rebecca saw Joel setting the table. That was the sort of thing Joel did these days: set tables, fold towels. Instead of play with Eddie or hound Trudi out of her room into the world with some godawful, impromptu song or ridiculous Joel dance. Once—not so long ago, though very far away, in a different life—he had been the person Rebecca trusted most. Her late-night online anagram-Smackdown competitor and Google Chat companion. Her music supplier. Almost her dad.

Now he was no one's dad. Without Amanda to reprimand him, to remind and reassure him of his role in the lives of the children they'd always surrounded themselves with but couldn't have on their own, Joel seemed to be melting into his own shadow. Of the six survivors inhabiting the Stockade (which was the name he'd given to Jess's compound), Joel was the one who'd recovered least. Every sight of him stabbed at her, like those tire shredders at the edges of parking lots.

Do not back up. Severe damage . . .

God, when was the last time she'd played 2 A.M. Smackdown with Joel? Had they tried that even once since coming to this coast? What did he even do *in his basement room, after dark?*

Not sleep, Rebecca was pretty certain.

Shaking her head as if this time that might actually help, Rebecca sorted the debris she'd scavenged and selected the shell fragment. It was hardest and smallest, the most likely to rouse Trudi without breaking her window. Behind and to her left, Jess moved off the patio and closer to the woods, peering into them with an intensity Rebecca didn't even want to acknowledge, let alone explore. And yet, here she was opening her mouth.

"Jess? Are you all right?"

The answer came slow and quiet. Pretend-casual. "Have you seen Eddie?"

"He's out again?"

"Probably down at the cove. I think his okras have come back."

"Then his okras will protect him," Rebecca said, immediately wished she hadn't, and was surprised when Jess glanced her way. She was even more surprised to see Jess smiling.

"His okras," she murmured.

If she'd been nearer, Rebecca would have hugged her. That was something they'd taken to doing, Jess and Rebecca, just sometimes. Like sisters. Like mother and daughter. Almost.

Rebecca let her own smile out, just for a second and too late. Already, Jess had returned to watching the woods. So Rebecca returned to her own task. Cocking her arm, she reared back, was about to let fly when Trudi's window popped open.

"Are you *throwing* shit at me now?" the girl said, glaring, her kinked hair raked and gathered atop her head in that way only Trudi could manage, like a clump of pine needles.

"Rapunzel," Rebecca called. "Rapunzel. Let down your hair."

Trudi snorted. "I don't want to crush you, ant."

"Aunt."

"You're not my aunt."

Rebecca waited for the window to slam shut. When it didn't, she said, "There's squirrel for dinner. Benny said to tell you."

"Benny's squirrel can go fuck itself."

"Watch it," Jess said from across the yard, not loud.

Trudi knew better than to backtalk that. Defiant, terrified, pissed, and lonely she might be. But stupid, never.

"Sock Puppet show tonight," said Rebecca, eyeing Jess briefly. For permission, she realized, which was silly. *Wasn't it?* "You could come, Trud. I'd take you along. You *should* come. We're loud. You'd like it."

Trudi held up her left hand. The yellow sock draped over her fingers was so threadbare that Rebecca could see the girl's skin through it, even from down here.

"I have my own Sock Puppet show *every* night," Trudi said. "And I never even have to leave the room."

Rebecca sighed. "Sometimes I think *I'm* your sock puppet."

"Those are your smart times."

"I think I feel your hand up my butt right now."

"Then why aren't you dancing?" Trudi held up her other hand, waving it back and forth in the air as though trying to drag Rebecca into motion.

Rebecca actually thought about dancing, and also about laughing. In the end, she just said, "Are you coming? Puppet master?"

"In a minute, I guess." She didn't even slam the window when she shut it.

Still gazing down the dirt path that led through the trees and along the cliff toward Eddie's okra cove, Jess moved to Rebecca's side. She'd exchanged her customary dinnertime sweatshirt for a paisley sweater and a long denim skirt that brushed the tips of the wet grass. The skirt was old and faded in patches, and so looked the same changeable blue as the sky on hazy days. She'd let her hair grow long so it spilled down her back, unstyled, lustrous and dark, with barely a hint of gray. The color of this island's earth, Rebecca realized. Jess *belonged* here.

What a sweet, surprising, sustaining thought that was.

Because if there really was a home for Jess, or even the possibility of one, after everything life had savaged her with, then surely, someday . . .

"You're so good with her," Jess murmured, nodding up at Trudi's window. As usual, she made no move to touch Rebecca. Usually, Rebecca felt grateful for that.

Something about hearing Kaylene talking to her mom, and the sight of Joel setting the table, and the realization that Jess had long ago started settling (or sinking) into this landscape pricked at Rebecca. She shook her head. "Meaning, I manage to get her to dinner? Most days?"

Jess's smile was her usual one, faint and faraway. It shed light, but not much warmth. "Baby steps, kiddo." She stopped watching the woods long enough to eye Rebecca up and down. Rebecca had to resist the impulse to spin away, Trudi-style, and burrow for the main house.

"What?" she finally said.

"Nothing."

"Something."

"Your clothes."

"My clothes?"

"They're not you, hon."

Surprised, Rebecca glanced down at her black sleeveless vest-shirt, black pants, black flat-heel boots which were neither ass-kickers nor come-hithers. Boots for pumping bass-drum pedals. "I think they're me. Sock Puppet me."

"I'm talking about the black."

Rebecca waited. To her annoyance, she realized she was holding her breath. When Jess didn't say anything else, she gestured back toward the house, up at Kaylene's window, and with a ferocity that surprised her. "Look at Kaylene.

Look at those stripes. Look at those *tights*. Are you saying that's her? Is that the Kaylene you know? Because the one I was best friends with—"

"She's wearing all that for herself," Jess said, not looking where Rebecca pointed. "What you're wearing is for everyone else. *At* everyone else."

Jess might as well have punched her. It was completely true, of course. Also—worse—it was exactly the kind of observation Crisis Center Rebecca would have made, once upon a time. The kind of observation her friends, and the people who used to call the Center, and poor Danni and Amanda, and pretty much everyone in her life back then had counted on her for. The only gift she'd ever been absolutely sure she had, which was now just another something she'd lost, somewhere.

She met Jess's gaze. As always, those eyes held tears that seemed on the verge of spilling over. Yet, not once, since that last East Dunham night, had Rebecca seen them fall.

The door to the windmill flew open and Trudi stalked into the yard, glaring but just for show. To stay in character.

"Come on, Mom," Rebecca whispered, so quietly that only Jess could have heard.

But Jess didn't hear. She had already moved away across the grass toward the woods, not the house. "I want to find Eddie," she said.

"He's fine," Rebecca called after her. "His okras will watch over him."

"Yeah, well, I want to watch them doing it."

Most times, these days, Jess stopped at the edge of the woods. But not today. Which wasn't like her. Not anymore, anyway. There was nowhere on the island for Eddie to go. Nowhere he *would* go except to the cove or across one of the grassy, rocky expanses of openness, chasing butterflies or collecting stones. There was no one else within a mile of Jess's Stockade, not even any actual buildings until the abandoned, century-old English army barracks and, past those, the overgrown meadows that wound down to the automated lighthouse on the isle's southernmost tip. Eddie had never shown interest in any of those, nor in the town where Benny had his diner and Jess her little donation center and charity shop.

"Don't make me come after *you,* now," said Rebecca.

"Tell everyone I'll be right there," Jess said, and vanished into the hemlocks.

Mist streamed from the trees like smoke Jess had generated while disappearing. Rebecca could smell its saltwater damp, and also Benny's chicken, the leaves dying overhead and underfoot, some far-off island neighbor burning other leaves somewhere. The season changing. Rain coming. She turned to start for the house and bumped face-first into Kaylene.

"Ow," she said. "Hi."

"Ready to go hit something?" Kaylene rubbed her own arms where Rebecca's elbows had bumped them.

"I'm ready to eat."

"No time. Vancouver. Early load-in, remember?"

"Goddamnit."

"That's right. Save that anger. Nurse it."

"Shut up."

"Where's Eddie?"

Rebecca glanced once more toward the trees. Darkness had closed off the spaces between them.

"Maybe we should go find Jess and Eddie," she murmured, and the shiver that perpetually lurked just under her skin got out, swept down her back.

"No time. We've got life to live. Screams to unleash." Grinning, ridiculous in her stripes and tights, Kaylene shrugged the waterproof guitar case strapped to her back, then held up the paper bag packed with whatever else she was bringing tonight.

"What's that?" Rebecca said, but Kaylene had already turned to leave, laughing as she went.

Fifteen minutes later, they were halfway down the hill, walking single file along the white line in the center of the road, the way they always did, to the rhythmic patter of a sudden rain in leaves. Sock Puppet, on the move. As usual, they kept clear of shadows. On either side, the woods rippled in the dark. Behind them, Jess's Stockade had already disappeared behind its hedge. Down below, less than a mile away—so close, and yet, from inside their compound, so remote that they could all imagine it was no longer there, could not be reached, could not reach them—the lights and houses of January Bay scattered over the headland. The town looked pumpkin colored tonight, orange and yellow and red. For Halloween, Rebecca remembered. The day held no specific associations for her. It was just another one of those occasions where children who lived in their own houses went to other people's houses. If she were going to be scared of anything, it would have been woods.

Or else the whole rest of the world, out there beyond the orange and black lights, the taverns and shuttered shell-and-fossil shops and seasonal kayak-rental sheds.

To prove, yet again, that she wasn't, she marched side by side with Kaylene, straight through town to the ferry port where their ferry was already docked, huffing smoke into the evening as it gathered up cars and pedestrians like an octopus combing a coral reef. In silence, with her drumsticks in her hands in her jacket pockets, she joined the rest of the boarding travelers, the homeless and aged and partying college couples, all edging up the plank toward the strange and solitary souls in shapeless rain slickers who seemed always to be on board already, at any time of day or night, hunched on the back benches of the passenger cabin or standing at their separate rails at the ends of decks to watch the rest of them coming.

7

Ironies, Emilia thought, shuddering into the moth-eaten sheet he draped over her whenever he left her down here in the dark. *So many ironies.*

The only place she was absolutely certain no one would ever look for her was in the library from which she'd vanished. That was a good one, for starters. To be fair, she wasn't technically *in* the library anymore, but underneath it, in the bomb shelter she'd never heard mentioned and suspected no one who still worked for the county even remembered was there.

But the Invisible Man remembered, or knew. He'd even known where to pull up the ratty green carpet in the back of the Records and Reference Room to reveal the trap-door, which probably hadn't been opened in decades.

The back of the same room, in other words, where the records of bomb shelter trapdoors were kept, and the history of the county catalogued and almost never read.

"Ironic. See?" she felt herself mouth into the scrupulously sanitized and deodorized blankets her abductor had provided, in the corner of the cement floor he swept clear of spiders and dust bunnies every single time he came back. She was too weak actually to vibrate her vocal cords. But her lips moved, and she was fairly certain word-shaped air still spilled from them.

Soon, he'd be back. Probably. Already, he'd been away a little longer than usual. She'd gotten surprisingly good at tracking passing hours down here, even without clock or light. Like a cat, she was. A feral, Piney Woods swamp cat, waiting for her captor to open the door.

Right from the start, from the moment he'd grabbed her, Emilia had decided to survive. Somehow. So she tracked hours. Counted ironies.

Here was another:

The person the District had installed upstairs as her replacement apparently possessed a sense of thoroughness and efficiency Emilia had never encountered in another Butterfly Weed county employee. He or she had pasted copies of the police department's HAVE YOU SEEN THIS WOMAN? flyer, complete with a faded, years-old, two-tone photo of Emilia, all over the library: not just on the doors to both bathrooms but inside toilet stalls; on cardboard bookstands, set up every few feet, all the way across the top of the circulation desk; in the empty end caps of each empty shelving unit.

Now if only the District could generate one plausible reason for anyone not employed by the county to *come* to this library anymore, someone might actually see those flyers. As it was, the only people Emilia was *cer-*

tain had seen them were Emilia and her abductor. They noted them together upon resurfacing in the Records Room every night, after the lights shut down and the air switched off.

Where had they even gotten that photo? she wondered, fingering the holes in the crooks of her arms, imagining playing herself like a recorder. Forming notes by opening and closing the holes, generating sound that way. She could still remember the fingering from elementary-school music class. D, E, A, C. She hummed inside her head, imagined playing a little Emilia's-arm steel guitar solo over the top of that goofy new Kacey Musgraves song, the sweet and funny one about family being family. The last new Kacey Musgraves Emilia was likely to hear. Unless she got out.

Until she got out, she made herself mouth even if she couldn't quite say it, pressing her back into the wall, playing the holes in her arms.

The police had gotten that picture from her parents. Obviously. If she thought hard enough—if she still had enough blood in her body to sustain memory—she could probably have called up the exact song her father was spinning on his record player at the moment he'd taken the shot, which had to be at least six years old. She knew this because Ursula, her turtle, was still alive, perched like a parrot on her shoulder. Was it the turtle, the music, her parents, or just habit that had once made her smile like that, sidelong and sly, whenever anyone snapped her picture? Apparently, the police had decided her Butterfly Weed ID photo wasn't distinctive enough. That no stranger just happening to glimpse her in some passing car or down some alley somewhere would be able to identify her from it.

Ironies.

Her parents were almost certainly in Butterfly Weed by now, Emilia realized. She wondered how long they'd stay, what they'd think up to do that wasn't already being done. A long time, and a lot, she suspected. They were those sorts of parents, always had been. The thought of them here . . . making nice to the asshole trust-fund Ole Miss dropouts downstairs who managed her building so they could get keys to her pathetic apartment . . . asking around the library and the Save-a-Lot and Hansom's Diner to find friends who might know where she'd gone, and slowly realizing that there weren't any . . .

The sound of her own sigh startled her, and she twitched, made herself somehow wriggle into a sitting position with her shoulders against the wall. Her voice was still in there, somewhere.

Thinking about her parents hurt. Even thinking about *Ursula* hurt. Not as much as the holes in her arms where the Invisible Man slurped at her every night, leaning across her lap and making little gulping noises like a five-year-old guzzling from a water fountain.

But it still hurt.

To distract herself, she curated and collated more ironies. In the weeks she'd been down here, she'd collected dozens more.

Ever since she'd taken this job, for example, she'd fretted over the emptiness creeping kudzu-like through the Butterfly Weed branch, the town itself, and by extension her own life, only to find herself somewhere even emptier.

Then there was the fact that she'd spent the better part of the last year—months and months, ever since he'd first appeared—trying to trick the Invisible Man into turning in her direction, looking her in the eye, and saying something. And now, she couldn't shut him up. All it had taken, in the end, was a single, exhausted, "What on earth happened to you," which had come out of her mouth sounding so much more gentle than she'd intended, simply because she didn't have enough air or fluid left after his feeding to expel anything but words.

Ever since, once he'd taken his nightly nibble, he just opened his mouth and rambled on and on and on. As though he were a vein *she'd* opened.

And the stories he told . . .

There was another irony, come to think of it. Perhaps the driving force behind her decision to become a librarian in the first place had been her love of Storybooktimes. How dearly had she loved her own, which had come complete with opening and closing theme music courtesy of her father and his magical, constantly detuning guitar? How often, in the midst of reading to the kids here, had she wished she could still have Storybooktime, too, find a lover or friend or surrogate dad to read or recite to her once a week, or every night, to help her sleep?

Well, now she'd found someone. And he had so many stories, all of them connecting to each other without beginnings or endings, that they seemed to stretch across her life like a freight train that would never finish its traverse.

That thought brought her to perhaps the worst irony she'd noted so far: if she ever did find a way out—*when* she did—she would miss the Invisible Man's stories. Because those stories . . . snow falling in sugarcane fields, children playing hide-and-seek there, and what they found in those fields on the night after the boat parade . . . and that other night, on the riverboat this time, amid screaming and shooting stars, when the Invisible Man first met his Sally, or Aunt Sally, or whoever she was . . . and what happened to them after . . . and dancing with his mother (or someone named Mother?) on the porch of the Pine Palace in Grace Holler, which apparently had been a real place . . . Emilia had always assumed it was made up, just a line in a song . . . and the lemon cake served on the sheets of men who'd come into the forest on horseback for a lynching, and found Aunt Sally's camp . . . and the months-long walks down the Mississippi toward its mouth with just a few companions, and sometimes none at all, only the Invisible Man and his Sally amid owls and bats and seabirds, with the offshore oil rigs rumbling and clanking in the roiling Gulf in the aftermath of a hurricane . . .

Mississippi had always seemed such a brutal, wild, wondrous place to Emilia. It turned out to be much wilder and more brutal than she had dreamed. Than anyone she knew had dreamed. As wild as the Colombia of her parents' childhood.

She'd been sagging down the wall, but now, using mostly her feet, Emilia pushed herself back upright. Even that slow-motion lurch made her nauseous, set her starved veins twitching like cello strings loosened on their pegs. Once she was sure she wasn't going to vomit, she took a deep breath, held it, went still, and listened. She wanted to be sure she'd heard correctly. Always, it seemed better to know he was here. That he was coming.

He was.

It had taken her a long time to learn how to hear him. The stairs out there, that led up through the trapdoor and back to the world, were concrete, free of creaks, and sheathed in dust, and the Invisible Man stepped so lightly. More lightly than a cat. It was almost as if he had no mass. As if he weren't really there.

"Close your eyes," he called softly, as he always did, so he wouldn't blind her when he pushed the door open.

Emilia slitted her eyes instead, so she could watch him come. He had his flashlight tucked under his arm, aimed upward, so that his bandaged head glowed like flame atop a candle. Outside-smells wafted off him, redolent and marvelous in this odorless room: burning-leaves smoke, wet earth, cigarettes (not his; he didn't smoke). With his free hand, he offered Emilia a white paper bag, and when she smelled that, her eyes welled, and she almost fainted.

"Catfish tacos," he purred, and smiled. "From that place you like."

From the Strawberry Side? She'd told him about the Strawberry Side?

And he'd listened?

How funny, she thought, as her trembling hands shivered awake, rose off her lap to flit to the mouth of the bag. She could remember so many of the stories the Invisible Man told her, but she barely recalled doing any speaking of her own.

Somehow, despite her nausea and sweating, there was

tortilla in her mouth, sweet and fleshy fish falling apart in her teeth, on her tongue, as tears spilled from her eyes and vinegar-cabbage tumbled down her sweater into her lap like confetti.

"Thank you," she heard herself saying, in her scratchy new not-Emilia voice. She hadn't meant to say that, hated that she had. But the fish taco had triggered gratitude, the same way it had conjured saliva out of the dry walls of her cheeks and throat. So, she had to admit, did the Invisible Man's manner, which somehow suggested courtship, the antebellum kind she'd only read about in books from half a century ago. Books that had lured her father to the American South.

"Shh," he said, and edged a straw between her lips. A bendy one, no less. Sprite shot up into her before she'd even closed her mouth around the plastic, like fluid from an upside-down IV, something over which she had no control whatsoever.

He waited until she was done eating, until the greasy paper wrapping fell from her fingers like a husk and the straw bounced along the bottom of the Sprite cup. Gently, he eased the cup from her hands, touched her face, let the flashlight catch in his eyes so she could see them. Sighing, crying without any tears—there wasn't enough Sprite in the world, she thought, to get her producing those again— Emilia slumped back against the wall, and her elbow fell open in her lap.

Like a bird at a fountain, he seemed to twitch, glancing around the empty room as though checking for predators. Then his head dove down, and his mouth was on her. In her. She felt herself gushing out of herself. Thought, hazily, that she had it wrong. *She* was in *him*. Her blood disappearing into his veins. She wondered if he ever considered using a bendy straw, sometime, just to change things up. With her eyes closed, she leaned into the wall and listened to him suck.

It didn't take long, never did. As usual, he came up chattering.

"You should have seen it," he said, wiping his lips with her fish taco napkin, spreading more of her across his mouth. He smiled through the bandages, again reminding her more of a suitor than a monster. "The woods where I found her. That's the kind of place one *would* find someone like her, don't you think? Of course, at the time, I didn't think anything like that. None of us did, because we didn't know she was someone like her, or even that there *were* someones like her. Sally *still* doesn't know, how could she? None of us would even have dreamed, not even the girl herself. That's why Sally did what she did at the last party, at our camp. Do you see? The circus, and the fire? It all makes sense. She thought she understood. But as usual"—and here he looked up, and his smile came slow, shy, and prideful—"only I do. Now. And oh, when I tell her . . ."

He was on his feet by this point, the flashlight on the floor, his hands steepled beneath his chin as he paced. He really did seem to glide on his own shadow, his posture perfect but his head bent. At one and the same time, he looked like a figure skater and a recently grounded teenager working through an excuse or apology. "When she understands, too . . . when I explain, and when she sees what I actually brought her, what I've done for her . . .

and what we have, now . . . what our responsibility is, to the child, above all . . ."

Emilia was as surprised as the Invisible Man when she burst out laughing.

He whirled, and she flinched, cowering deeper into her corner, shivering beneath his gaze like a cotton stalk in a late-summer wind, watching pieces of herself detaching, floating away. All he said was, "I know. Right?"

That made her laugh harder. The phrase sounded ridiculous in his bandaged, cultured, Faulknerian gentleman's mouth. He'd have sounded more natural wailing a *cumbia*.

She laughed so hard that actual wetness spilled down her cheeks. Sprite-flavored, no doubt, since she couldn't imagine she had enough of her own fluids left to spill.

What stopped her laughter, finally, was the tilt to the Invisible Man's head, the sudden lifting of his eyes. She could feel his gaze penetrate her pupils, twisting and setting like a hook in the softest place in her brain. She stopped shivering, except for occasional, volition-less twitches, like a fish yanked from a river and hoisted in the air.

"I've never actually tried this, you know," he murmured. His cadence was his own, now, buttery as Gulf Coast moonlight, old as the Delta. "Nightly little tastes, instead of occasional feasting. It feels so much more . . . civilized. Humane, too, don't you think? For me, of course, I'm not so insensitive as to imply . . . I mean, I don't know how it feels to you. Or what it's doing to you. Can you tell?" He cocked his head, now, studied her face.

"Tell?" she managed. She wasn't sure what either one

of them was asking, or whether this even qualified as sentient conversation.

"Are you different, do you think?" he asked.

As in, less liquid? Entirely drained of hope? Closer to dead?

That was the moment she grasped the richest, most appalling irony of all. The curse of her name, bestowed at birth by her father, had come true after all, but in reverse. Apparently, in the Restrepo version of the story, the corpse turned out to be the one walking around chattering. Emily was the motionless thing on the bed. Or, in her case, mattress pad.

"I don't know," she finally said, because the new laugh building in her throat wasn't one she dared—or could bear—to unleash.

The Invisible Man nodded thoughtfully, touched her cheek, and smiled again. "I understand. If it helps, I don't know, either. We're going to find out together. Isn't it exciting?"

Then, abruptly, he was pulling her to her feet and dragging her out of the shelter, up the cement stairs. Emilia kept tripping, not quite getting her feet over the lip of the next step, but he yanked her along anyway. At the mouth of the trapdoor, she had to control an urge to lunge through the opening, though not to escape; even the thought seemed ridiculous. She knew he'd taken something essential from her, or drooled something into her, because she didn't even *want* to escape, anymore. She just wanted to clutch carpet in her fingers, cling to the top of the ground. What her captor had really done to her, she realized, was bury her alive. Render her invisible.

The Invisible Man dropped her on the floor in a heap. Moving to the table next to the microfiche viewer, he started gathering folders and papers. He showed no concern whatsoever about whether she might scramble to her feet or crawl to a computer terminal and alert someone, somehow. He didn't even glance her way.

Madre de Dios, *was she* jealous? *Because he was paying more attention to his papers?*

Eventually, he sagged into a chair. When he finally did return his attention to her, he was no longer smiling. His bandaged hands quivered atop the pile of folders, but not with excitement. In their paleness, in the slivers of light from the computers, they reminded Emilia of the wings of a smacked moth. Tiny, desperate things. His gaze slid into hers again, but instead of hooking or smothering her, it just settled in her skull this time, seemed to curl into that soft place like a cat.

"Five years," he whispered, and his beautiful voice rippled in the air, swirled the dust motes. "I have so much to tell her. But I'll never find her again. In the end, all of this . . ." He tapped the stack of folders, gestured at the machines and reference volumes. "This was easy. Because it had all already happened, do you see? The pieces were all there. I just had to find them, recognize them, figure out whether they fit. And now I have, and they do. And I can't tell her, because I don't know where she is. She doesn't even know I'm . . ."

Actual sound drained from his voice, though he went on speaking, his lips still glistening with whatever he'd sucked from her tonight. Eventually, his eyes slid away, too, toward the floor, and his bandaged head sagged into his hands. Her Invisible Man. She was on her knees, then her feet, before she realized what she meant to do.

Weaving on weakened legs, she settled before the nearest computer and poked it awake.

Why was she doing this? Not because she wanted to. Not quite.

He wasn't even watching, was too busy muttering into his lap, tapping his stack of file folders as though they were telegraph keys. It would have been so easy for Emilia to call up her Gmail, snap off a tweet. Check in on Facebook or Google locator. Surely, that alone would have alerted someone. Eventually.

Yet she didn't.

Because she couldn't.

Because her hands were his. The impulses directing them were hers, but directed now by other impulses atop them. She could feel them in her head and under her skin, now that she knew they were there, warm like the Invisible Man's mouth never was, gentler even than his voice. Like her father's hands curling her finger around the trigger of the pistol he'd taught her to shoot when she was ten, or the handle of the ax he'd taught her to chop firewood with, more because that's what characters in American novels did than because their cabin was cold. Decades ago, in another life. When she was another person, a dusky-skinned Mississippi girl who'd been christened Emilia after a malevolent story by Colombian parents who loved her.

Maybe this is *me,* she thought dully, watching her fingers trigger keys, her browser accessing databases the Invisible Man wouldn't even know about, so how could he be directing her to them? Despite his clearly formidable research and organizational skills, the Invisible Man would have never have thought to check where she was checking. He had never asked her to connect the bits she was connecting, which she'd scavenged from all the stories he'd serenaded her with over these past weeks as he slowly, slowly killed her. The "parties" by the river with his Sally, the massacres at Grace Holler, the whistling young fool in the hat who'd fled for the North with his Mother, or someone named Mother. He'd never seen or even looked for the trail there would have to be, wherever these creatures went, once anyone stepped back far enough and realized what they were looking at.

And now, just like that . . . there it was.

There she is, Emilia thought. It could have been any of them, she supposed. Assuming there were more of them, although somehow, she hadn't gotten the impression there were.

But this was the one. Her trail. She was sure of it.

She stared at the screen a little longer, skimming once more through the headlines she'd collected, the snippets of story no one else apparently realized was unfolding. The most recent one, from just a couple days ago, recounted the discovery of a half-decapitated, exsanguinated corpse in a pasture, way out on the Wyoming plains, being nibbled by sheep. The incident was being investigated as a hate crime.

It wasn't, she knew. It was worse.

Or was that better, *because at least there was no hate in it? As far as she'd gleaned, there was no feeling involved whatsoever.*

With a smile that didn't feel like hers, and communicated absolutely nothing she actually felt, Emilia turned the screen to her captor. The motion surprised him, and he jerked up his head. He stared at her, then the computer, her again, before bolting to his feet. He loomed over her with his bandaged hands in the air in the greenish, gloomy Records and Reference light, which made him look like a giant rabbit. His mouth remained satisfyingly agape.

Emilia felt herself smile. "This her?" she said.

Fifteen minutes later, as he hustled her out of the library and into the open air for the first time in weeks, the Invisible Man was still atremble, practically bursting from his bandages like a butterfly from its pupa as he muttered and planned and scurried ahead. He did retain enough focus to order Emilia to turn off her monitor as they left.

But not enough to check whether she'd turned off the computer itself. Which she hadn't. Just in case the next user—if there was one—actually turned on this machine before the library closed down for good, actually looked at what was on the screen before x-ing out of it, and somehow recognized her little breadcrumb trail—or, single breadcrumb—for what it was.

Afterward, Rebecca would never shake the idea that Kaylene had caused it all. That she'd gotten careless, let Jess's Stockade and the San Juan Island mists lull her into believing she was safe or invisible, and so uncovered a little too much of her light. And her light had lured the world back to them, and restarted everything.

Of course, that was ridiculous, and Rebecca knew it even at the time. Down deep, she knew the world had always been coming, is always coming. And nothing ends until everything does.

But until that moment, savaging her drums on that garishly green dive-club stage, she'd let them both pretend they'd forgotten. She'd stopped admitting having the dreams, even to Kaylene. She'd never mentioned the three separate instances during the past two years, all on late-night, rain-swept ferry crossings, when the water churned in the wake of their slow passage and the misty, landless night seemed to suspend them in the Strait, when she'd glanced up from the rail or the cabin bench where she'd huddled and saw . . .

Thought she saw . . .

What?

A ghost. A hint of wet, blond hair under a hood. A glimpse of a pale, too-wide face, smiling, wreathed in fog, as though hiding behind a curtain. The face she'd smashed to pieces. The one inside the other face she'd smashed to pieces. The face of the woman who'd warned them about monsters, saved them from monsters, and was one.

But she wasn't here. She could not be here, even if she'd survived. Which she couldn't have. Not through the hailstorm Rebecca had unleashed, the back of the shovel slamming down, down, *through*, smashing and splinter- ing. Mashing and pulping.

Even if Sophie had survived that, how could she possi- bly have found them? Why would she want to?

She couldn't be here. Rebecca knew that. And so she'd decided that imagining her presence, or worse, admitting those imaginings, *naming* what she'd imagined, could only give the ghost power. Saying aloud what she thought she'd seen would poison what Jess had so miraculously salvaged. What she'd rebuilt and reclaimed. What they all had. No one in Jess's compound had ever made a rule about not men- tioning monsters. But that was only because none of them imagined it necessary. Because they all understood.

The Stockade was a Monster-Free Zone. More, actually. It was a zone where monsters had never actually been, or even existed. Joel, Jess, Eddie, Benny, they all instinctively clung to that.

Kaylene, too. Maybe Kaylene most of all. She'd done battered-women's shelter work, after all. Gotten training. Kaylene, more than any of them, knew the role of sanctuary space in recovery.

That was why, at the moment it happened, Rebecca was probably thinking less about Halfmoon Lake woods, or Halfmoon House, or the friends and loved ones she'd lost there, or the creatures she'd killed there, than at any other moment, waking or sleeping, in the five years since.

They were, mid-show and mid-song at the Caiman Club, way down at the still-ragged edge of the Drive, with the Vancouver rain they could no longer hear battering the roof overhead, and the green and gold Caiman Club lights strobing and spattering the stage. Rebecca had her sticks whirling and pummeling *(not like her killing shovel, or just like that shovel, but she wasn't thinking that),* her mouth streaming words Kaylene was shrieking up front in the dry-ice whirl. She was watching the stripes on Kaylene's dress suck light into themselves, watching Kaylene's tights pumping like pistons as she caught Rebecca's rhythm and stomped it down into the stage and through the crowd. There really was a crowd when Sock Puppet played, now, so many wild-eyed teens and Simon Fraser girls and Hewlett-Packard office escapees still in their office wear, almost all of them shrieking along. Some even knew the words, and every single one of them rattled and shuddered and smacked into gobs of light that broke over their faces like eggs, colored them caiman-skinned, remade them new and strong and wild. Like sock puppets Rebecca and Kaylene had knitted out of nothing, out of notes and air, and shaken to life. Like a whole new species, mostly but not entirely female, fierce and armored and numerous enough to be safe, savage and joyful enough to be free.

Kaylene had brought her bag onstage, but Rebecca hadn't asked what was in it. She just kept working her arms, driving the drums, herding the beat harder and faster ahead of her. She was hunched low on her stool to ride it harder, still, and when Kaylene spun momentarily out of the lights, the lights followed, chasing, but couldn't catch her. Rebecca laughed, delivered another cannonade on her snare, shout-sang and laughed as her best friend—the last one she had, the one who'd made it, and with whom she'd made *all of this*—dropped to her knees.

In slow motion, it seemed—in jerky, flipbook lurches through the strobing smoke—Kaylene slashed down at the strings on her guitar, freed a buzzcloud of a chord, and fumbled at the mouth of the bag. The bag fell away, spun off on a current of air, and Kaylene rose, her hands rising with her, unfolding as they came, reshaping. Resurrecting.

The thing in her hands rose on its own. Seemed to. Like a winged thing. It flew up over Kaylene's head, darting and bobbing through the shafts of light, and settled in her hair. Grabbed hold there.

The Whistler's hat.

Before Kaylene had even straightened her guitar on her shoulders, Rebecca was off her stool, off the ground, sailing through and over her drums, light streaming from her skin and screams from her throat as her hands rose to meet it.

9

nother day gone, or at least, Aunt Sally assumed it had gone. This had been an unusual one, because apparently she'd slept. Not just dozed off, but conked out. Why? she wondered, twisting deeper into the scratchy motel sheets, trying and failing, as always, to find a warm spot. A spot warm enough.

Because Ju knew, now? Because Ju had seen? But what did Ju know, and what had she seen? And why that silvery laugh, wild as wind? You think I don't know? *That's what she'd said.*

Cryptic little witch-girl. Orphan thing, as alone in the world as poor Sally herself.

My witch-girl, *Sally thought, and shivered. Actually shivered. In pleasure. In alarm. Or because she was cold.*

"Shhh," she heard, as though on wind from far away. "Don't!" Then came that laugh, so bright Aunt Sally could literally feel it on her skin like a sunrise. Like she

96

imagined a sunrise feeling. Maybe even remembered one feeling. What she remembered next surprised her: the bloom of fire from the circus tent, on her very last Delta summer night, when she'd said good-bye to her monsters and lit out, at last, into the world, with Ju. A girl she hadn't Made but wanted to be with every waking second, more than she had ever wanted anything in her long, blood-river blur of a life. Just so she could bathe in the shimmer of her laughter.

What a night that had been! Those first hours gazing at Ju, feeling Ju gaze back, in ways she shouldn't have dared or been able to. The sunspot eruptions of the fires Sally had set. The screaming, disintegrating souls of her monsters like a penumbra around and over the camp, over the river, distorting the night. Transforming it. Transforming her.

That had been a sort of dawn, hadn't it? As near to a sunrise as Aunt Sally was ever likely to experience, and maybe more like a genuine awakening than any other creature on this planet had actually experienced.

Yes.

"A hundred Jus between teeth," she heard now, that singing whisper floating through this grungy, terrible room, this hole in the Wyoming wind, just the latest terrible room of the last five years, complete with burred sheets and heavy blanket-coverings that weren't ever heavy enough. They lay atop her in the dark like the broken-down sides of cardboard boxes, made her feel cheap and lonely, neither aunt nor queen nor even companion, just a wandering thing. A hobo.

Or rather, that's how she would have felt without Ju shimmering beside her.

"I'll bring some booooyyys in," Ju whisper-sang, sang-laughed. Even Aunt Sally recognized the misquotes, now, the lyrics Ju loved to tease apart like a cat shredding yarn. "Some skin paraded like the moon."

Shivering with the cold she never could escape, Aunt Sally smiled.

Then she bolted upright in the bed, eyes everywhere. She took in the dresser, with Ju's emerald-green hairbrush and iPod and rainbow scrunchies and one sock scattered across it; the puffy purple coat flung over the back of the chair, because the girl was genetically incapable of putting anything away (because, in fairness, nowhere and no place was hers, or ever had been, and they were never staying); the other bed, so unrumpled it could have passed for un-slept in, except for the corner of sheet Ju always peeled back as she slipped from it, leaving no imprint, just a purposeful trace, so anyone who happened by would know a ghost-girl had lain there once.

But wasn't lying there now.

Was no longer in this room.

Panic—Aunt Sally recognized it, though it was still a new sensation for her, or so old she'd forgotten she could feel it—flared in her guts. Flinging back her own covers, she swung her feet off the bed, grabbing for the coat she always laid neatly across the bottom, a trick for snatching warmth that Caribou had taught her back in their Delta camp. Because she'd actually slept, today, she had no sense whatsoever of what time it might be. The slit of white-yellow all the way around the edge of the grimy green curtains could have emanated from streetlights or cloud-shrouded sun. The humming wind outside the door gave no clue; that wind hummed day or night, here. The ceiling and walls around her ticked and tapped. Maybe it was raining. Maybe those sounds were paint flaking, the room falling apart.

She glanced toward the digital clock, forgetting she'd unplugged it; the red blare of the numbers got under her eyelids, kept her awake, stirred the bottomless pool of Aunt Sally's thoughts in ways sunlight through tent wall never had, back when she'd slept (or not slept) alone in her tent on the Delta. When Caribou was always a command away, and never, ever left her, except when she ordered him to.

Where the hell was—

"Even coma toes," came Ju's whispered singsong, tinting the air. "They won't dance and tell."

Then her laughter, a barked donkey bray.

From where?

To Aunt Sally, surfacing fully inside her own skull felt like clawing up out of a grave. Was this really how not-monsters slept, every single night? What hard work it was resisting the pull of the void, getting all the way awake. No wonder they always seemed so tired.

In the bathroom, she finally understood. Ju was in the bathroom.

With someone else. The laughter had been someone else's.

The second she thought that—as though to confirm the conclusion—the other person brayed again, more quietly. As though he were laughing through a hand.

Swaying by the bed, Aunt Sally marveled at the strangeness of it all. The nerve *of it all. That girl had actually slipped out, while Sally slept? Had brought someone back?*

Had Ju done that before?

Aunt Sally launched herself toward the bathroom door. In her mouth was a metallic taste, sticky and sharp, and her cheeks prickled as though she'd been slapped. Unless she was smiling? Oh, yes, she was smiling. Because she was angry? Because she was laughing? How did one tell? She had her hand on the door to throw it open, but didn't. Instead, she eased it silently back, just enough so she could see.

The boy—some ranch-tanned, ropy thing with yellow hair and delicious eyelashes, in a navy shirt with a flaming skateboard emblazoned across the chest—was in the bathtub, one blue-jeaned leg flung over the side. His eyes were wide and his smile wider as he watched Ju dance, lean and tilt in front of him. Her hair poured loose down her back. Under her skirt, her bare legs looked so long, all of a sudden, so thin. White as new teeth. Her movements were ridiculous, all wavy-armed and poky-hipped, except they were Ju's movements, and therefore mesmerizing. Each wiggle seemed instinctive and specific to this creature, inimitable as the shivering of leaves on a particular tree.

"We're in each other's teens," Ju sang, mangling the line, charging it, so that it sparked as it left her mouth. "We're on each other's teens." Then she leaned over the tub, over the boy, whose eyes seemed to be peeling themselves to get wider before giving up and falling closed. She settled over him. Aunt Sally felt the moment their lips met, that thousand-tipped tremor of nerves awakening, startling, surging toward sensation like blooms toward sunlight. Ju was still singing, straight into her boy's open mouth.

Aunt Sally supposed she should be angry. She thought it might be her job to announce herself, now, put a stop to this, though she wasn't sure why, exactly. She didn't actually move until Ju gasped and stopped singing—though not kissing—as the boy rose off the fiberglass, closing his arms around the girl's back. At first Aunt Sally couldn't make sense of the sight, but then their faces turned slightly and she got a better look at their lips. The redness bubbling out of the corner of the kiss, across Ju's cheek.

Where he'd bitten her?

Aunt Sally was on them so fast, even she never felt herself move, was simply there. Ju half lifted and half scrambled backward with her skirt flying up around her hips like the bell of a fleeing jellyfish and her hair flailing in the air like tentacles. The boy never even made it up on his elbows. The sight of Sally slammed him back against the fiberglass even before her hands engulfed his thin, teenagey shoulders. Of course, he understood more quickly than Ju just how much trouble he was in.

"I . . ." *he started, and that was all she let him manage.*

"Never speak," *she hissed, staring down.*

"Aunt Sally," *Ju murmured, neither singing nor laughing, now. At least the girl still knew when to stop testing.*

"In a minute. Quiet."

In the tub, the boy stirred, tried to, and Aunt Sally flattened him with a glance. She let one hand slide off his shoulders, slip down the open buttons of his shirt onto his chest, which was so warm, flat and hard as a pebble baked by the sun. Smoothed by that relentless wind.

"Just what do you think you're doing?" *Aunt Sally murmured, to the kid and to Ju behind her. Letting herself enjoy herself, momentarily. What an addicting sensation enjoyment turned out to be, even at her age.*

"Get off him," said Ju.

Aunt Sally straightened, let the kid drop, and stood still for a second. Just to make certain she'd heard correctly. Then she turned.

Ju stood with her back against the wall, her fingers at her reddened mouth. If she'd sounded snottier or angrier—any of those things Aunt Sally had somehow learned that girls Ju's age generally sounded—Aunt Sally might have slapped her. Or maybe laughed, and pulled Ju to her.

Instead, Aunt Sally stood and swayed, barefoot and uncertain in this drafty, urine-saturated bathroom. She felt suspended between the girl she'd claimed and raised—partway raised, at least, and shared life with, kept company—and her girl's crush. Conquest. (Victim? she thought, then dismissed that thought.) The feeling spilling through her wasn't new; it was, in fact, the oldest feeling Aunt Sally remembered, quite possibly her first one. But she hadn't experienced it in at least a hundred years, and it took her a moment to recognize it:

This was terror. Plain and simple. Now, after all this time.

And the cause, she realized, was that more than anything, just now, Ju had sounded bored.

"Honey," she finally started, and Ju laughed. Her silver-shimmer laugh, sizzling down Aunt Sally's veins like electrical current, burning like sunlight but cold as the moon.

Mercifully, the laughter stopped. The girl rubbed hard at her mouth, seemed to shudder as though she were the one electrified. "I'm sorry, Aunt Sally."

That was all it took. Instantly, Aunt Sally was beside her, reaching a hand toward Ju's hair, her face, not know-

ing, as usual, where to touch. "You don't have to be sorry. You just surprised—"

"Uggh." *The girl leaned away, almost slammed herself back against the doorframe.* "Could I just get one hour— how about ten minutes?—of actual privacy? What do you think of that?"

Aunt Sally felt herself sway again. "What do I . . . ? Why—"

"Ten minutes. Just so I can get an idea of what it's like to be alone? I hear some people like it." *Suddenly Ju had tears in her eyes. They shimmered, like the rest of her.*

Beautiful fairy-girl. For the millionth time, Aunt Sally wanted to grab her, cup the girl's chin in her hands, touch that light. Tonight, the shimmer glowed even more fiercely than usual, turned the girl positively wavy right there in the doorframe.

Unless it was her own tears, doing that? Was Aunt Sally actually crying? Was that a thing that could happen?

"Oh, baby," *she finally said.* "You don't need privacy to be alone. I can tell you everything you'll ever need to know about what being alone is like."

Except—and the question jolted Aunt Sally so hard, she actually grabbed the edge of the rust-riddled sink to hold herself steady—could she? Because when, really, in all her endless eons of nights-as-days, had Aunt Sally ever been alone? Certainly not in the tarpaper cabin where she'd been born. Not in the slave-child bunkhouse where she'd been raped the first five or eight times. Not in the years after her . . . awakening . . . however that had happened, when she'd whirled like a hurricane through the South, collecting and dispatching and, just occasionally and accidentally, creating *companions. Lovers and listeners. Sycophants and slaves of her own. Not during the decades in the Delta, either, when she'd had Mother and Caribou and all their monsters.*

No. *Not until she'd met Ju—become a sort of mother, at last, the only role she could think of that she hadn't yet played—had Aunt Sally ever been alone. Felt alone.*

"We're living ruuu-ins," *Ju sang, the words emerging new, transformed, from her mouth.* "In palaces we've dreamed."

"And you know," *Aunt Sally answered—sang!* She was actually *singing!—while Ju touched her tongue to her bloody lip, blinked through the tears in the corners of her eyes.* "We're each other's—"

Ju's laugh silenced her. It sparkled cold between them like frozen breath. "Just stop, Aunt Sally," *she said.* "Don't ..." *She turned away, straightening her skirt on her little bird-hips as she walked into the blackness of the bedroom.*

Dimly, Aunt Sally felt the boy stir behind her, rising out of the tub. She was aware she'd left him alone too long. But Ju's laughter echoed in her head, seemed to attach to corners in her brain like spiderwebbing and wrap up her thoughts. All she seemed able to do was watch the girl move to her bed, switch on a light, grab her latest stolen phone off the nightstand and start perusing. If she even remembered that she'd brought a boy to this room while Aunt Sally slept, she gave no sign.

Aunt Sally felt the boy's footsteps behind her, now, silent as he could make them, which of course wasn't anywhere near silent enough. She could have turned on him at any moment, halted him without so much as lifting a finger. But she didn't seem to be doing that. She seemed, instead, to be letting him creep closer. Right up behind. If he had a knife or some other sharp thing, he could actually annoy, even hurt her. And she seemed to be allowing an opening for that. Waiting to see what he'd do.

To see who he was. What sort of boy Ju brought home.

Not a boy inclined to stab her, apparently. And smart enough to plaster himself against the door as he edged past, and to keep his head down. He really was just a boy, it turned out. A coltish, hay-colored thing, sand-skinned and bright-maned. Sticking out all over himself, too, of course, because even if he was trying not to look, he was in Aunt Sally's presence, after all. Close enough to touch, if he'd dared, or she'd invited him to.

Unless it was being near Ju that had done that to him?

He hadn't buttoned his fly or his flannel shirt, and he just kept shuffling determinedly toward the door, the world out there, the wind still whistling from nowhere to nowhere, relentless as Aunt Sally's Mississippi had always seemed but so much emptier.

By the time she spoke, she'd half forgotten the kid was even in the room. "Ju. Tell me what you like about this one."

The boy jerked to a standstill, trapped between Aunt Sally and the bed, as though he'd been lassoed.

Ju glanced up from whatever she'd been reading or looking at, swiped to the next page or contact list or whatever, swiped again, and only then bothered to look up. The second she did, Aunt Sally felt the challenge radiating from her. The . . . not quite defiance . . . not yet, but . . .

"Who?" Ju murmured. "Oh. Him?"

It was the tone as much as the words that infuriated

Aunt Sally and alarmed her still more. Leveling her gaze, she bore down, burrowing into and through Ju's eyes as though directing a table saw. With satisfaction, she saw the girl flinch and tear up again. And then, with admiration—and also something much deeper, richer, and more hurtful—she watched Ju straighten again. The girl even tried lifting the phone to block Aunt Sally's glare before dropping it back to her lap.

What had the girl said the other day, back in that alley outside the coffee shop in Laramie? You think I don't know?

"Urrrgg," Ju burst out, startling Aunt Sally and breaking her hold. "See?" And then, "Oh, okay, right, that's right. Do the eyes, now. Here it comes. Do the hurt *Aunt Sally look."*

The fact that Aunt Sally had no idea what Ju was talking about made her want to throw her arms in the air, or dance for joy. She couldn't have explained any of that, even to herself.

"Come on, Aunt Sally. Give me the lecture. You tuck me in, you get my meals, I'm your fairy girl. All you ask is that you get to watch me walk, eat, sing, and sleep, every single second of my life. Go ahead. Say you love me again."

I say that? Aunt Sally couldn't remember saying that, and then she did. She had *said it. Only once or twice, both recently, but yes. At least twice. Surely that meant she actually did . . .*

"The truth is, though, Aunt Sally," Ju said, slipping under the blankets and pulling them up toward her throat. For protection, maybe, or to make herself vanish. "Really, you just want to be me."

And that, at last, was what did it. Throwing back her

head, Aunt Sally erupted into laughter. Never in her life had she laughed like this. The sound, the feeling swelled in a giant bubble from her guts, splitting her ribs, expanding her until she thought she might burst from happiness or amusement. Possibly, other creatures—the ones she preyed on, the ones that dreamed, that walked in daylight—knew the difference between those things. Aunt Sally neither knew nor cared. She just laughed while the girl stared and the boy shuddered between them like a wedged log in a whirling eddy.

"You know what?" she finally managed, still laughing, holding her own stomach, feeling her formidable self inside herself. There was just so much of her, now. Inside, anyway. "You know what, my fairy girl? Witch-light of my world?" She stopped laughing, but only long enough to wink. "You could be right."

In response, Ju glared. Then she let the covers drop and stared back. The smile that crept across her face was almost shy; certainly, it was sweet. Definitely, there was love in it; Aunt Sally was all but sure.

"So," said the boy, and the fact that he could speak was a surprise, possibly to all three of them. "You're like her nanny?"

There was a moment—right after her teeth punctured his temple and the side of his face, but before his cheekbone exploded in her mouth—when Aunt Sally experienced yet another brand-new thing. She hadn't even meant to be looking at the boy, because even as she'd struck, she was aware of what would be new to Ju, right then, no matter what the girl claimed she already knew. And Aunt Sally wanted to see the reaction.

But she was *looking at the boy, partly because his arms kept flopping around, still trying to encompass her, his body surging against her torso and his brain twitching and firing even as she slurped it from its pan, churning with all those dreams she'd dredged up in him, the ones they all seemed to be born with, of finally finding that one love or fuck or flickering connection profound enough to shatter their shells, free them from the very hungers and sensations and skin that triggered dreams in the first place.*

Because she was looking at him, she saw his eyes. They were positively ablaze with terror, but also with a welling, bubbling sadness as they bulged, side by side, toward the sills of their sockets. Like jumpers, *Aunt Sally thought as she chewed and slurped and sucked.* From the top of a burning building.

Was that *how they felt as she finished them? Had it always been? She'd just assumed, somehow, that the dreams she stirred anesthetized or at least distracted them.*

The boy bucked hard once more, spasmed, flailed his weed-stalk arms but without purpose, then crumpled as she rode him to the ground. Even as she did that, Aunt Sally forgot the boy entirely. Her attention returned to the girl in the bed even as her teeth found the seams in the sides of the kid's throat, parted him like a curtain. She could feel those fairy-eyes on her, light as light. Ju wasn't looking away. She wasn't even blinking.

You think I don't know? *Ju had said.*

She knew now.

With that certainty came liberation and relief. But also—and here was yet another new thing, the fifth or

*five-thousandth of the last five years, after a century of vir-
tually no new things—a pang of some emotion Aunt Sally
had never felt, yet recognized almost immediately. She'd
heard it sung about, often enough, heard Mother and her
Whistling Fool mewling on and on about it. She'd even
seen it in the bulging eyes of the boy beneath her.*

So this is regret, *she thought, sucking her gums, though
it took her a bit to realize what she was regretting. As it
turned out, tonight marked the end of a dream she'd had.
Not a healthy or desirable one, maybe, and she didn't
even know where it had come from.*

*Aunt Sally had dreamed that Ju would never know.
Would not need to see. That to Ju, and Ju alone of all living
things, Aunt Sally could be something other than slave,
master, meaning-maker, monster, deliverer, destroyer. That
to Ju, Aunt Sally could simply be . . .*

Well. That was done, now.

*When she'd finished devouring, Aunt Sally straightened,
then stood. She licked her lips to clean them but didn't
bother wiping her dress. The stolen phone lay faceup on
Ju's lap, but the girl wasn't looking at it. She just sat, her
back against the headboard, eyes wide open and full of
tears. Her mouth was shut. If she was feeling any surprise,
about any of this, Aunt Sally couldn't see it.*

*Stepping carefully over the corpse, Aunt Sally moved to
the bed, feeling Ju watching, drinking in her gaze. Did Ju
understand the bond of trust they'd just sealed? How Aunt
Sally did hope so. For both their sakes.*

*Just once, as she lowered herself to the bed next to the
girl, stretching out her legs atop the coverings, did she feel
Ju flinch. Not away, she just flinched, or maybe that was a*

shudder. Aunt Sally could understand that. Why shouldn't Ju shudder? Even if she really had known, or thought she'd known . . . it was different to see. It had to be.

Settling beside the girl but not touching her—not yet— Aunt Sally rested her own back against the headboard, which vibrated with the shaking of the girl's shoulders.

Still—and oh, how Aunt Sally loved her then—Ju didn't duck away. She didn't wipe her tears, and eventually, after a long time, she turned, of her volition, toward Aunt Sally. The full force of those green, winking eyes met Aunt Sally's.

I should hold her, *Aunt Sally thought.* I should wipe her tears. Say, "there, there." Try to explain. *Wasn't that what mothers did?*

Instead, Aunt Sally reached across Ju's lap and picked up the phone. Naturally, it displayed one of those purple-bannered, catch-phrase-littered music Web sites she loved. All those brightly colored, spiky-haired, furry-bearded kids waving guitars and middle fingers at a world they'd only begun to realize was way too big for them. This page was regional, apparently, called Pacific Northwest Grrrrrrl-Thing, whatever that meant. Apparently, it meant lots of stage shots of boys with beards and girls with guitars, their lips bared in snarls they would never really own. There were also lots of crammed-together words, as meaningless to Aunt Sally as pebbles from a beach she'd never been to.

She was in the midst of yet another new feeling, this one without precedent in the entirety of her experience and without any name whatsoever, when for some reason she swiped with her finger and scrolled down the Webpage and saw the giant green headline.

RIOT GRRRL RIOT!!
THE NORTHWEST'S SAVAGE NEW DARLINGS TURN ON EACH
OTHER.

Then she saw the photograph, and everything—her thoughts, her blood, the boy's blood trickling down her gullet—froze inside her. For one moment, for the first time in five years, Aunt Sally even forgot about Ju. She just stared at the picture. Taken with my iPhone 6, *it proudly proclaimed. The resolution really was impressive.*

The picture showed a little ropy brunette sailing over the top of a drum kit, her sticks raised like swords, or truncheons.

The oblivious oriental girl in the stripy dress, in the cone of stagelight, was just starting to turn. Aunt Sally could almost make out startled, dark eyes peering out from under the brim of her hat.

How many thousand hats in the world were just like the one that girl wore? Yet Aunt Sally knew this one instantly. Would have known it anywhere. Those smudges of Delta earth right where she remembered them, straight across the sagging brim. That particular shapelessness, that droop so utterly akin to its owner's, mirroring its owner's posture, which had always masked insouciance as submission.

That was the Whistler's hat.

10

Shifting her aching body yet again, trying to find an almost-comfortable spot on the closed lid of the toilet, Rebecca leaned into the ice pack the shaggy bartender had given her, wedging it against the side of the stall with her face. The cold seemed to grab the new bruise where her cheek had met crash cymbal on her way over the drum kit toward Kaylene, squeezing it as though it were a tennis ball. Which, Rebecca suspected, was about right, sizewise.

"Ow," she said.

"Hurts?" said Kaylene from the next stall.

"A lot."

"Good." Of their own volition, Rebecca's lips twitched, trying to smile, until Kaylene added, "Because I don't like being hit."

Because of where she has worked and what she has seen. Because she's Kaylene, and lives to laugh, and spread laughter. And mourn.

"I'm sorry," Rebecca murmured again.

Outside the bathroom, in the Caiman Club's all but empty main room, Mr. Shaggy Bartender—Sean—had cranked the jukebox again, working through the same shuddery, sensational setlist he always played at the end of the night. Roxy Music's "The Bogus Man." The great Kate's "Hounds of Love." Some Canadian jazz singer's version of "Trying to Get to You," which Joel would have absolutely flipped for. The songs vibrated in the walls, rattled the whole building. Every single one of them, Rebecca realized, was about someone on his way. Someone coming. Hounds hunting.

It occurred to her that Kaylene hadn't apologized back. That was okay. This apology had been about Rebecca attacking her—Rebecca going batshit crazy—plain and simple. Kaylene had already said everything that needed to be said, by anyone, ever again, about that goddamn hat.

The fucking monster's hat.

"Oh, shit," said Rebecca, bolting upright and banging her elbow, now, against the toilet paper dispenser, which brought all-new pain tears to her eyes. "The *hat*."

"What?" Kaylene sighed.

"The hat! Where's the hat? We left it out there. It's *loose*. Kaylene, we have to . . ."

There was a rustling, a sliding sound, and then the hat appeared under the wall of the stall, pinned to the floor by Kaylene's boot heel. Its straw—if that even was straw, it might have been cheap plastic, but Rebecca sure as hell wasn't going to touch it again to make sure—had darkened, and it was splitting in several places. It should have seemed menacing, wrapped around her best friend's foot.

Instead, it looked about as threatening as a scrap of newspaper.

"Oh," Rebecca said. Her mouth made no move to smile again, but something inside her did. Briefly. "You could have stuffed it in the van."

"If I dropped my amp and at least two or three of your drums on top of it, right? Wouldn't want it attacking the equipment."

"You're mocking me."

"You fucking bet. *Ow.*" Kaylene lifted her foot and stamped down, splitting the hat still more. "God, I miss Marlene."

"Oh, me, too," Rebecca whispered.

"I want a strawberry Twinkie."

"From her backpack."

"Nice and squashed, so you can't even get it out of the wrapper without Twinkie-ing yourself."

"Imprinted with her Orgo Chem notes. Like edible Silly Putty."

"Silly Putty *is* edible. God, Rebecca, who even taught you the essential food groups?"

Sister Dierdre, maybe, from Orphanage Number Three? Mrs. Collins, Foster Mom Number Two, the one with the cauliflower ear and the bipolar son? Rebecca had liked Mrs. Collins, actually. Or felt sorry for her. At the time, she hadn't distinguished much between the two.

"Amanda," she said, after too long a pause.

"Strawberry Silly Putty . . ." Kaylene murmured.

Without intending to, Rebecca had slid sideways on her toilet lid, away from the hat. She made herself edge back, recenter. She was going to stamp her own foot down right next to Kaylene's, but she couldn't seem to get her leg to lift. At least she found she could take her eyes off the floor. Briefly. If only to think about Mrs. Collins's long-fingered hands, perpetually dusted in flour, and her apologetic eyes, which she flashed every time she made chocolate drop he's-sorry cookies to make up for her son punching Rebecca.

Baby steps.

"I miss Jack," she said, and for a moment half imagined him bursting into the bathroom, waving a squirt gun or playing a pennywhistle he'd dug up somewhere. Grinning at everything.

"Fucking Jack," said Kaylene.

"Which neither one of us even got to do."

"Hey, now! Rebecca! Is that actually you? Wow. I don't think I've ever heard you . . ." Finally, for the first time since the fracas on stage, there it was. Kaylene's laugh. Rebecca's smile got all the way onto her face this time, and clung there for a little while.

"I really do miss Amanda. Her tea, and her towels. Oh my God, her towels, Kaylene. I swear she had her own private dryer setting. Amanda-warm . . ."

"I miss Mrs. Starkey's pizza."

"Her pizza sucked! It had fruit. Canned fruit."

"What's sucking got to do with pizza?"

Out in the club, Shaggy Sean had Joy Division rumbling. Some ghostly, tumbling, gorgeous thing about walking in silence. In the next stall, Kaylene was no longer laughing, but possibly still smiling.

It's still okay, Rebecca was thinking. She wasn't just wishing it, either. *We're still okay.*

"I miss my mom," Kaylene murmured. She rarely said

that aloud, though Rebecca knew she felt it constantly. *To be thoughtful,* Rebecca realized, and was amazed to be realizing this only now. *Because of my mom . . .*

"I wish I missed mine," Rebecca said. Mostly to make it okay for Kaylene. "I wish I *remembered* mine, actually." After a while with neither of them talking, she added, "I miss Danni. That girl the Whistling Asshole snapped in half. She was awful to Trudi, but I think she was all right, really. I think she was *going* to be. I think she was on her way to being . . . amazing . . ."

More silence, now, terrible and sad and comfortable enough. The silence they always shared, when they weren't Sock Puppet, and screaming.

"I miss Oscar," Rebecca said.

"Who's Oscar?"

Here were her tears again, massing, as usual. A few even crept out. "No one. Grounds crew at UNH-D. Just a guy I knew."

The next silence lasted longer. Eventually, Kaylene stirred, stood up but didn't exit the stall. Rebecca imagined her standing there, hands flat on the wall as though searching for a secret panel. "My dad," she whispered. "I can't believe how much I miss my dad."

"You almost never mention him."

"I know," said Kaylene. "My mom always pops up first. She's the one who calls. But . . . his laugh, Rebecca. Someday, I need to get you in a room with him—or, no, in woods, where there's packing snow—so you can hear what he sounds like when you bean him in the face."

The next question came effortlessly, bubbling out of

her UNH-D Crisis Center training or maybe just her own still-twitching instincts. "What else about him?"

The litany spilled from Kaylene's mouth as though she'd been chanting it all along. Storing it up for years. Baseball gloves, a lavender tie that went with nothing else he owned and that her mom hated, a viola he never played but played astonishingly, a handful of stolen, predawn diner break-fasts they were supposed to pretend Mom of Warm Bao didn't know about at the IHOP around the corner from their house, where they got cardboard American pancakes and coffee the color of cheap engine oil.

Even after Kaylene went quiet, Rebecca suspected that her mouth was still moving, still chanting. Weirdly, Kay-lene's chant was proving at least as comforting to Re-becca as it hopefully was to her.

Eventually, after who knew how long, Kaylene sighed. "Thanks, Rebecca. Thanks for letting me talk about him."

"Thanks for talking about him."

"I miss him. I miss *them*. I'm too old to miss my parents this much."

"I'm pretty sure they miss you that much, too."

"I miss *you*," Kaylene whispered, and Rebecca startled, sat up straight.

Then she stood. "I'm right here."

And I've forgotten again, she realized, her glance plum-meting to her feet as she took an instinctive hop back. But the hat was gone. Retracted. As if on cue, Rebecca heard the rustling of a paper bag as Kaylene squirreled the hat away again.

"At least, I think I am," she murmured.

"Well, come on out, then," said Kaylene, and popped open her stall door.

When Rebecca emerged, there was her friend, paper bag half stuffed in her pocket, lips swelling where Rebecca had inadvertently driven her shoulder into them in her headlong grab for the hat. Reaching out slowly, Rebecca put a finger near but not quite on Kaylene's mouth, then brushed matted strands of hair back behind her friend's ear.

"I'm so sorry," she said again.

"You should be," said Kaylene. And then, "Me, too."

They looked at each other in the mirror. "Good God. We're going to have to explain this to Jess."

"Can we do that tomorrow?" Rebecca whimpered, and Kaylene actually laughed, then winced as her own fingers flew to her mouth.

"That sounds like a plan."

"Except we don't have any money."

"We have a little. From the club tonight."

Glancing up at the mirror again, Rebecca found that she didn't even want to meet her own eyes, let alone Kaylene's. "I'm surprised they paid us."

Kaylene shrugged. "Sean says if we ever play here again, we'll probably sell out, after tonight. He said it was no skin off his face, only ours."

"Still. We'll barely have enough for gas."

"Yet another thing I miss," Kaylene muttered. "Having a little money."

It surprised Rebecca how quickly she nodded at that. "Yep. That's getting old."

"My God, Bec. Are we here?"

Rebecca knew immediately what Kaylene meant. But it felt better, just for a few seconds longer, to pretend she didn't, even as she felt her heart thump. Her blood actually leapt down her arms and legs. "Where?"

"At the night where we come back? Meaning, the night we don't *go* back? The night we finally start life over?"

Kaylene's voice had broken, but whether from excitement or terror or pain or plain old exhaustion, Rebecca could no longer tell. She'd lost at least a few of her instincts, at least for tonight. But she touched her friend once more, gently, on the elbow. "I'm not. Not quite. Based on the evening's evidence."

That earned her one more chiming Kaylene laugh. "Got to agree with you there. But . . . let's stay in Canada tonight, okay? Even if we have to find a park and sleep in the van. I'm too tired to deal with Jess."

"Me, too. We better call her, though."

So that's what they did, once they got out in the main room. When Rebecca told her they'd decided to stay over somewhere and would be home tomorrow, Jess sighed.

"Be safe," she said. Not quite like a mom. But not like she was kidding, either.

"Everything okay there?"

"It is now. Eddie got out again after dinner. Disappeared for almost an hour, I had to go corral him near those crazy trees on the cliff. He's doing that almost every damn night, all of a sudden. It's like he's got a secret okra girlfriend."

Rebecca grinned. "I wouldn't put it past him. He's a resourceful little bugger."

"Dugger," Kaylene corrected, staring out the front window of the club at the rain that seemed to hang permanently from every awning in Vancouver like translucent curtains.

Already, the two of them were the last ones left except for Shaggy Sean and the hulking Tsimshian bouncer who always grooved, with his shoulders, to whatever music was playing, whether live or recorded, and never seemed to look anyone fully in the face. Right now, he was at the bar, dipping and bobbing to "Dancing Barefoot."

"This song always scares me," Rebecca said after hanging up.

"Hell, yeah," said Kaylene, dropping the hat bag onto the top of the table nearest the window. "All-time fave."

"The part about being taken over. Spooky."

"Yeah. But then *she* comes on. Like a heroine." They hummed the chorus together when it came.

When it was over, Rebecca ran her fingertips over her bruised cheek. "We need to ask where there's a rest stop. Or a campground."

"We will," said Kaylene, and sat down.

Rebecca joined her. After a few seconds, her own shoulders started to dip and bob to the music, and Kaylene's did the same. In the window, just hovering there, was her friend's reflected face. And there was her own, bruised and shadowed.

For way too long, until Shaggy Sean asked if they were really okay and then kicked them out, they just sat together, holding hands across the table, watching themselves in Canada, alone and bereft and free, floating in rain.

11

The night before, as usual, Sophie had followed the two of them all the way to the ferry. As usual, the one in the stripes sang as she moved, swayed more than walked, while Rebecca, the Little Orphan That Could—and had—trailed behind, hands and drumsticks in her pockets. Even now, Sophie sometimes had trouble believing that those compact, girlish hands had killed the Whistler. Or finished killing, after Sophie had done the hard part. The pouncing and skull-sucking.

Sophie's plan, as usual, had been to follow them to the show. As far as she knew, she'd been to every single Sock Puppet performance without ever being seen. At least not by Sock Puppet. She'd been seen plenty by the moshy, screaming, fist-pumping girls and their sweet, reedy boys. They all considered themselves so next-gen evolved, immune to their longings, at least until Sophie made eye contact with one or five. Just for fun. By this point, going to *Sock Puppet* shows had become practically a ritual. A way of marking time. By most measures, after all, Rebecca and her striped, long-haired bandmate constituted Sophie's closest remaining friends on this planet.

True, as far as she could remember, she'd never actually spoken to the stripy one. And true, Rebecca had tried to kill Sophie after she'd bashed in the Whistler's head. Except, maybe she hadn't. Maybe, as she'd slammed that shovel down over and over, onto and through both faces until Whistler-pulp positively floated like mist above the forest floor and shaded the scent of all that pine resin even sweeter, Rebecca had simply considered Sophie collateral damage, expendable in order to achieve the desired end. Sophie could respect that.

Either way, the reality remained: these were the living things Sophie knew best. Almost the last living things she knew at all. Except, she supposed, for Jess. And Jess hardly seemed a safe friend choice, these days.

Idly, as she'd watched them pick up that rusting, white van full of their stuff from behind the diner where they both waitressed and earned whatever pathetic money they earned, Sophie had let herself wonder, yet again, whether this would be the night she'd let them see. She wasn't exactly planning on revealing herself or anything. Her plan, to the extent that she had one, remained the same: to trail along, slip in amongst the surprising crowds, and just be with everyone. She'd bump up against a few unsuspecting concertgoers, flirt, mesmerize a somebody or two if she was in the mood.

Right before the encore, she'd fade away into the night and head back to the island ahead of the band. Maybe do *a bit of Ferry Godmothering. In ways that still surprised her, these evenings had started to feel amazingly like the ones she and Natalie had shared in the years before they'd had children or met the Whistler. There was literally almost no difference. Except for Natalie not being in them.*

Last night, she'd become aware of how closely she was letting herself follow, now. She'd actually stood out in the open across the street from the diner, right in front of the nautical-trinkets-and-taffy shop. Positioning herself just outside the cone of perpetually misty yellow streetlight, Sophie had waited for the van to emerge from its alley. When it had—right after it had turned toward the ferry dock—she'd waved.

The Stripy One's window was open, but Sophie hadn't called out. Not yet. On the day she did, they'd all have a decision to make.

Why, last night, had she let them go without her? Why had she stayed behind on the island?

It had taken her hours to work it out. She'd just stood rooted at first, watching the van edge onto the deck. After the ferry had gone, Sophie whiled away the hours lurking in mist that became rain just outside the tavern she had never entered, and the market she had no need to enter. Finally, just after two A.M., when the last ferry of the night docked and disgorged exactly three passengers, none of them Sock Puppet, Sophie had set herself on a bench in the empty parking lot of the post office that connected everyone on this island (except her) to everyone else in the world. And that's when she'd had her first revelation:

It wasn't that she had no one to write to or call or connect with now. It was that she almost never had. Even before the Whistler, if she was going to be brutal and honest with herself, and why not, at this point? Who had there ever been for Sophie?

There'd been her mom, sometimes. Her mom had taken vacations from heroin, periodically. Some of those had lasted weeks, even months, and during the longer stretches, her mom would get sudden bursts of energy and take her daughter all the way to Southgate mall. Maybe buy her an Orange Julius, if they were splurging, and she could dig enough cash out of the sleeper-couch that took up most of the east wall of their trailer.

There'd been Elainey, a New Jersey cousin Sophie had met exactly once but emailed and later texted all the way through high school.

She'd had her share of boys, of course, a few of whom she'd even liked.

She'd had her Roo. But for so few days. Barely a year. Hardly a lifetime at all.

Most of all, she'd had Natalie, and yes, godfucking-damnit, Natalie's mother, who was marooned on this island, too. And who quite possibly blamed and hated Sophie. Possibly, she'd hated Sophie all along.

Sitting there in the post office parking lot, as invisible and inanimate as the bench on which she rested—except for her constant, relentless shivering—Sophie brooded deep into the night. Just as she was about to get up, skulk back to the abandoned barracks in the grasslands, Sophie's second revelation slammed into her:

Those girls. Women. Sock Puppet. Huddled in their awful van on the loading platform, one of them singing, the other laughing in spite of herself.

In spite of herself.

That was the thing that triggered understanding, finally made clear to Sophie what she was still doing here, and why she'd been following those two people for years, now.

It wasn't only the late and careening nights, the deafening music and swarming lights in the dumpy clubs where they played, or the wide-open, warehouse-district emptiness of the areas outside those clubs that reminded Sophie of Natalie. Of all her nights with Natalie.

It wasn't just the thousand glancing interactions between those women and the people they played for, not one of which bloomed into so much as a conversation, let alone a connection.

It was the women themselves. Those two: Stripy Laughing Thing and the Little Orphan That Had. They might as well have been Natalie and Sophie. Even the music they made—savage but surprisingly bouncy, something you could sing even as you screamed it—was music she and Natalie might have concocted if their lives had lasted just a little longer, been just a little different. If they'd had more usable time in the time they'd had, a tiny bit more money, access to instruments to learn and play.

Watching those women—hopping a ride on their lives like a hobo in a boxcar—was like hopping the ghost of her own life as it rocketed away from her. Taking Natalie with it.

Where are they? Sophie had thought then, shuddering to her feet, rattling in the cold and dark. *Why the fuck aren't they back? She'd been watching the docks since midnight without even realizing what she was doing. And they hadn't come home.*

Their absence itched her. Chattered in her brain. That wasn't healthy or helpful. Time to go, *Sophie realized.*

Go she had, back up the hill to the dusty, empty barracks where, instead of lying on the pile of sheets she'd stolen and formed into her resting-place nest, she'd spent the whole day pacing.

She was still pacing now, almost twelve hours later, as the murky, gray daylight leaking through her papered-over windows finally darkened. When it got just a little darker, out she'd burst like a bat from its treetop, and whirl off into the world to get some shit sorted. Get her own shit sorted, because this was not *how she planned to spend her eternity of days.*

Ferry Godmother, she thought, and winced. Because really, who had haunted whom? What had she really done for the past five years but trail in thrall behind her own ghosts? The ghosts of herself?

That's who those women were, in the end. Right this second, maybe, they'd be stomping down the gangplank exactly the way Natalie and Sophie would have stomped as they returned home. They'd be singing at precisely Natalie-Sophie volume, and wearing the same . . . well, no. Not even Sophie would have tried rocking those stripes. And Natalie would never have dared a worry-scowl as deep set as the Little Orphan's, because Sophie would have danced it right off her face.

Throwing open the door to the barrack, Sophie stared out at the grasslands that swept toward the cliffs. The twilight mist seemed to be lifting rather than thickening, today, leaving just a little too much light for comfort. Just enough to hurt, and Sophie had had quite enough hurting for this particular epoch of her lifetime. So she'd have to stay here a little longer before heading out to discover whether Sock Puppet had come back, and then deciding what to do about that, either way. How to jettison those women once and for all. Because ghosts, like light, fugged up her nights. Also, they hurt.

All at once, here it was: rock bottom. Not only had she just had her worst thought yet, but quite possibly the worst thought possible: not only would Natalie and Sophie have been these women, if they'd gotten the chance. They would be these women still, right this second and forever, if only Natalie hadn't gone and gotten herself dead.

Chosen *to get dead, instead of staying with Sophie.*

The coward. The sulking, selfish bitch.

Sophie's fury stunned her, almost tipped her right off her perpetually trembling legs into her nest of sheets. Five years it had taken just to acknowledge how angry she really was. Now the words spun in her mind, spattering over memories of the only best friend she'd ever had like dirt on a coffin lid. Or, in Natalie's case, tarp, because that's what Sophie and Jess had lain her in, under that tree in those Maryland woods, holding Sophie's murdered son to her breast.

Sulking coward. Selfish bitch.

How was it that Natalie—brooding, blazing Nat Queen Cold, the most brilliant and beautiful person Sophie had ever known—had taken the Whistling Shitfuck at his word? How had Natalie actually believed that she would somehow, inevitably, become like him, simply accepted what she'd been told, that the way his life (or not-life) was and felt was the only way hers or Sophie's could ever be or feel?

But Natalie had believed it. And so she'd chosen to exit life entirely, with the help of her hypocrite, aren't-we-brave-now gnome-mom, leaving Sophie marooned and alone in the middle of a million other lives that could never be hers, dangling like a hanged thing from the one question Natalie had left unanswered. Had barely bothered to ask:

Was the monster right? Was the Whistler's way the only way there was?

Dark was crawling in across the cliff tops, slowly, so slowly. But it was coming. Sophie could edge all the way out into the open doorway now, let the last light lap at her feet. Soon, she could go. Stop thinking, start moving. Get the world sorted.

Was the monster right?

Looking back over the last few years, Sophie had to admit that there was at least one deceased surgeon, a few unlucky strangers she'd met at precisely the wrong moment (for them) in her travels, and a handful of now-vanished ferry passengers who would no doubt have said yes, assuming they could have said anything, anymore. No doubt, Jess would say so, too, if anyone asked. So, probably, would the Little Orphan That Had, judging by her indiscriminate wielding of shovel.

So. On Natalie's side, there was the Whistler, plus everyone Sophie had met since the night they'd met the Whistler, and, if she were honest and weighing clearly, almost everyone she'd met before, in her first life, too.

And on the other side . . . somehow . . . maybe . . . there was one Sophie. Who remained unconvinced.

The trembling in her legs had subsided to ordinary, permanent quivers, which always made her feel as though she were a walking sapling. Something new and young. And the sky had darkened enough for Sophie to slip from her doorway. She started across the grass toward the edge of the cliffs. The ferries didn't come to this side of the island, but sometimes she saw ships out there. Tonight, though, there was nothing but sea spray and whitecaps. As though the world had emptied. As though she were indeed Ferry Godmother, and had gone wherever ferry godmothers go when no one's wishing.

Turning away, Sophie lurched along the edge of the cliff toward the path down to the sea cave where she sometimes slept, marked by the tree she'd taken to climbing to wait for Eddie. To play at being Eddie's Cheshire cat. Usually, she waited until full dark to do this, though almost no one but that kid ever came up here. But tonight, she didn't care who saw her.

Her legs seemed to solidify under her feet, and the last fog fled before her. Overhead, stars spilled across the newly dark sky like jacks from a bag. The billion shiny bits and pieces of a whole universe to play with and in, if only she could remember how. Hadn't that always been the key to days worth having, life worth living? Keeping it all feeling like play?

Even in her life before—from her first conscious days tossing peanut shells and her mom's discarded syringes across the floor of their trailer—Sophie had intuited that.

Natalie hadn't. But she'd known Sophie did. Natalie had given Sophie meaning, and Sophie had given her joy. And that was why they'd been such good friends.

By the time she reached the edge of the woods, the mist had cleared entirely. The stars positively billowed in their brightness, and Sophie was practically skipping. Refurbished-Sophie skipping, anyway, an arhythmic hop-stagger-straighten that made movement itself into a never-ending hopscotch game, a series of leaps from point to point. She hadn't meant to head for the woods, had no conscious intention of skirting so close to Jess's compound. At least, not so early in the evening, when everyone there would be awake, maybe even outside. In the moment, she barely felt conscious, was simply listening to her own motion, the wind of the world in her ears reminding her she was awake and alive. Only at the last possible second—when it really should have been too late—did she realize she'd been hearing Jess's voice from the moment she'd entered the forest. She didn't see Jess until she'd almost plowed straight through her.

Even more astonishingly, Jess didn't see Sophie. She was standing between two towering firs just inside the tree line, a few steps past the edge of her yard, her back ramrod straight and her hands near her mouth, like a chattering gopher up on its hind legs. Her scratchy yell poured through those hands, and it sounded so familiar: the same yell that had once unfurled across her trailer park, calling her daughter and Sophie home for dinner.

Except this time, Jess was yelling a single, stretched-out name.

"Eddddiiiieeeeeeee . . ."

Diving off the path—with that sensation, again, of coming off her legs, though she never actually did—Sophie half fell, half plunged into the brush to Jess's left and lay still. It was that stillness, most likely, that kept Jess from spotting her. That, and the fact that Jess was focused entirely on finding Eddie, calling him back from the cliffs or coves where she clearly assumed he'd gone.

One of these nights, instead of calling for him, Jess was going to follow him out there. And if that was one of the increasingly frequent nights when Sophie happened to be there, too . . .

That could have happened tonight, *she realized. Unless Eddie had been out all day, she must have just missed him. The realization made Sophie's skin tingle all over.*

Because she was about to see Natalie's son again? Or because she might finally, finally, get to confront Natalie's mother again? Or both?

Who knew? Who cared? The tingle became a shudder. So delicious.

For what seemed whole minutes, Sophie lay in the dirt and fallen needles, grinning right up to the edge of giggling, as though she and Jess and Eddie were playing Kick the Can, Ghost in the Graveyard. As though Jess were It. And now—same as then, way back when Jess had played those games with Sophie and Natalie, crawling under and behind trailers full of scary or stoned neighbors—Sophie had a sudden and surprising urge. She'd had it five years ago, too, in the New Hampshire woods, crawling across the roof of that tipped-over trailer at the moment she realized she really had done it, rendered herself invisible, so that no one, not the Whistler, not Jess, not even the Little Orphan That Hadn't Yet, realized she was there:

She wanted to be found. Right now!

Staring through a curtain of pine needles at that stunted, sanctimonious little powerhouse of a woman—a piston with nothing left to drive—Sophie almost couldn't keep from launching to her feet, dropping on Jess like she had in those other woods where each of them had lain the bodies of their children. No doubt that would have earned Sophie one last bath in Jess's icy eyes, which somehow warmed as they enveloped. Surrounded you like a snow-bank.

Then Sophie would say hello. Because here, incredibly, was another discovery, something that she should have known already and hadn't, because at the time of their last actual interaction, she just hadn't lived long or hard enough, yet:

Jess was as lonely as Sophie. Maybe even lonelier. Maybe—even when she'd had Natalie—she always had been.

Maybe Sophie really should spring up? Sneak around behind, throw her hands across those ice-eyes and whisper, "Guess who?"

And after that . . . what? Did she really imagine Jess would invite her back to the compound? Lecture her over Cheerios while some playoff baseball game played on the radio, the way Jess liked, and Benny, her fuzzy man, baked pies?

Benny. Who'd actually loved Sophie, in a way, when Sophie was alive. And whom Sophie had loved in a totally different way—or else raped, it depended on perspective, maybe—once she was dead. Different-alive. Whatever she was.

Certainly, Benny did not and would not love her now, or ever again.

Jess, either.

So. Probably no actual sneaking up behind, then. The urge to get found evaporated like the last of the mist. Jess called, "Eddie, come on," but not angrily, and then stalked off to her right toward the cliffs.

She'd sounded much more annoyed than afraid, Sophie decided, sitting up.

Because she doesn't know how afraid she should be. Because she doesn't know I'm here.

Lurchy legs and all, Sophie sailed to her feet, feeling like one of those giant balloon-phantoms floating up off a lawn. Even as she jerked into motion, she was grinning again, because as usual, Jess had everything just a little bit wrong. She was right about the kid's intentions, but wrong in the specifics. Yes, he'd headed for the cliffs and coves. But not the ones Jess had headed for.

Skipping along the path, Sophie checked that Jess was well away to the right, then darted left toward the twisty tree, which had long since become Sophie and Eddie's meeting place.

Sure enough, there he was, swinging his stubby legs in his baggy, shiny pajama bottoms. His down coat puffed around him like a floatie, more suited to preventing drowning than freezing. His scrunched little face was aimed toward the Strait and the cove where his beloved killer whales sometimes surfaced. Tonight, though, the cove was silent except for the barely there lap and slap of water on rock. When Sophie got close enough, she saw the boy's dark hair hanging straight across his own ice-blue eyes.

This was Natalie's son, all right. And that made him Natalie and Sophie's, by right and by design. That was the way they'd always thought of and treated both their kids, when they'd each had one. When Sophie's Roo and Eddie's mom were still in the world.

Unlike Jess, Eddie somehow sensed her presence, probably because he'd come here looking for her. But he didn't turn around. Not until she was right underneath him did she note the crinkles at the corners of his mouth as he fought for control of his smile.

And why was he smiling? She knew that, too. The smile was because he'd come looking for exactly this. He'd wished for Sophie to appear, conjured her up, and she had.

Maybe she was a Ferry Godmother, after all.

"Are you a cat?" she said.

Eddie remembered, knew what she was echoing, and lost control of his smile. It broke over his face, and he laughed, but not loudly or for long. He was—as he'd have to be, growing up amid all those grief-ravaged people—cautious with joy. As mistrustful of and curious about it as though it were a beehive. Which, as far as Sophie had ever seen, was exactly what joy was.

"I called you," Eddie said. "I waited."

Far across the cliffs, Sophie could just make out the shadow of Jess's retreating back. There wasn't any mist, were already billions of stars, and yet Sophie felt as though she and the boy were cloaked in darkness, invisible and protected. Even if Jess turned around, she'd never find them.

"*Want to see my cave?*" *she said. She offered her hand and helped him down, gesturing in Jess's direction and holding a finger to her lips.*

"*You're freezing,*" *Eddie said.*

"*Shh. Always.*"

Eddie grinned.

Hooking her elbow through his, careful not to touch any exposed skin and make him colder, Sophie hustled him into something approaching a trot. Off they rushed along the cliff and down the secret path only she knew, hunching and racing together as though outrunning an incoming storm.

12

Even from the darkness of his tiny room, where he'd waited for over an hour behind his half-closed door for the living room to clear, Joel sensed that something was wrong the second the girls came home. Something other than Eddie staying out even later than usual on a mistless, moonlit night. Almost certainly, Eddie was fine and nearby, crouching behind rocks in one of his okra coves or maybe under cover of a fir right at the edge of the yard, loving that he'd scattered adults all over the top of the island hunting for him again.

Slipping his headphones off—he hadn't been playing anything, anyway, just using them to seal himself into his own silence, keep him resolute and committed to the decision he'd made—Joel zipped them into the packed duffel on his bed and crept to the doorway to listen.

"Where is everybody?" he heard Kaylene murmur, in nothing like her usual singsong. If Rebecca answered,

Joel didn't hear. The sink turned on, then off. No one else spoke, and he heard no other movement.

Which could mean nothing. It probably meant nothing other than that they were tired, except that being tired rarely stopped Kaylene from singsonging or Rebecca from answering. Benny and Jess and possibly even Trudi were still out in the woods, apparently, which meant Eddie was still out there, also.

Which meant that this time, something really could have happened to him. Probably, it hadn't. But it could have.

And if it had? What did that change?

That was something Joel had learned from his life: something could always have happened. His being or not being here wouldn't change that. He'd meant to disappear before the girls came home, because saying good-bye to Rebecca, in particular, seemed not just hard but unthinkable. But then Eddie had slipped off, and Benny and Jess had swept up Joel in the search, and so for a while, he'd done what he'd been doing since he came to this island. He trailed along. Helped where he could. Closed himself down to just the moment right in front of him, because there was no hurry to get anywhere, and nowhere, really, to go. And nothing he wanted to remember ever again.

Until lately. Suddenly, with increasing regularity, he did. Suddenly, he was thinking all the time about Halfmoon House, which he'd partially built and completely rebuilt himself. About his wife, forever retreating from him even when she'd been alive. About the children they'd never managed to have, and the lost children of other people they *had* had, for brief whiles. And the fierce, fighting child they'd lost for good, that last night in the woods.

His woods. His and Amanda's.

And Rebecca's. At least she was well on her way to becoming someone else, now. Or, becoming herself. The self her life was going to allow her to be. That's how Amanda would have put it. As usual, she'd have been right.

Maybe someday he could call Rebecca from wherever he'd gone and reintroduce himself. Somehow, that conversation seemed easier to imagine than the one where he stepped out this door, stared into her silent face, and said, *Gotta go. See you sometime.*

Nope. He couldn't imagine doing that. He would wait until the girls went upstairs. The fact that they'd come home from Vancouver a day late and weirdly silent changed nothing.

Nevertheless, here he was creeping closer to the door to listen. He knew what he wanted to hear. Every single time Rebecca and Kaylene went off to play a show—no matter where it took place, or what time they got back, or how it had gone, or how exhausted they were—they came back singing, in spite of themselves. They did it through clenched lips, softly, as though afraid of waking something. On the rare occasions when they didn't sing, they gossiped about some guy in the crowd, or some teen- or tween-girl wolfpack who'd bumrushed the stage, or another garlic clove and kalamata olive pizza some local had told them about. Apparently, kalamata olive pizza was Sock Puppet's after-performance meal of choice.

Once or twice, especially lately, they'd even come in giggling, and also fighting their giggles with their hands

over their mouths, like teenagers creeping home past cur-
few. Like the teenagers Rebecca had never been or been
among, or the college kids they'd both been all too briefly.

But tonight, they were silent. Neither of them had even
started up the stairs. As far as Joel could tell, they were just
standing in the kitchen in the dark.

*Did they realize Eddie was gone again? Probably not.
And why would that have silenced them, anyway? It was
hardly the first time, and seemed barely worth worrying
about, given the things those girls had had to worry about
in their lives.*

For one moment—a sweet one, something to treasure
later, because even thinking he might be of use again had
to mean he really had been, once—Joel hovered with his
hand above the doorknob. He was strongly considering
abandoning his plan and moonwalking right out into
their line of vision. He'd throw his arms wide, sing something, and make Rebecca laugh just once more.

How he had loved—how challenging and how reward-
ing it had been—learning how to make that silent, lost,
loving person laugh.

How much Amanda had loved him for being able to do
that. Possibly, it was the last thing his wife had loved him
for. And he had loved her for the permission and encour-
agement. And resistance.

His eyes filled with tears.

Out in the living room, Rebecca spoke, and the tears
froze in his lashes along with the ridiculous hope in his
heart. Because in all the years Rebecca had lived at Halfmoon House while he and Amanda had nursed her through
the loss of her parents and into adulthood, through all the

late-night check-in phone calls after she'd moved out, Joel had only heard her sound like this once before. On the day she'd told him he should leave Amanda, because Amanda was strangling him. That she sounded this way now meant something really *was* wrong. Something worse than Eddie playing hide-and-seek.

"Kaylene," she said, dead flat.

"Oh, come on," Kaylene said, or slurred, the words blurring together as though she were drunk.

Or speaking through split lips?

"I'm not fighting. I'm not mad at all. I just don't . . . why would you even keep that thing?"

"We've been through this. Stop giving that fucker power, Rebecca. It's a *hat*. That's all it ever was. Now it's *my* hat. Our hat. Sock Puppet's hat. Because that's all *he* is, now. He's our sock puppet, to make do whatever we want. And the only thing I did onstage last night was—"

Even from behind his door, with a thousand mixed-up memories whirling in his head, Joel heard the change in Rebecca's tone. He could feel her magic, practically see the gesture he knew she was making right that second: the little shake of the shoulders, the settling in behind those quiet, brown eyes as they flared gently, grabbing and warming anyone close enough to notice. Because whatever she was furious or upset about, her friend needed her.

"I'm not talking about last night anymore, K. It's done. I get it. I think. I'm just asking, okay? I'm not criticizing. I'm literally . . . I don't understand how you could even *pick it up*. *When* did you pick it up? Did you lift it off his head after I smashed his skull in? How could you have—"

"I love you," Kaylene said.

"I love you," Rebecca snapped back, so savagely that Joel clutched the door, leaning into it while holding his breath. He wanted them to stop talking, now. This was the sound he wanted echoing behind him as he vanished. Those were the words.

That was his girl. His and Amanda's last and best, and she sounded so fierce and fine. So loving and loved.

Although—of course—Rebecca wasn't their last. There'd been two more after her: Trudi, still teetering on the edge of her own abyss with only Jess and Rebecca holding her back, now; and Danni, whom they'd all just started to reach, and who'd died broken-backed and gasping on the pinecone-littered ground of Halfmoon Lake woods.

"Sorry about your face," Rebecca murmured. Whatever that meant.

"Sorry about your soul," said Kaylene, and Joel couldn't help it, he barked out a laugh and then froze. He held the door, kept still while his memories settled to the extent that they ever did. Loneliness rocked and slapped inside him like rainwater in a reservoir, filling him so completely that it had practically become him.

Finally, at least one of the girls stirred and started up the stairs. *Yes,* Joel thought, nodding. *That's right. It's time. This is good. Go.*

It really was good. He was all but sure. Rebecca no longer needed a middle-of-the-night online word-game partner, because she either performed or slept through nights, now, or at the very least stayed offline during them. She didn't need a surrogate father anymore, either, not with Jess as a very-nearly-mom. Kaylene and Rebecca had each other. Jess and Benny had each other, plus three almost-daughters and a for-all-intents-and-purposes son. Collectively, they had Trudi for a project. Trudi had Jess to resist, and Rebecca to fight and ultimately give in to. And Eddie had all of them.

They were all okay, now, or at least as close to okay as Joel suspected anyone could get after what they'd experienced. Eddie would turn up because he always did. And if he didn't, Joel *still* wouldn't have any role to play, just more grief to bear. And he didn't think he could do that. He couldn't imagine where he would put it.

Or maybe he just didn't want to grieve anymore. That was okay, too. It really was. It would have to be.

For a few breaths more, he waited, listening to the house, the owls in the woods, the late October wind rattling the patio screen. Rebecca could still be in the living room, he knew, just sitting, the way she once had at the long, wooden worktable in the kitchen at Halfmoon House, or at her desk in the Crisis Center room at UNH-D. Waiting for someone to need her.

But he didn't think she was. If she'd realized where Jess and Benny had gone, she'd already be outside joining the search. And if she hadn't, she'd have headed up to her room to take care of herself. That was something she'd finally learned to do in the last five years, though not from him.

Easing open the door, Joel stepped into the hall with his bag over his shoulder. Sure enough, the living room and kitchen were empty, the patio outside white with starlight, crosshatched with pine shadows. At the front door, he turned once more, put his fingers to his lips, and blew a kiss no one would ever catch to the house and everyone who lived in it. A voice popped into his head, the one from that insane Web-radio show he'd loved in the last days of his marriage. The voice of Jess's actual daughter, as it had turned out.

"*L-l-l-love me,*" he murmured along, then hummed the opening riff of the crazed, sixty-year-old song that voice had been mimicking.

He opened the front door and the cool air sucked him out.

Right away, he detoured off the road into the woods, partly to keep anyone who happened to be looking from spotting him, and partly to scan the brush one more time for Eddie, just in case the kid had decided to hole up somewhere in this direction this time instead of in the backyard or with his okras.

Okras, Joel thought, smiling faintly. His lungs clutched, clinging to the breath he'd just taken. *He's all right. Be all right, kid.*

All the way down the hill, sliding through ground cover and pushing back curtains of pine branch, Joel kept his eyes on the woods, and so was surprised to realize he'd walked right past town to the water's edge. Cutting back to the road but keeping to the gravel and the shadows—not that anyone down here would notice his leaving, or care if they did—he made his way to the little one-room, workerless ferry terminal where would-be riders could wait out the rains. His goal had been to catch the last boat of the night, but one glance at the clock told him he'd dawdled too long. So be it. He wasn't going back to Jess's Stockade. This was as good and private a place to wait as any.

The room was too bright, lit by buzzing overhead

fluorescents, furnished with a row of green rusted standing lockers, two splintery wooden benches, a coffee machine, a cigarette dispenser, and some twenty-year-old posters for whale-watching tours and cruises to Victoria and the Haida Gwaii Islands. The very few times Joel had been down here at this hour, he'd found at least a couple homeless people or dangerously drugged-up runaway teens from the mainland sacked out around the room. But tonight, mercifully, the terminal was empty.

Settling on a bench, Joel opened his duffel for his headphones, then left them where they were. Instead, he listened to the seabirds and sea wind, water rolling up to and onto the land. Everything felt so blank, as though he were between showings at a movie theater, watching the white screen, thinking next to nothing. Feeling next to nothing. Awaiting the start of the sequel no adult in his right mind would ever want to be part of.

Did he sleep? Could he even tell the difference, anymore?

Dawn came so softly that he didn't notice the change, hardly realized the time had come—that time still moved at all—until he glanced up and saw the 5 A.M. ferry, the first of the morning, already shuddering up to the dock.

Hustling to his feet, he realized he wasn't even going to be the first passenger aboard. Abramowicz, the venture capitalist with the sleek, olive suits who'd built the turreted McCastle on the promontory at the far end of the island, was already on the gangplank, having slipped under the chain in his tailored trench coat. A redheaded mother and her teenaged son were getting ready to head up, too. Joel had seen them around the diner many times, knew them to nod to but not by name. They were leaning on the low sea wall with Styrofoam cups of coffee in their hands.

Barely bothering to button his jacket, Joel hurried into the brightening pink of the morning. For the first time in years, he had an urge to shout something ridiculous, wake everyone up and get them laughing. Poke that brooding redheaded kid right between the shoulder blades, whisper, "Tag," and race away past Mr. Abramowicz up the gangplank.

He was about to do just that—it was the best start to his next life that he could think of on short notice, and he was out of practice—but he stopped to watch the ferry's only two passengers disembark arm in arm: a gliding black woman in a shiny, silver rain shell with the hood drawn despite the absence of rain, and a long, lean praying mantis of a girl who also had her translucent rain hood drawn but her head up. Her stunning green eyes seemed to absorb all the light, literally gulping it into themselves, like stars imploding.

Along with everyone else at the dock, Joel stood aside until the two women reached the chain. Then, on impulse, he lurched forward and unhooked it for them. He meant to say good morning, tip the cap he didn't have. Then tag the redhead kid and race him onto the boat deck.

But something froze him as they passed. The woman brushed him with the edge of her rain shell, hustling the girl along with her other arm. Right as that happened, the feel—no, the *scent* of her—ghosted over and through him:

Old, wet leaves. Leaves that had lain for decades under

other leaves on the floor of a forest, liquefied, retained their shape but not their substance.

It was an odor he'd inhaled all his life, in every woods he'd ever known. But only once before on a creature in motion.

Just like that, he knew.

The woman in the rain shell . . . *Had she felt him, knowing?* She turned. Her gaze danced down him. Then she was gone, hunching as she crossed the street toward town.

Abramowicz bumped him aside without so much as a nod, as though he'd never seen Joel in his life. The mother and son swept past, too. The boat horn bellowed. And still, Joel stood where he was. He stared at the ferry, then behind him at the two hooded figures disappearing into the terminal. For another half hour, that would remain the only open door in town. Not long after that, the nautical-trinket shop would open. Then the gas station. Then Benny's diner . . .

Do it now, he heard himself think, almost say. *Attack her now, before she knows you know.*

He blinked, and there it was under his eyelids: the image he would never again be rid of, no matter what other life he somehow managed to find or build: Amanda, shooting him a last cryptic glance as she flung herself at the whistling demon in the sombrero in the very last seconds of her life. Joel watched those moments replay. Watched flying bits of Amanda explode into the air around him.

The ferry horn blew once more, drowned out the humming whimper he knew he was making but could barely hear. That horn was for him, he knew.

Last call. *All aboard.*

So be it.

Turning his back on the boat, the sea, and all his possible futures, Joel ducked around the side of the terminal. When the woman in the rain shell and the praying mantis girl finally left, slipping from shadow to shadow to keep away from the light, he went inside again and stored his suitcase in one of the lockers.

"Be right back," he heard himself tell it, in the voice of someone abandoning a child.

Then, as casually and inconspicuously as he could, he edged out the door, off the road, away from town, and into the woods.

13

Her moment came, as Emilia had known it would, and sooner than she could have hoped.

In his excitement, the Invisible Man had declined her suggestion that they make the trip in segments, over a period of days. He also denied her the fifteen minutes it would have taken to search up a well-timed red-eye that might have gotten them across the country under cover of darkness, protecting his skin and her increasingly light-sensitive eyes. He wanted the first thing in the air.

And so, less than twelve hours after Emilia had sniffed out the trail of his precious Aunt Sally for him, their flight jostled through a states-wide thunderhead that stretched across the empty, rolling plains below like furniture covering in an abandoned house and touched down in Laramie just after dawn. They still might have made it to the terminal before sunrise, but for some unimaginable reason—their plane seemingly the only machine awake, their wing lights the only illumination on the ground that didn't emanate from the spreading pink overhead—they idled almost an hour on the tarmac while the Invisible Man fidgeted in his seat like a five-year-old and Emilia soothed and shushed him the way a mother might, or a sister. Or lover.

That was his first flight, after all, she thought. *All those things he claimed to have done and seen done, but he'd never before left the earth and returned to it.*

Unless you counted dying, however and whenever he'd done that, if he actually had. Did that count?

Thoughts like those didn't even jolt her, anymore. But the next one did:

My first flight, too.

A long time ago, late in the evenings when her mother finally coaxed her father into turning down his record player, he'd come and sit on the edge of her bed in her tiny room and tell her how, one day, he'd whisk her off into the night sky and take her to his childhood haunts in Bogotá. Together, they'd hunt old forty fives and seventy-eights in the market stalls on hot, buggy weekends, nosh *dulce de leche obleas,* and dodge the jugglers and acrobats. Somehow, her notions of flying had conflated with imaginary Colombian wanderings with her father. Until tonight, whenever she'd imagined air travel, she'd envisioned more singing.

Right before their plane finally moved toward a gate, Emilia began to worry. Every time she stopped murmuring, the Invisible Man resumed squirming in his seat. She had kept their shade drawn, but everyone else seemed to have opened theirs, and now sunlight poured through the cabin and down the aisles as though hunting. The cowboy in the Nordstrom tie across the aisle had stopped bothering to keep his glances sidelong; he stared openly as the Invisible Man twirled a frayed edge of bandage at the bottom of his neck like a little girl with a hair curl. Way back in his throat, he'd started to grunt.

He's going to lose it, Emilia knew. *If we don't get inside soon.* Why that thought made her feel guilty, she had no idea. None of this was *her* fault.

Except maybe not standing up right now, and screaming a warning. Getting the exit-row passengers to pop the door, trigger the slide, jump, run.

To calm herself as much as her companion, Emilia forced herself to lean in closer, murmur faster. She didn't even know what she was saying. All the while, she fingered the holes in her arm, playing the notes. *D E A C. D E A C.* She'd done this so often now that she'd started recalling whole songs from fourth-grade music class, which was the only one she'd had before her school district cut arts instruction for good. At the end of the year—in her honor, Emilia was convinced, possibly even after a complaint from her father, though he'd never mentioned doing that—they'd learned "La Cucaracha." So she played that, now, on her open veins. On the air whistling over and into them.

Finally, inevitably, the Invisible Man popped open his seat belt, started to stand. Emilia grabbed hold, pulled hard, and was surprised when he yielded, folding back on himself and dropping his head onto her shoulder. He whimpered like a puppy appealing to its master.

Only then did it occur to her that she might be exactly

that: his *master*. At least, she might become that, one day. He clearly wanted, even needed one. So she grabbed him by the hair as hard as her fingers could grab, which wasn't very hard, in her weakened state. Hard enough to surprise him, though, and the surprise kept him quiet just a little longer. Holding tight, she serenaded him, singing along to the notes she alone could hear emanating from her arm.

"Shall I tell *you* a story, for once?" she said, when she'd finished the song.

He didn't answer, but he went more still. The plane, mercifully, started to move toward the terminal. She told him about her name. About her father's lifelong Faulkner fixation, which only intensified after he finally got the glamorous opportunity to be the first-ever South American–born hire—as an adjunct, teaching half Introductory Literature Survey and half in the adult education extension—at Delta South-Jackson University. He'd demanded that his only daughter be called Emily, in homage to the Great Mississippian, and to bind her to his adopted homeland of magnolia trees and soft-spoken julep sippers who mopped sweat from their brows and swayed to the sweet breezes and didn't seem to hate him.

It had taken most of the pregnancy, as Emilia's mother told it, to convince him that using that name might be bad luck. She even got him to scour the entire Faulknerian oeuvre for a more suitable choice. And when the twenty-six hours of labor had ended, and their baby lay quiet and squinch-eyed and squirming on Emilia's mother's breast, her father had grinned down at both of them, softly weeping, and said, "The problem is, they're all bad luck."

So her mother had suggested Emilia.

The whole time she'd been telling the Invisible Man this story, Emilia had slowly lowered her head, feeling her companion—*captor*—go still against her. She was all but kissing his ear when he suddenly straightened, gazing at her out of the holes in his bandages, over the ridges of his charred and ruined skin.

"It's a very musical name," he said in a slow-honey drawl her father would have loved. No: *recognized*. Because this drawl was learned, just like her father's. Another imitation, an even more skillful one. Whoever the Invisible Man had once been, he wasn't Mississippi gentry, either.

At any other time, Emilia's eyes might have filled with tears. She half expected them to, anyway. But she had no tears in her, just a permanent, floating fug that had cleared for one sweet second.

She made herself gaze straight back at the Invisible Man, and sure enough, she could see him in there. She was there, too, floating in his irises like a little bluegill behind aquarium glass. Slowly, sadly, from far away, she felt herself smile. "My mother was a fish," she said.

To get him off the plane, past the wide-open windows, she had to drape him in his coat and her coat, then borrow a blanket for his head. They waited until even the old couple a few rows ahead were wheeled off by the ground crew. Then, huddled together, they hurried up the jetway. They were a few feet from the building when a gust of wind battered the walls as though trying to get at them. The Invisible Man jerked his head up, catching a pinprick of light on one exposed ridge of cheek before gasping and ducking. As though from inside the terminal, Emilia heard herself laugh. As she did, her arm tightened around his long, bony shoulders.

At the car rental counter, while her companion lurked on the far side of the baggage carousel, Emilia procured their transport using the driver's licenses he'd procured or had forged somewhere and a credit card he gave her but that she suspected wasn't his. The license with the picture that looked a little like hers bore the name *Debra Billingson*. Emilia wondered—without any emotional response she could detect in herself—if that was a real person. Or had been. She kept expecting the terse, college-aged African-American woman behind the counter to pause as she stared into some alert on her computer screen with her startling blue eyes.

Was it possible that someone back in Butterfly Weed, in her old life, had found the trail Emilia had left? Recognized it for what it was?

Oddly, Emilia still felt little beyond curiosity. She also didn't seem to be opening her own mouth, leaning in to beg for help or to warn.

Still too risky. Still not the moment.

Instead, she waited, stealing glances at the rental agent's eyes. That astonishing color. As though all the sky outside the glass sliding doors had swept in and filled her. Maybe what had happened in the Butterfly Weed library—what the Invisible Man had done to her there—wasn't so rare as she'd imagined. Maybe it happened all the time, to everyone. Sooner or later, the world you lived in permeated your skin like light, like air, not so much changing or claiming as reminding you:

You belong to me. You are made of me . . .

"Anything else?" said the rental agent, snapping off words as though popping a gum bubble. She handed Emilia keys and a map shaped like a paper place mat with horseshoes and saddles decorating the edges. Already, those eyes were moving to the customer behind Emilia. The Nordstrom cowboy.

Emilia almost blurted out everything right then. The whisper rose in her throat. *Help me. Get help.* But she turned away before the words could escape.

Why?

Because if she said those words, the woman with the eyes was going to die. Emilia couldn't have explained how she knew this. She had never actually *seen* the Invisible Man do anything, except to Emilia herself.

But she did know. So she waited. Made herself bide her time.

Barely five minutes later, her moment arrived.

The car, of course, was *out there,* in a lot a good two hundred yards away, across a wind-whipped, shimmering lake of weak October sun that, to her companion, might as well have been a lava flow. Once he'd circled the baggage claim and rejoined her, she offered him the keys. He took them, then immediately offered them back. As she'd known he would.

"Could you get it?" he said, sounding like an infirm grandfather, not so much afraid or weak as overwhelmed. He stared through the glass, no doubt picturing the winking chimera of a woman—creature—he had dreamed, for years, of finding again. His world had come for him, too, after all. *Savagely. And more than once,* Emilia realized,

with a spasm of something very like . . . though of course
it wasn't . . .

He pushed the keys into her palm. Her fingers barely
trembled in the taking, the trembling as much from weak-
ness as any effort to disguise her intentions or keep herself
from grabbing and running. At the threshold, just as the
doors whisked open, Emilia hesitated for a single moment.
Until then, she'd somehow kept from glancing back to
check whether he was following, but now she let herself
look.

Had he intuited her thoughts? Did he know? He was
just standing there, watching his . . . *companion? Blood
cow? Valet? What was she, now, exactly?* . . . melt into all
that terrifying daylight.

He'd made his choice. He would take his chances.

Out she stepped. She almost hesitated again as she
passed from under the overhang above the taxi queue
into the sun, half believing the light would hurt her, too.
But it didn't. It just poured onto her face, not warm, so
much drier than any sun she had previously known, and
yet so *alive*. Her steps accelerated.

Keep going, she thought, and went on thinking it. *Get
in the car. Don't hurry.* There was no need to hurry. She'd
simply climb in, head straight to the back of the lot and
onto that open, empty access road. Then she'd disappear
into the plains or up the mountains. He would never
find her.

He wouldn't even bother looking. She wasn't what
he'd chased, or would, ever.

She shuddered as she clicked the key button, watched
the little green Cougar blink awake and chirp almost like

an actual cat. Like a living thing, welcoming her back to her real life.

Go, she was thinking. *Drive!*

But even before she'd settled behind the wheel, other thoughts blew through her.

He was her responsibility. She couldn't just leave him in this airport, huddled and hooded and scared. Unsupervised and close to panic. She would not be able to live with the consequences.

Also—though she didn't want to examine this thought at all—she didn't appear to want to.

Backing the Cougar out of its space, she turned toward the exit to the lot, which turned out to be on the terminal side. That postponed her decision a few more seconds. The Invisible Man had emerged through the sliding doors and was standing by the empty taxi queue, in the dip in the pavement down which people wheeled rolling bags, right at the edge of the shadow provided by the overhang.

Her Invisible Man, small and scared and hopeful amid all these Stetsons. All this sky.

In spite of that thought, or maybe because of it, and with a bang in her heart as though someone had set off a firecracker under her ribs, she pushed her foot down on the accelerator. *Go!* she was still screaming inside her head. Her tires squealed, and the Invisible Man looked up, right at her. He knew. She was sure of it, realized that she was accelerating rather than stopping, understood that she was going to blow right past him. His eyes grabbed hers as she approached, still accelerating. Unless—wait—were *her* eyes grabbing *his*? She watched him twitch in his bandages, felt him *know.*

Then he made his own decision and stepped off the curb into the road.

Go-o-o, Emilia's mind shrieked and went on shrieking even as her foot leapt to the brake and slammed down. The Cougar bucked beneath her like a rodeo horse as it skidded to a stop.

Through the windshield, she watched the Invisible Man stare at her. At *her,* in spite of the sun on his skin, which had to be sizzling even through his coat and her coat and the airplane blanket and his bandages. He was staring at her, and never mind his precious Aunt Sally, hovering forever over his life like God. A god that had abandoned him.

He'd stepped out to her. Right into her path.

To make it easier for her to run him down? As a challenge?

Or in a sign of trust?

He *trusted* her, she realized, astonished. Partly, she was sure, because he had no choice. He would not be able to get where he needed without her. But at this second, this pathetic, monstrous creature needed her more than any living thing had needed her, ever. She had, at last, made herself indispensible to someone.

Some part of her, way down in the depths of her brain, kept screaming, but she was no longer listening. She watched the Invisible Man move for the passenger door. Watched her fingers pop the lock to let him in. When he'd settled in his seat, hidden as much of himself as he could under the coats and blanket, he peered at her sidelong out of the cave of hoods he'd made. Emilia felt tears on her cheeks again. She couldn't have expressed—and didn't want to examine—why she was crying, or for whom. But every time she did it, she found the fact that she still could a sort of comfort.

Once they'd reached Laramie, they made stops at three motels, two coffee shops, and a library to leaf through the last week's local papers. Within an hour, they had the confirmation they'd come for. The trail was obvious, in the end. The traces unmistakable if you knew what you were looking for, and accepted that it was real.

"They won't still be here," the Invisible Man announced, once they'd pieced together all the bits of fact and anecdote they'd collected: the redheaded fairy girl no one had seen before, who'd sung one song at the little folkie joint downtown and then vanished; the two mutilated corpses found fifteen miles apart within a week of each other, one in a motel room no one could remember renting to anybody, the other washed up against a fence way out on the plains. That one was mostly bone, like something buffalo hunters might have left if there still were such things as buffalo hunters, and if they hunted things other than buffalo.

Before leaving the library, they used a computer terminal to comb the police blotter for stolen-car reports, then checked the Greyhound and Amtrak stations. Finally, safe under cover of darkness once more, they returned to the airport, where the Invisible Man showed the one photograph he carried of his precious Sally to every desk agent he could find.

By midnight, he and Emilia were on a flight to Bellingham.

14

The first text of the day dinged Trudi awake at quarter to seven. Blinking in the Sunday-morning dark, she rolled over, cleared sock puppets off her pillow, and pulled her phone from underneath.

The texter was Eliana, naturally, back already from her first-thing-everyday swim practice, having apparently just read Trudi's final barrage of messages from the night before, chronicling the latest round of Stockade insanity: Eddie hiding in the woods somewhere; Jess and Joel and Benny scurrying in and out of the compound shouting instructions to each other, none of which were *hey, he's done this before, why don't we just hang out and wait for him.* At one point, Benny had even put out a plate of mushroom-eggs and ketchup, Eddie's favorite, on the picnic table, as if the kid were a cat.

Much later, around ten thirty, Jess had remembered Trudi and called up, "Hey, keep your eyes open, huh?

Keep watch? Call me the second he comes back. I'll be . . ." Then she'd gestured at the trees, as though that were some sort of destination or plan.

To her own surprise, Trudi had tugged the window open to answer, mostly because Jess always managed to look so goddamn small. It was a knack she had. "He'll come back. He always comes back."

"I know," Jess had answered, in that voice of hers that actually said, *I almost know.*

That seemed fair enough, given Jess's life. And so, despite her being sure—nearly sure—that Eddie really would be back, Trudi had done as asked. Instead of going to bed, she'd sat at her window, talking to her hands. Sometimes, she put her puppets down and used her thumbs and her phone—the portal through which she communicated with the mainland, that magical other dimension where people lived with parents and didn't get devoured in woods—to talk to her friends. She watched the yard and the back of the main house while everyone else swept into and out of the trees. Around one thirty A.M., jerking out of a cliff-dive in her chair, it occurred to her that tonight's Jess-overreaction might not be so overreacty. That's when she'd unleashed her final volley of texts about her "family," which wasn't the way she thought of the people she lived with, just the closest she could come with any words she knew. *Family* was closer than *keepers.* By a little, anyway.

Sometime after two, feeling only slightly guilty, Trudi had given up, crawled into bed, tucked her phone into its permanent depression at the top of the mattress, and fallen asleep. She'd dreamed of other woods. Of the circle of trailers near Halfmoon Lake, and what she and Rebecca had found there.

Sometimes, Trudi really believed it was only her phone, always charged and perpetually alert under her pillow, that kept her from waking up screaming every single morning of her life.

Today Eliana's first text read, *Jesus, Tru, U liv w wood sprites!!*

Before Trudi could clear her brain and sit up and settle back among her puppets to answer, Raj chimed in.

& witches, bitches!

Snorting, Trudi glanced toward the window and considered creeping over to the main house to see if everything was okay. She wouldn't actually have to go in, probably. Only after a few seconds did she realize she was praying again, in her way. At least, she thought she was praying. No one she'd lived with—either in Jess's Stockade or Amanda's house at Halfmoon Lake—had ever taught her how. If there was a how.

She prayed that Eddie had come back. She prayed that hard, even though she rarely talked to the kid. Probably, she realized, and not without regret, she spoke less to him than to her mainland friends, whom she only spoke to when she was at school and had never once invited to the Stockade because she couldn't imagine them here.

Because it wasn't safe here?

She read Raj's text again, could practically hear him crowing the words in his defiant, fag-boy singsong.

Only guy I know who can txt gay, Trudi typed. Floating behind the words, she could see the ghost of her own reflection in the viewscreen. There she was, superimposed on an actual conversation. Practically a real person. Almost present out there in the world most people lived in.

Had ur rampion? Raj responded.

Trudi scowled. That joke had soured the first time Trudi herself had made it, way back in fifth grade, in the aftermath of her very first 5 A.M. foray across the Strait to Bellingham Harbor School. The teacher, Mrs. Kobenberg, had decided to read them "real" Grimm stories, for an opening-day treat, because they were "older now, and should start to understand the world as it actually is." When she'd gotten to the end of "Aschenputtel," and the little cooing crow in the story started going after eyes, Trudi had shot to her feet, hurled her backpack into Mrs. Kobenberg's face, and fled the room, screaming.

After that—after a few days, when the school had decided she could try, once more, to return, under strict probationary conditions—Trudi knew she had to turn what had happened into a joke. It was only a matter of which fairy tale her classmates would select her nickname from, so she'd done it for them. Picked the character least like her that she could possibly imagine, so that maybe the name wouldn't stick for too many years. And since she lived on an island, up in a minitower, imprisoned and cared for by a woman who wasn't her mother . . .

I'm letting down my hair, Trudi texted, silenced the phone, and dropped it facedown on her nightstand before it could alert her to Raj's or Eliana's answer. Then she lifted her hands to her head, fingering the tight cornrows along her scalp. If she shaved off all six of them and stitched them together, she'd still have more of a friend-ship bracelet than an escape rope.

Her fingers slipped for the millionth time to the fraying band of black and red thread around her wrist. Here was the only friendship bracelet anyone had ever given her, and it hadn't come from a friend, but from Danni, the bitch-tormentor who'd traumatized her life at Halfmoon House, then suddenly—on her last day on Earth—knocked at Trudi's door, handed her this bracelet, and herded her out to the woods. So Trudi could watch her die.

On the nightstand, the phone buzzed, vibrated closer to Trudi like a little winged beetle. Ignoring it, she flung the covers back, slipped out the other side of the bed, and went to the window.

What had she expected to see? A big banner, maybe? "Welcome Back, Pain in the Ass Kid?" A cake with can-dles where the mushroom-eggs had been?

There was none of that, of course. In the creeping morn-ing gray, the only things moving in the yard were the light and the mist. The house itself stood dark. Rebecca and Kaylene appeared to have come back from their latest shrieky-music-for-shrieky-girls show, because the curtains in both their rooms were drawn, now.

But Eddie's curtains . . .

Slipping fast into jeans and one of her two blue BELL HARBOR KELPIES hoodies—the only sweatshirts she owned, "gently used" school uniforms having replaced Amanda's bargain-catalog orphan-wear in Trudi's half-empty dresser drawers—she grabbed her phone, then checked Jess's bedroom across the hall. The door was closed. Maybe

Jess was in there sleeping instead of still out hunting. Maybe everything was okay now.

But if she opened the door and Jess wasn't there . . .

Instinctively, or maybe superstitiously, Trudi decided not to do that. Instead, she tiptoed down the staircase. Whether Jess was in her room or not, it seemed better neither to wake her nor to know, at least for a few more minutes. As she stepped out into the wet grass and pooling mist, Trudi realized she was praying again. *When had this started?* she wondered. *And how did you stop, once you start?*

Then she wondered why was she so sure she *shouldn't* pray? Which of her caretakers had taught her that?

Halfway across the yard, shivering in the chill, Trudi slowed, then stopped. At first, she thought the morning bird sounds had halted her. Not the shrieking gulls—she loved shrieking gulls, almost considered them her spirit animals—but that breathy, humming moan. Click-and-moan. Somewhere back in the firs that ringed the yard, or in one of the little rock mounds in the woods, was a pelagic cormorant's nest. This according to Rebecca, who for some reason researched such things. Whatever it was, it made noise mostly in the early morning, and mostly, it moaned. Occasionally, like now, it squeaked low, like a baby rolling over in its crib during a nightmare.

But that wasn't what had stopped her. Nor had the white mist swirling around her ankles like a river of ghosts. The mist here never stopped or scared her. All mist could do was make her cold.

Even after she realized what she'd seen, she stayed put a few moments longer, staring at the main house's patio doors. Or, more precisely, at the single square of crumpled green paper pinned halfway up the door. As Trudi watched, it lifted slightly, straining against the strip of tape that held it in place. It could have been a grocery store receipt, or—yes—a check from Benny's diner.

That's what it had originally been. Now it was a note written in black marker. Just a few words Trudi couldn't quite read from where she stood.

Like, *Bye, Trudi*. Or, *We've had enough of you*.

In the woods, the cormorant clicked, then squawked, triggering a riot of louder hoots and screeches all over the woods.

"Now you've done it," Trudi murmured, lifting her hands. Letting her hands talk to each other. "Woken the whole family. Stupid bird."

At least the racket spurred her off the grass onto the patio. She edged up to within a few feet of the darkened house, until she could read the note:

HE'S FINE. KNOCK OFF THE RACKET.

For a few seconds, as the world seemed to slide from under her feet and leave her suspended in mist, Trudi stared. Then she whirled, throwing up her arms to swat away whatever she was suddenly certain was lunging for the back of her neck. In that instant, she was sure she really did see something—someone—melting back into the shadows of the firs.

Unless what she'd seen was the shadows of the firs shrinking as the rising sun erased them.

Whirling again, she confronted the note, stared it down as though she could make it blink or melt it like a shadow in sunlight. But the note stayed where it had been taped sometime last night, right under Trudi's watchful eyes, which were apparently less watchful than she'd always convinced herself they'd become.

How was that possible? When had this happened?

Abruptly, she had another thought which was actually more of a vision: of herself stomping into the woods right now, scattering shadows and cormorants like a ferry churning wake, rousting everything in her path until she found Eddie and stole him back from whoever had written this note.

Then she had an even crazier thought.

Could this be from one of her friends? Raj or Eliana? As a joke and a hello? For one moment, in early morning sun, that seemed right on the edge of plausible. The exact sort of prank Eliana and Raj might concoct, having had enough of Trudi never inviting them to see where she lived.

Had she even told them which island, though? She didn't think she had.

Probably not them, then. But being the first one to see this note, take action, locate Eddie, and bring him safely back ... wouldn't that make her, at last, an undeniable and indispensible member of ... whatever it was they had here?

"Stupid bird," said one of her hands to the other, or maybe to her.

Before either hand could say anything else, Trudi turned and walked straight back across the grass, past her tower and into the woods. Her gaze flashed everywhere, boring into the shadows. She didn't waste much time in the trees; if Eddie were here—wood rat though he might indeed be—

someone would have found him by now. Anyway, that note suggested he wasn't hiding. Someone had him. He was where *that person* was.

Bursting onto the cliff-side path, she stopped momentarily, startled by the colors. Mist had unrolled like a giant futon on the surface of the ocean, which shaded gray and blue as the watery sun lifted like a tousled head off its surface. All around her, blue rye grass shimmered gold, dusty purple, and green as it shifted, settling and resettling. In that instant, suspended above the Strait as though at the prow of a ship, Trudi felt the island behind and beneath her, so much more teeming with life than it seemed from her tower. Too vast and shadowed for anyone ever to search or know, just like every other square mile of miraculous land on the planet.

In actuality, the island wasn't vast all. And she wasn't so very small anymore, either. Jess and Joel and Benny would have looked in all the places Eddie usually went—his orca cove, his wood-rat tree stumps—but not in places the leaver of that note might have taken him.

Assuming, then, that that person was neither okra nor wood rat, and also unlikely to be hanging out for pancakes and coffee in Benny's diner, there were only a few places left where he or she might be. All of those places were clustered off to Trudi's left, between where she currently stood and the abandoned barracks.

Goddamnit, Eddie, she thought, then thought of Danni again. Danni escaping with her into the Halfmoon Lake woods, shrieking and laughing, on the day Danni died. Which had also been the only day she'd been Trudi's friend.

"I'm coming," she murmured. "Little fucker."

She started left along the cliffs toward the low, crumbling, stone and wooden buildings of Hornby Camp. She was pounding the ground with her feet, hands up, palms and fingers chattering to each other inside her head as she plowed forward. Birdsong dropped away behind her. The Strait went quiet, barely even brushing the rocks below. A single gull broke from its yammering companions overhead to wheel behind and sometimes ahead of her, in case Trudi was headed for food. It shrieked sometimes, and Trudi found herself glad of its company, of any noise that wasn't her own feet in the softly switching grass.

That proved especially true as she crested a rise and the blue rye thinned and she found herself looking down the gently sloping edge of a caldera-shaped depression in the rocks and grass. The hollow marked the place where, a hundred and fifty years earlier, a handful of English soldiers had established their own Stockade, planted a Union Jack to express solidarity with the only slightly larger British platoon over on San Juan Island proper, and claimed these cliffs for a few more years for England.

She'd learned that history tidbit during her first year at Bellingham Harbor. The fact that the event was taught at all amazed and amused her. In New Hampshire, she'd learned about Minutemen and abolitionists. Here, teachers recounted the Pig War, a years-long "conflict" between camps of soldiers who rarely even saw each other, named for the only creature—the one pig—that had died in it.

In the thinning mist and creeping light, the four remaining structures of Hornby Camp—only two with roofs, and only one with all of its walls—barely looked like buildings at all. They were more like kicked-over cairns, their stones spilling across the dirt, not even substantial enough to haunt, let alone hide a kid in. And what would haunt them?

She'd been wrong. Had to have been.

"Spectral ghost pig . . ." murmured one of her hands to the other.

"Oiiink," the other whispered back.

The circle of abandoned trailers in Halfmoon Lake woods had been scarier—*much* scarier—even before the whistling freak in the hat had broken Danni's back over his knee, then shredded Amanda as though pulling apart string cheese.

Yet standing atop the slope in what constituted full sunlight in this place, at least in early November, Trudi couldn't get her feet to move. She also couldn't seem to get her mouth open wide enough to shout, *Eddddiiiieee . . .*

The girl below didn't so much emerge as appear. Suddenly, she was simply standing in the grass, halfway between Trudi and the barracks.

Where had she come from? How long had she been there?

Hands still up, riveted in the air as though they'd been nailed there, Trudi stared. The girl's flowing red-and-pink-striped hair seemed to stream from her scalp, sweeping and swishing around her as though she were made of grass. She'd seen Trudi, too, and was gazing up the rise, looking as surprised as Trudi felt.

But less alarmed. And smiling.

Too soon, Trudi thought, then wondered what that even meant.

Smiling wider, the girl in the grass floated uphill. Her

gaze held Trudi's. Trudi didn't try to look away. Part of her wondered why she thought that would be hard. She considered stepping back but didn't do that, either.

Couldn't?

Get away, Trudi snarled, but only inside her head. Even her hands had gone silent, sagged to her sides. Dimly, she wondered how it was possible that she'd never seen this person before. Sure, Trudi had made it her business *not* to know as many of her fellow islanders as possible, but she'd ridden the ferry hundreds of times with every single other kid on this island. All twenty or thirty of them. She did it every goddamn day.

Then she wasn't thinking at all, just floating, as though on her back in a pool, gazing into the cloudless aquamarine of the other girl's eyes.

An arm's length away, the grass-girl glided to a stop. She swayed, and the rye swayed around her like the hem of a skirt, as if she were a *Wizard of Oz* witch who'd dropped out of the mist. In the part of her brain that still felt like her own, Trudi hoped this witch was the good one.

Slowly—beautifully—the grass-girl smiled wider.

Not like light spreading, Trudi thought without thinking. *More like darkness pulling back. Like tide receding.*

"I was supposed to stay put," the girl said.

Trudi seemed to be smiling back without smiling, or at least without intending to. "Me, too."

"I didn't feel like it."

"Me, either."

It was like one of those mirror exercises actors did, Trudi thought, as the smiles on both their faces stretched wider. *Which of us is leading?*

"Ju," said the girl.

"Tru," said Trudi.

"I like your hair." Ju lifted a hand as though to touch Trudi's cornrows, then dropped it again.

"I like yours," Trudi heard herself say.

"She's going to be mad."

"Yep."

Which "she"? *And how would Ju know?* Trudi was sure she should care but didn't.

"I found a cave," said Ju. "Want to see?"

Side by side, then single file once they reached the cliffs, they made their way down an all but obliterated path, past the abandoned nests of dozens of seabirds long since flown, toward the silent, surging water below.

15

Rebecca had been up since before dawn—in truth, she hadn't slept—and when she heard the cormorant in the woods and creeping footsteps in the yard, she got up, threw on sweats and socks, and started for the bathroom. She didn't bother looking out the window because she didn't care which of her Stockade-mates was awake. If it was Eddie, she'd make him oatmeal with a grape jelly swirly-smile.

If Jess, she'd sit down beside the older woman at the chipped dining room table, sip scalding coffee, and admit, eventually, that she'd been afraid to sleep. Jess would glare at her and say, "Everything worth being scared of happens while you're awake." Rebecca would glare back and answer, "What's your excuse, then?" And they would share another of those one-second smiles they reserved for each other.

If Trudi, Rebecca would murmur, "It's a miracle," loud enough to get a sock-puppet snarl, then drag the girl to the

172

couch and demand to know who she'd been texting lately, so Trudi could have the pleasure of not answering.

If Benny, she'd order up blackberry pancakes, and he'd blink through his thicket of eyelash like a tomcat giving her the slow, we're-old-friends wink and say, "Two dewberry wonder-wheels," and then—over his shoulder as though as an afterthought, with the carton already out and the eggs poised in his palms—"Coupla chicks to ride 'em?"

And if Kaylene . . .

Probably, it *was* Kaylene, Rebecca realized as she swept a toothbrush, hard, through her bruised and swollen mouth. Kaylene wouldn't have slept much, either. As far as Rebecca knew, Kaylene still hadn't slept two consecutive hours in five years, ever since the moment she'd clawed out of unconsciousness to find herself soldered by her own blood to the ice rink in Mrs. Starkey's barn. Unless the blood had been her best friend's. Or her other best friend's.

All of which made what she'd done onstage the night before last that much more inexplicable. Except not really. At least, it didn't seem so inexplicable to Rebecca anymore. Emerging from her room, she tiptoed downstairs and glanced toward the coat closet where she and Kaylene had stuffed the Whistler's hat upon their return, in its mashed paper bag behind the galoshes rack and the scarf pile. It was Rebecca, in the end, who'd decided that they had to bring it home and dispose of it themselves, as soon as Kaylene decided she was done with it. In the meantime, here it would stay, quarantined with the rest of them.

Rebecca very much hoped it was Kaylene wandering around. She wanted to give her friend another hug. There was no need to talk about the fight or the hat anymore because there was nothing else to say. Kaylene had been right after all. The hat was a hat. Now it was Kaylene's hat, to wear with stripes.

The living room was empty. Rebecca glanced toward the kitchen and through the sliding doors into the yard, but there was no one in either place. For a few seconds, she stood by the couch with her hands on her hips, tonguing the bruises Kaylene's guitar pegs had left when they slammed into her mouth. In truth, Rebecca had slammed into them while hurtling onto Kaylene's back. All she could really remember of that moment was shrieking—her own—and then the monstrous feedback roaring out of Kaylene's amp, the geysers of surprised shouting from the audience, and the feel of the Whistler's hat squirming in her hands. Oily, *juicy,* like a giant centipede she was popping.

Trying to pop.

Joel, she realized. That's who must have been moving around. The fact that she hadn't even thought of him before now provoked another ache, from a much older, deeper bruise.

Joel. Or rather, Ghost-Joel who lived under the Stockade stairs. The only resident of the place who'd shown no sign whatsoever, as far as Rebecca had seen, of resurrecting or recovering or even remembering himself.

Whirling, she grabbed her laptop off the counter where she'd left it two days ago and jabbed it awake. *Why had she never tried this? What if Joel had just been waiting— exactly the way he used to, back in their East Dunham lives—for Rebecca to surface on his screen and tell him she needed him? Call him out to play?*

SMACKDOWN? she typed. She wasn't even sure that game

existed online anymore, knew neither of them would remember their old passwords even if it did. She also knew
that wouldn't matter. What mattered was her message in
his morning, scrawled across his computer window like a
word traced in dew. Their private code for *Hello, old
friend. Almost-dad. I'm sorry I've been so . . .*

He didn't answer. He wasn't on his computer or even
awake, most likely. Pushing back from the table, Rebecca
started to stand, then froze. That old sensation—her Spider sense, or "trick," as Jack and Marlene had called it,
back when there'd been a Jack and a Marlene—sizzled
through her skin and paralyzed her. For a second, she literally could not breathe.

It had been so long that at first, she couldn't remember
what to do next. She felt herself casting about inside her
own head as though riffling her desk back in the UNH-D
Crisis Center for the ALWAYS DO/NEVER DO instructions on
how to handle suicidal callers. Instructions she'd memo-
rized and never once consulted or needed. She'd always
just intuited. Known. She knew now.

What did she know?

Whatever it was, it hurt. Horribly. As agency returned
to her limbs and she got herself moving down the little hall
toward Joel's door, the hurt softened, rounding into something richer, something strangely *right*. Almost like the
faint, flickering ache that came with memories of her parents. Because in truth, ever since the cataclysm in the woods,
and even before, maybe since the day Rebecca had moved
out of Halfmoon House, right on time and in just the way
she was supposed to because she'd grown up, she and
Joel had been floating inexorably away from one another.

They'd kept calling back and forth across the void, but they'd gone on drifting, like the doomed astronauts in that Ray Bradbury story he'd insisted on reading her once, at bedtime, no less, because he was Joel, haunted in the dark but singing by dawn.

There were tears in her eyes and a sort of smile on her face as she tapped gently, for form's sake, before pushing open Joel's door. For a breath or two, she stood, absorbing the room's new emptiness, feeling it fill another pocket she'd never known she had inside her. *That's what we really accumulate,* she thought, to the extent that she was thinking anything. *Not experience, not memories, but holes. We are places to put empty places where people we loved have been.*

"Off you go," she said. Even to herself, she sounded like a mom saying good-bye to a child. Already, she could picture herself brewing coffee, starting pans for Benny's eggs, and telling the rest of her Stockade-mates the news, one by one, as they awoke and came down to start their days: *Joel's gone.*

It wasn't even a new role for her, she realized, wiping her cheek. The whole time they'd lived here, she'd thought of this place as Jess's Stockade. They all had. Yet it was Rebecca who dealt with Trudi. Rebecca who'd bought the battered drum set, on impulse, at the monthly San Juans flea market, started bashing it on a nightly basis, and eventually badgered Kaylene into forming Sock Puppet. Rebecca who did most of the playing with Eddie, because Joel wasn't up to it, anymore. She could feel her housemates above and around her, attached to her, as though she were the trunk of a surprisingly sturdy tree. So much more deeply rooted in this world than she'd imagined.

Suddenly, she remembered. Shuddered, straightened, and spun around, glancing everywhere. There *had* been someone down here this morning. In this room, or skulking around outside, peering through the glass.

Back in the living room, she stared into the yard but saw only mist and milky morning sunlight. There were no lights in Trudi's or Jess and Benny's windows in the tower out back. Rebecca was already half across the dining room, preparing to throw open the door and yell for Jess without being sure why, when the knock came.

Came again.

Rebecca froze. Eventually, she turned toward the front door, simultaneously taking a step away from it. She was trying to remember if anyone had ever knocked on that door. Surely, someone had: a mailman, although they hardly got any mail; Benny after forgetting keys; someone. The sound seemed completely out of place, superimposed from some other house in another dimension, where a different Rebecca lived with an actual family to which she'd been born. If the cormorant from the woods had popped its head out of the kitchen-sink drain and hooted at her, that would have seemed more natural. As though dreaming, she felt herself stumble forward. She opened the front door.

The force of the gaze that met her slammed into Rebecca like hail, hit her so hard and fast that for a second, she thought she'd been blown off her feet, sent flying backward. The woman's face was shaded by a heavy umbrella—there was no rain, just misty early-November morning sunshine—and a gauzy veil that obscured everything but the blaze in her eyes. She lifted the veil and let Rebecca see her face. Her skin was perfect, shimmering black. The night sky walking.

Rebecca knew what she was looking at before the woman so much as smiled or said one word. She remembered this feeling, would never, *ever* forget it. But what she'd felt before barely even qualified as the same experience. Was the kiddie-ride version. There would be no leaping back from *this* gaze, the way she'd managed to when Sophie had shivered up out of the sheets in the attic bed where Jess had hidden—and imprisoned—her. There would be no leaping toward it, either, the way she had with her shovel when she'd murdered the thing in the hat.

No. The best she could do this time was stagger back a single, shuffling step and drag her head into a half turn. Her gaze didn't pop free. But at least it slid sidelong. A little. That was something. A very small something.

It was more, apparently, than the woman expected, because as she stepped into the house, she said, "Huh." Lowering the umbrella, she released Rebecca long enough to glance around the living room, up the shadowy stairs toward where Kaylene slept, down the hallway toward where Joel mercifully didn't.

That was something, Rebecca thought, *and not so small a thing, either: Joel had gotten away. With luck, he might never even know what happened after he'd gone.*

Thinking that triggered a new revelation. A little one, and hardly surprising, all things considered: she was preparing to die. She had been, really, since the moment the monsters had come to East Dunham.

Maybe even before that. In truth, she'd been preparing for this moment since the instant she'd opened her childhood bedroom door to another knock, in the middle of the night, and found not her parents nor her babysitter but a police officer. Such a tired face that woman had had. Almost featureless, worn smooth like a beach stone. There had been no pull or power whatsoever in *her* gaze. She'd had a surprising, gentle voice, though, all whisper, more mama-librarian than northern New Hampshire cop. Rebecca could still hear that voice, though the only words she could remember it saying were, *Get dressed, honey.*

At her sides, her fists curled uselessly, except maybe as silent signal. Reminders to herself: she was going to die. She did not want to. Not even with all these pockets sewn into her skin, overflowing with people she'd already lost.

The woman took a single step forward, and her face blotted out everything else. Eclipsed Rebecca's whole world.

Rebecca forced her mouth open to scream. But she didn't. *Not couldn't, didn't.*

She stared, though. *The eyes on this woman.* They were somehow churning and still all at once, like the surface of a great river and also the river underneath. The smile on her mouth never got near those eyes, but it glittered, fleeting as sunlight sparkling on water.

"Don't worry, little fighter," the woman said, smile sparking brighter and then fading as she rummaged in the pockets of her heavy coat. Her voice seemed to probe at Rebecca, latching onto memories and instantly poisoning them. This voice was almost a perfect opposite, or negative, of that New Hampshire woman cop's voice. So purry-soft, for a creature with *that* mouth.

No longer smiling at all, the woman held up an old, creased Polaroid.

Before her visitor could ask her question, Rebecca gasped. She felt as though she might literally fall *into* the photograph. Or as though she were emerging from it. The sight of the hat was not what upset her, this time. It was the face underneath: the papery skin, the jack-o'-lantern grin that sang, had kept singing even as Rebecca slammed her shovel into and through it. Over and over and over.

Finally, she understood. It wasn't the monster's face that had haunted her all this time. It was not what the bearer of that face had done to her life and loved ones.

It was what she'd done to *it*. To *him*.

What she'd had to do.

Creased as it was, the Polaroid seemed to overflow with color, though the scene was shadowed in darkness. River reeds flowed in all directions and a swollen moon flooded river and earth alike with whiteness.

The hat was there, all right, but not where it belonged. It wasn't on her monster's head, but slumped—almost curled, like a cat—on the head of the grinning woman draped over his shoulders. At first, Rebecca assumed that woman was her current visitor, then saw that it wasn't. The woman in the photograph was heftier, with dustier skin and lighter eyes. Same mouth, though, or at least the same sort of smile, hovering by the monster's ear as though she'd just finished whispering or was about to whisper. Like a lover, or a mother.

How could something with that *mouth love? How could any mother or lover love that thing?*

That boyish, grinning, monstrous thing.

"You *have* seen him," the woman hissed, snatching

back the photo, advancing so fast that Rebecca half expected to feel her reaching inside her skin, rifling her as though she were a trunk.

"I . . ." Rebecca managed, trying to squirm back but managing only to drag her head a few inches farther away. The woman's breath smelled surprising. Mint and apples. Yet it stank.

"Out with it, missy. Is he . . ." The woman stopped, mouth open, hand raised and cupped as though she were about to grab Rebecca's chin. Or scoop out her eyes.

But she looked startled. Stunned, even. As though something had just occurred to her. In that single second, watching this new monster's terrible, beautiful face, Rebecca thought she recognized something in her visitor's expression. Something she'd learned never to trust and always to dread.

Hope? Was this creature hoping? *What was she hoping?*

"Are . . . *they* . . . here?" the woman whispered.

"They. They're . . ." Rebecca's tongue felt wrapped in cotton, too slow and clumsy for words. "He's . . . her . . . I've never seen her."

Her visitor's face seemed to snap like a bowstring, hope shooting away and that other expression—the killing one—locking back into place. "No," said the woman. "I thought not. Stupid of me." She grabbed Rebecca's face and began to squeeze. "How about him?"

Even as her cheekbones started to bend, Rebecca experienced a surprising surge of relief. She could feel her *self*—her whole self, everything she'd been and done and everyone she'd ever known and helped, counted on and loved—erupting out of wherever it had all been hiding. Flooding through her. What a relief it was, she thought, to die as she had lived. To be who she'd been at the moment she stopped being.

"He's dead," she said. "I killed him."

"*SALLY!*" called a new voice, out of nowhere.

Instantly, the pressure on Rebecca's face released, as though she'd been sprung from a trap. She staggered back, banging against the dining room table, her hands flying out to steady herself, then up to her face to feel the cold the woman's hands had left. Had *imprinted*.

By the time she'd steadied herself her visitor was already out the front door, heading straight down the little drive. At the edge of the Stockade's outer fence stood two more people Rebecca had never seen. A tall man dressed in what looked like a fifty-year-old seersucker suit and bandages that completely wrapped his head and hands, and a wan Hispanic woman with a pince-nez and beautiful, long black hair. The woman seemed to float beside her companion, trembling like a sapling in the morning breeze, shading him with a green-flowered parasol.

"Boo?" Rebecca thought she heard her invader say, in almost—but not quite—the same tone she'd used to ask if the monster and his mother-lover were here. "Is that really you, Boo? Well, I never . . ."

With a lurch and a cry she almost managed to bite back, Rebecca leapt to the front door and slammed it shut.

16

For hours, it seemed, Sophie just sat against the slick, cool wall of the cave and watched Eddie crawl, climb, and perch among the rocks at the back. He moved like a crab and at a crab's pace, scuttling over open spaces, freezing, peering down into some crevice or pool at a sea star or pebble or swirl of water. Occasionally, he'd call out to announce a discovery, but his words blurred in their own echoes, and Sophie simply called back, "Uh-huh," and went on watching. Even more occasionally, he'd remember the game they were playing, take out the dead cell phone she'd given him, and stick it to his ear. Then she'd lift the shell in her lap to her own ear as though it had just rung, and he'd say whatever he said into the phone, and she'd tell him, "Eat." Those were the only times he remembered the apple in his sweatshirt pocket and took a bite.

Mostly, though, the kid forgot she was there. Indeed, he

seemed to forget everything except the rocks, the water, and whatever he thought he glimpsed in them. Sophie, for her part, had temporarily forgotten everything but him. Once, apropos of nothing she could discern, the boy swung his head around, looked right at her, said absolutely nothing, and grinned.

That was the best moment.

"Like my cave?" she'd said then, but he hadn't heard or hadn't understood and had gone right back to exploring. And that was only right, and the reason she'd brought him here, though this place had never felt like hers and barely qualified as a cave, really. It was more a deep, womblike indentation in the rocks, into and out of which the green salt water of the Strait flowed and sloshed like amniotic fluid. Sophie had never lugged belongings here, never set up a tent or anything. Even today, all she'd brought were the groceries she'd stolen for the kid.

Watching Natalie's son prowl, though, she realized how much time she must have spent on these rocks during the past five years. She liked the slap-and-settle of water in its pools, and the occasional sea lion bark or snuffle of something larger surfacing out in the cove. Even more, she liked the spatters of green light playing over the rocks and the piles of kelp strewn about like dirty clothes in a little girl's room.

Not that she'd had that sort of little girl's room, not in the trailer where she'd been a little girl. Sophie would have been terrified to leave clothes on the floor for fear of accidentally stepping on one of her mother's discarded needles.

Soon, she knew, she'd have to take Eddie back. If she

was still planning to take him back, which she assumed she was. What else was she going to do with him?

Except look at him. Watch him slip through curtains of green light and slide his hands into rocks and talk to sea anemones.

Without consciously intending to, Sophie lifted the shell to her ear. She even made dialing motions in the air with her finger, to no one watching.

"Mission Control to Vanishing Boy," she murmured. Her voice hummed in the cave, sounding like breath across an open bottle. Even in her own ears, the words blurred, so she spoke a little louder. "Mission Control to Vanishing Boy. Come in."

It took three more tries before Eddie realized she was calling and turned around. "Huh?"

Sophie gestured with the shell. For a second, the kid looked baffled. Wide-eyed, red-cheeked, dead earnest. Natalie's boy. Then he scowled because he'd been interrupted, and that made him even more Natalie's boy, even though he'd hardly known his mother and certainly wouldn't remember her scowl.

That sweet, savage Natalie scowl.

Fumbling in his pocket, Eddie withdrew the dead phone and accidentally flipped out the apple core along with it. Not that he noticed or cared. For some reason, he shook the phone as if that would wake it before putting it on his ear.

Then he grinned at her again.

From nowhere, a laugh seized Sophie. It was like none she could remember, or rather, like the actual laughs she'd stopped having almost exactly five years ago. The vibration of her ribs jiggled the ghost-weight that was always there on her chest, and for one ridiculous second, Sophie actually thought that she would look down at her body, and there, in his sling, blinking goggle-eyed, would be her own boy.

Her Roo. Who was not asleep on her chest but on Natalie's, in the cave in the ground that Sophie and Jess had dug for them. No matter how often Sophie lifted a shell to her ear and called, her Roo would never answer.

She stood. Eddie did, too, and slipped. He slid on his butt toward the water just as the orca glided into the cave.

It came so smoothly, so naturally, heading right for Eddie, that Sophie had the crazy thought that he'd called it on that dead phone she'd given him. Summoned it like a water taxi, so he could ride across the cave to her side. An image flashed through her head from some old nature TV show—God, TV!—of a whole pod of orcas tossing a screaming kid back and forth between them. Hurling the kid so high in the air, it was as though they were flying him.

Dolphin, she snarled inside her head. Not a kid.

"Eddie," she hissed to startle and alert him. He looked up, looked at her, looked down and saw the whale.

Five years, she was thinking as Eddie froze, his little sneakered feet inches from the edge of the water. Five years, and she'd hardly seen so much as a crab in this cave. Not even a bird.

For a long few seconds, both she and Eddie seemed to hang suspended over the water, not quite motionless but rooted, waving in place as the orca surfaced. Its rubbery skin looked blacker than anything Sophie had ever seen except for the black in its eyes. At least its skin reflected the green of the cave, which seemed to flicker across it and become imprinted in the white patches. The cave, painting itself. The whale's jaws unhinged. The teeth inside were slimed with something dark and glinting that dripped into the cavernous well where its pink tongue lolled. Nothing about that face seemed to be smiling. Slowly, slowly, the whale rolled all the way over on its back. It kept rolling until it was upright again, as though it were bathing in this shadowy light. Taking a shower.

"Sophie . . ." Eddie said, softly—in awe, and fear, but not enough of either. His expression triggered the memory, and the memory flattened her against the rocks:

That night in the Okefenokee, when Natalie had made them turn around, stop running, head home to try to reclaim and save their children. And Sophie, still drunk and giddy in her new body—which was actually the body she'd always had, it was her that was new inside it—had slid out of their flatboat into the brackish, heavy water to float with the alligators.

So reckless. So stupid.

But their skins! Bumping against her. All that cold, throbbing, knobby weight. How impossible it had seemed that anything that heavy and hard could be alive. And yet the alligators were unmistakably, impossibly alive, and old-seeming. Like tipped-over tree stumps, swimming. Hunting.

Insane, Nat had called her. Shouted at her, actually, while demanding that she get out. So Sophie had, eventually. So that Nat—the sane and supposedly less reckless one—could send them screaming right back into the hands of the Whistler and his Mother and Natalie's mother, who had turned out to be the most ruthless, reckless, and murderous of all.

Abruptly, Sophie was off the wall of the cave, scuttling around the rocks toward Eddie, and not slowly, either. "Hang on, kiddo," she murmured, possibly to the kid, possibly the whale. Both of them, she thought, had better listen if they knew what was good for them. Interestingly, no part of her seemed to want to slip into this water.

Eddie, though, was leaning way out over it. If it was possible to teeter while lying flat atop rocks, he was doing that. "Hey," he said. There was no doubt about it. He was talking to the goddamn whale. "Hello."

In the shallow water of the inlet, which barely covered its back and left the top third of its fins jabbing into the air, the whale glided closer. It's going to leap, Sophie thought, and lunged across the last bit of rock to grab Eddie's wrist. He cried out while she yanked him to his feet and all the way back against the wall, which wasn't nearly far enough.

When she let herself—made herself—look down, the whale was still gliding past them, turning lazily, almost as if it hadn't seen them, except Sophie was positive it had. It looked enormous, wilder and even more alien than her alligators. It flowed past, less a thing in the water than of it. Water with teeth. Finally, like an inkwell emptying itself, it flowed back out of the cave into the Strait and vanished.

"Wait," Eddie croaked as Sophie pinned him against the wall. When she was sure the whale was gone, she pulled *him around to the safer, wider ledge of rocks along the right-hand side of the cave. His little shoulders shuddered under his coat. His hands seemed to be pushing against and grabbing onto her stomach at the same time. He might have been talking to her or the orca.*

She brushed his head, felt his silky little-kid hair. It wasn't downy like her Roo's had been, but still so soft. "Yeah, yeah," she muttered, pulling him closer. She didn't so much see as feel the shadow shoot up her back.

Whirling, she shoved Eddie behind her and almost lost her footing, imagined both of them plummeting right into that black, dripping, unsmiling mouth. But she didn't fall, and there was no whale in the water anymore.

There were two girls standing in the cave mouth, haloed by light, staring in. One was a long-haired, willowy thing who was weaving back and forth without moving her feet, the other a squat, cornrowed teen with her fists curled. Sophie felt a surge of panic, and underneath that, guilt. And underneath that . . . nostalgia? Because as far as she could judge, the sensation she had now was the exact one she used to have when Jess caught her and Natalie smoking cigarettes. For a single, crazy moment—for the second time that morning—Sophie almost felt like herself again. Like actual-Sophie. Or, Sophie-before, assuming she was some sort of Sophie, still.

Which she was. Wasn't she?

An all-new dread seized her, this one an entirely Sophie-now experience. Because even squinting into the light, and even though she'd hardly ever seen the cornrowed girl when she'd skulked around the perimeter of Jess's compound, Sophie knew her. That girl had been in the New

Hampshire woods on the night of the Whistler. She'd been there to watch Sophie bury her face in the back of the Whistler's skull, filling her teeth with his cold, weirdly crusty brains (and sure, Soph, right, most brains are wetter, it's the *crustiness* that was weird about that experience).

Her next thought landed softly; it wasn't a prayer, barely even a wish. She simply hoped the cornrow girl hadn't recognized her. Sophie just wasn't in a hurting sort of mood.

The girl was peering hard into the cave, shading her eyes with her hand. She stepped inside. Eventually, inevitably, she squeaked, "Eddie?"

"Hi, Trudi," Eddie called from behind Sophie's back, then marched right past her. The little traitor.

"Where the fuck have you been, you brat? Everybody's totally freaked. Get over here!"

Eddie didn't look back, nor did he bother keeping to the safety of the rocks. He sloshed through the shallow neck at the top of the inlet, right past the place where the orca, less than thirty seconds before, had waited with its black mouth gaping. The cornrow girl scuttled forward to meet him.

The other girl now caught Sophie's attention. She'd stepped forward, too, but only enough to fold herself into the shadows at the cave mouth. More interestingly, she appeared to have eyes only for Sophie. Her head was cocked, and—from what Sophie could discern at this distance—there was a sort of flatly curious expression on her face. It reminded Sophie of something, but she had no idea what at first.

Then she did.

That was the look—the exact one, right down to the angle of the head and compression of the mouth—that Sophie imagined on her own face as she'd studied the alligators drifting around the flatboat that night in the Okefenokee. It was the expression she was almost sure she'd been wearing as she slipped into the water. It communicated curiosity, she supposed, and was also a sort of greeting. A tentative Hello?

As the cornrow girl reached out and tugged Eddie to her side, Sophie glanced away from the willowy girl. She watched green light rippling on the rock walls. She didn't so much remember all the endless, empty hours she'd spent in this place these past few years as retreat toward them like an alligator into its estuary. She no longer had anything to do for the foreseeable future. No one to talk to or stalk or study or hunt.

"Hey, Eddie," she called abruptly. "Should we show your friends around?"

Instead of answering, Eddie spoke to the cornrow girl loudly enough for Sophie to hear. "I want to stay!"

A brand-new smile broke over Sophie's face. This one was equal parts Sophie-then and Sophie-now, Roo-haunted and Natalie-derived and ferry-godmother-fueled and her own. The moment had come, she realized, to make some changes. Set some ground rules. It was time to have a come-to-Sophie chat, for starters, with Queen Jess and all her fearful little Jesslings. Sophie had had enough cave-phantoming and forest-skulking for three lifetimes.

Well, two, anyway.

The willowy girl was well inside the cave now, crouching to run her fingertips back and forth over the surface of the water like lures. As far as Sophie could tell, her pretty, pouty mouth wasn't moving, but she looked like she was making a wish.

Be careful with the wishing, *Sophie thought, and experienced a surprising twinge of something warm, almost pleasant, deep inside her chest.* Watch out for whales.

Moving slow, making sure the cornrow girl saw her coming while keeping her own face averted, Sophie started toward the entrance to the cave. Beyond it, sunlight spangled the surface of the Strait like glitter. What she had in mind was going to hurt, all right. How come, every time she had to deal with Jess's minions, she had to do it in daylight, and therefore burning?

Keep not recognizing me, Cornrow Girl, *Sophie thought. Wished. Just let me go. And by that, what she meant was,* Let me let you go.

"You guys want to watch the kid a bit?" she purred. Super-casual.

Too late, she realized that that request was just weird enough to cause exactly the reaction she didn't want. Which was exactly what happened: the cornrow girl jolted upright, pulled Eddie tighter against her, and looked straight into Sophie's face.

Oh, don't, *Sophie thought. Willed, really. Could she control their memories, too, or just their movements? Five years into her new life, she still didn't know basics like that. She could see the struggle on the face of the girl in front of her. That still might not mean the girl knew who Sophie was. It could have been an automatic reaction* to meeting Sophie's gaze, a sort of terrified-cat crouch. Probably that was all it was.

Maybe that was all.

Five feet away—well within lunging distance—Sophie stopped. She had to squelch a sudden impulse to crouch at the girl's feet and roll over in place like Eddie's okra. To see what the girl would do, and also for fun. Because it would be fun.

All right, *she thought.* Spit it out.

But the girl said nothing. She might have been fighting to say nothing, or she might have had nothing to say. As a test, Sophie let her own gaze drop to the girl's throat. Upon deciding that might not be so reassuring, though, she glanced instead toward the cave wall. Then she made herself wait.

The girl didn't run or challenge or say anything. She just stood there.

"There's plenty of food," Sophie murmured, gesturing toward the indentation in the rocks where she'd stored the groceries. "Just make sure he eats one piece of fruit per Cheetos bag."

"Boooooooo," said Eddie, squirming in the cornrow girl's grasp.

The girl didn't seem to be letting him go. That was a less good sign.

The way Sophie saw it, she only had a couple options, at this point. And only one of them ended with her possibly seeing Eddie again. Or at least, ended with her seeing Eddie without destroying the rest of Eddie's family. Then she wondered if she wasn't at least as much Eddie's family as they were, except for Jess.

The question really was whether he *would think so?*

She made up her mind. "Okay, then. See ya later, Cheshire cat–kid."

"You're *the cat,*" *said Eddie, right on cue.*

"Damn straight." *Sophie was moving, now, steeling herself to deal with the daylight. The willowy girl finished wishing and stood up right in her path. Sophie made to brush past, and the girl grabbed her arm.*

Not hard. But the fingers felt funny, chalky-dry despite having dangled in the water (although Sophie wasn't sure they'd actually touched it).

"You live here?" *the new girl said, and met Sophie's eyes.*

Just as she should have, the girl stiffened. But . . . what's this *I'm* feeling? *Sophie wondered.* Not a jolt. More a tickle. So strange . . .

"I live nowhere," *Sophie answered, without meaning to answer.*

"Me, too." *This girl's eyes were a different shade than the green in the cave. Deep-woods green, and full of shadows.*

Sophie realized she had no idea what to say next, yet her mouth opened anyway. What came out was, "Well, in that case. Howdy, neighbor."

The girl smiled, or at least, a smile ghosted over her face. That was enough distraction to free Sophie—no, that was ridiculous, the smile had simply broken the weird and clingy mood—*and she edged past the girl toward the cave mouth. One more time, she stopped to stare out at the Strait, with its everyday accompanying clouds way out on the horizon, gaseous and imaginary as islands she'd never reach.*

Feeling those deep-woods eyes on her back again, Sophie turned.

"Can I come?" the girl said.

Her instincts told her to flee right now. But Sophie made herself take a good, long look. It was as though this wispy teenager had somehow attached herself with a single touch, as if she were a spiderweb Sophie had walked through. Or, better—assuming she was sentient under that blank stare—a remora. A parasite, awaiting scraps.

But the stare wasn't completely blank. And underneath the blankness was something familiar. In Sophie, that something was a loneliness so old, it predated Natalie's death, or even their encounter with the Whistler. Was probably exactly as old as Sophie was.

How on earth had this kid come by it?

"Take care of the boy," she said. "Of Eddie. Please? I'll . . . be right back."

Was that a shrug? A smile?

Whatever it was, it sent a shiver of pleasure through Sophie. Maybe, in some way she couldn't begin to understand yet, her luck—her lifelong luck—had changed. Just now, in the instant this girl had walked into the cave. Maybe this weird, willowy creature was way more fairy godmother than Sophie had ever been. Maybe this girl was her *fairy godmother.*

"I'll see you soon," Sophie said, and stepped into the light.

17

To Emilia, trembling and tingling in the single shard of sunlight between two towering firs, it was like coming out of a coma. Although she could remember every single thing that had happened since the moment the Invisible Man had turned on her—reached out and claimed her, let her *see* him—the weeks since then felt like home movies of someone else's life or dreams. Not recent dreams, either, and not whole ones, but fragmentary bits that had somehow escaped into daylight to flutter at the edges of consciousness like ash from some long-ago campfire.

She was Emilia again, or very nearly: Butterfly Weed spinster-in-training, or in-residence; catfish taco and Kacey Musgraves lover; Colombian-Mississippian only child; Storybooktime mesmerizer of local kids with nowhere else to go. Standing here blinking and prickling in this weak, almost wintry morning sun, this air so much lighter and more gossamer than any air she had previously known.

Apparently, her coma-dream had been all too real, though, because not five feet away, sheltered in the shadow of the firs, bandaged hands waving and head bowed, her Invisible Man was still talking. His companion—that regal, magnificent woman with the black, curly hair bubbling over her shoulders and down her back like just-tapped oil and eyes deeper and darker than the river back home—was still listening. Her mouth was slightly parted, and sometimes parted a little more. When it did, Emilia felt surges of inexplicable, sickening . . . *what? Pride?*

Because this woman was his Queen? Maybe everyone's Queen? And Emilia's man had pleased or at least amazed her?

Wriggling where she stood, turning back and forth in the light, Emilia felt threads of dream stretch around her but not tear or melt. Indeed, they seemed to be expanding, wrapping more of the landscape like a cocoon. The longer she stayed in the dream, she somehow knew, the more she would change. She had to get free, return to the world she was almost sure she was still part of. If she could just shake her shoulders a little harder, stop leaning forward to hear more of the Invisible Man's tale and observe the Queen's responses . . .

Abruptly, she went still, holding her breath. *How long, exactly, had the Invisible Man* not *been talking? When had he stopped?* He was just waiting, hands folded in front of him yet fumbling over each other in eagerness while the Queen stared. Incredibly, only now did Emilia realize she had no idea what any of this was actually about. And that was proof, more than anything else she'd thought or done, that the Emilia who'd emerged from the Butterfly Weed basement and wound up on the other side of the country in the company of a man whose face she'd never actually seen was no one she knew, or at least no one she'd been.

The Emilia she knew was a finder-outer. A records riffler, a nosy parker. One way or another—through reference materials, dogged research, or just up and asking—Butterfly Weed Emilia would have found out what was going on here long ago.

When the Queen finally moved—straightening, running an absent hand across her cruel, gorgeous mouth—Emilia startled, and the Invisible Man stopped fumbling. Somehow, he seemed to lean in with his chest and away with his waist, moving forward and back at the same time.

The Queen threw back her head and laughed. Not in delight or amazement. Oh, Emilia knew that laugh. She'd heard it all her schoolyard life from white boys and even more often, for some reason, from black girls on the cracked blacktop four-square courts of her dusty, rural Mississippi school. She'd started hearing it right around the time her classmates had given her her first nickname. *Spic-Chick*. The better, nastier name came later. *Chica de la Nada*.

This was *their* laugh.

"Oh, 'Bou," the Queen said, while the Invisible Man bowed his head and dug his feet into the matting of pine needles as though trying to hold his spot in a floodtide. "I never knew you had a dreaming side."

"I don't," he murmured.

Untrue, Emilia heard herself thinking, *you do! Tell her!*

Then she thought she might vomit.

"I always thought you were so practical. So . . . rigorous. That's what I"—(Emilia could see her fashioning the next word, attaching the barb to it; an arrow not just pointed but poisoned)—"*loved* about you."

"It's true," said the Invisible Man, exactly like a kid caught in a lie. But he wasn't lying. "I was. And I am."

"Dutiful 'Bou." The Queen reached out as though to caress or pet, then slipped a single, crooked finger into the tiny gap in the bandages at the side of the Invisible Man's mouth hole. Still sporting that terrible smile, she slid the finger along the side of his face and deeper under the bandages.

Emilia swallowed a yelp. The Invisible Man turned his head into the touch and bumped against it like a cat rubbing its scent on someone. If she wasn't so sure he already knew—*had* to know—Emilia would have warned him: there was no love in that touch. Curiosity, maybe. Cruelty, definitely. Yet he was practically purring.

The Queen tsked, pursing her full, perfect lips. "My poor, glowing boy. Look what I did to you."

What she'd *done? She'd done this to him? And was he really not hearing the self-satisfaction in that question?*

"It's okay," the Invisible Man murmured, squirming at once into and away from that probing, poking touch. "You couldn't have known."

The Queen burst out laughing. "When I lit you on fire, you mean?"

Even then the Invisible Man only bristled, started to

lift a hand to his face to stop that finger. But the hand dropped back to his hip, and his voice came out a sigh. "None of us knew who Ju was. Not even you." Now he wasn't just squirming, but dancing. "You still don't. It's . . . that is, it *was* . . . unimaginable . . ."

Under the bandages, the finger seemed to be pulling, puncturing. The Invisible Man winced, and tears filled his eyes.

"What are you babbling about, 'Bou? I'm amazed and honored that you tracked me down. Truly I am. But then, that was always your particular—"

"You're not going to believe it," the Invisible Man said.

"Tell me." Under the bandages, the Queen's finger stopped moving, curled like a snake under a rock. Way down in her deep, dead eyes, something stirred or reflected.

As though she were emerging from a coma, too? A much older and deeper one?

Waking this woman up, Emilia suspected, was not a good idea. Was an even worse idea than finding her had been. Almost unconsciously, she took a step back at last. But only one.

"The thing is, Sally," said the Invisible Man, smiling off one side of his face, "you'll say I'm mistaken. But I checked. And then I rechecked. The way you know I do."

Sally. What an absurd name for such a magnificent, malevolent thing. Emilia watched her just standing there, regal, listening to the Invisible Man's story.

"I didn't start with any theory. How could I? I was just looking for an explanation of what we all felt, as soon as we laid eyes on her. You felt it, too. It might even be why you felt you had to—"

"Don't ever tell me what I feel. Or felt," said the Queen. Sally. She did something awful with her finger.

The Invisible Man gasped, talked faster. "For the longest time, I couldn't find anything about her. I don't just mean sealed court records from the orphanage. I couldn't find anything about Ju at all. Not one mention."

Ju. Emilia recognized that as a name, somehow knew it was a girl, realized the Invisible Man must have mentioned her at some point in his musings. But none of the research he had let her conduct had had anything to do with any girl. He'd had Emilia focus on tracing his Sally.

Again, Emilia experienced an absurd pang of jealousy, which made her angry. She edged one more step back, deeper into sunlight. She was barely fifteen feet from open road, now. Probably, she realized, her Invisible Man wouldn't even care.

The Invisible Man seemed to puff up as he continued. "But I found her mother's name. Eventually. It's on documents the orphanage ladies went to their usual great pains to secrete away. She's just some local teenager, no one we know and not important."

"'Bou," said the Queen. She leaned forward, almost giving his bandaged nose an Eskimo kiss. "You better get to what is important. I'm not at all sure I like you talking about Ju."

The Invisible Man was smiling again, at least with the side of his mouth that wasn't hooked through the cheek. "What's important, Sally, is that before she got pregnant during her senior year and lost her scholarship to Mississippi State to run track, Ju's mother loved to dance."

"Last warning," the Queen murmured.

The Invisible Man shuffled his feet, folding his fingers together and then apart as though pulling a pin on a grenade. "She loved dancing at the New Grace Holler Hop." He gave a hop himself.

The Queen stood still, stared blankly.

"The New Grace Holler Hop," the Invisible Man whimpered again, all but stamping his foot. "The ones they held in 2003? Those stupid hip-hop barn dances for 'at-risk' teens in that warehouse way out Route 49? Sally, *New Grace Holler.*"

"'Bou, goddamnit."

"The place all your monsters went back to, remember? The place some of them had already been going back to, even before our little Policy game directed them to. To prey on the people there. To *play* with the people there . . . toy with. Dance with. Maybe even . . ."

The story had lost Emilia. *Was Grace Holler another girl? No, wait . . . she'd heard of Grace Holler. Somewhere . . . in a song . . .*

For the first time—not just in this conversation, but possibly, Emilia sensed, in years—the Queen startled. She took a long step back without withdrawing her hand from under the Invisible Man's bandages. There was a wild glimmer in her eye, too; it could have been amazement. It could also have been terror.

"It can't be," she finally said, low and hard. "You *know that.* It's impossible. Not once has one of us impreg—"

"You already know it's true, Sally. You're just having trouble admitting it. The ramifications are too great."

This time, the probing finger didn't just tweeze or tighten; it twisted, and the Invisible Man cried out.

To her astonishment, Emilia felt herself stepping back into the grove, hands lifting as though she were about to interfere. She had to force herself to stop. There was a brand-new voice in her head, or rather an old one, so faint that it took her several desperate blinks to realize it was her own.

Hello, she thought, all but crumpling where she stood. *I thought I'd lost you.* Tentatively, softly, Emilia slid one foot back, then the other. She even navigated a half turn toward the road.

But she didn't run. Not yet. She knew she could, now. She wanted to hear the rest.

"'Bou," hummed the Queen. "I'm about to tear your face off your face."

Through his pain, still grimacing, the Invisible Man drew himself up. Even more hideously, he grinned. "Sally," he said. "She's *ours.*"

"Whose?"

"Ju! Is ours. Half New Grace Holler poor kid. Half monster we made!"

"*I* made." The Queen twisted again, and the Invisible Man screamed. Held his ground.

"Yes. You. Of course. But she's ours, Sally. She's *both.* Did you know that could happen? Do you realize what this means, for all of us?" The Invisible Man threw his arms over his head, open to the sky. "She is something brand-new in the world. Together, we can—"

With a savage downward rip, the Queen dragged the Invisible Man to his knees in the pine needles.

But she was also trembling, Emilia realized. What a miraculous thing, to see this woman shake.

The Invisible Man had not stopped chattering. Through his tears, he blinked up at his queen, holding out his hands. "Sally," he gurgled, "we've had so much wrong. Or maybe something in us has changed. *Evolved.* I don't know. But now, together, you and I can usher in a whole new age! Can you imagine? We can *raise* her. We can . . ."

The next moment was the strangest of all. The Invisible Man glanced away from his queen toward Emilia. The bandages at the tortured corner of his mouth had unraveled and hung from his cindery lips like shredded spider-silk. His whole body trembled, and his eyes—those winking, desperate eyes—leapt for hers. *Like a little boy reaching for its mother,* Emilia thought. As if the Invisible Man were the last of her lost Butterfly Weed library boys, abandoned by fate to whatever worlds he could create inside himself and then hold up for her to see.

"That's what you imagined," the Queen purred. With the hand that wasn't in the Invisible Man's mouth, she patted his head. Stroked it. "That's what you dreamed all these years under your bandages as you learned all of this, then tracked me down." She made a kissing sound with her mouth. "That you—my sometime pleasure-toy, it's true, and my very favorite crawling thing—would become my partner at last. The companion to help me usher in this bold new age. Ju's . . ." The woman shuddered. Then, to Emilia's horror, she giggled. *"Father."* She erupted into laughter.

With a jerk—really more a flick of her wrist—the Queen yanked the Invisible Man to his feet, pulled his head around, bent forward, and—her finger still in his cheek—kissed him full on the mouth. A squeal burst from Emilia's lips. Even she had no idea what it signified. But she staggered back, her eyes locked on the clenched creatures in front of her. The way they scrabbled and grabbed at each other, they might have been climbing one another, fucking, or fighting for their lives. Whichever, that kiss just kept coming, the Queen somehow *burrowing,* her face driving into and up under the Invisible Man's bandages. The noises they were making—low and constant, half feral cat and half incoming hurricane—blended together, filling the grove as their faces mashed deeper into one another. Only slowly—but *before* the blood burst from between their lips, spilling down the Invisible Man's bandages into his collar and spattering across the Queen's cheeks—did Emilia realize what was actually happening. What the Queen was doing to her Man.

No! she realized, with a tremor so primal it seemed to stem from the very center of her, from the ghost of umbilical cord that had once tied her to her own mother in the only way anyone is ever actually connected to anyone else. *It isn't just the Queen. They're doing it to each other.* The Invisible Man, it turned out, had had an entirely different ending to his quest in mind. Even as she thought that, the moaning and yowling from across the grove got *wetter,* filled with horrid, sucking, burbling sounds. She saw the Invisible Man's arms float up. They encircled his queen as the long, silver, serrated blade he'd probably had secreted against his skin for years slid from its sheath of gauze. And as his hand rose to strike, and his face caved in—dry as dust after that first blood spatter, like old drywall crumbling to paste under the bandages that had held it in place—Emilia had one wild idea, and an even wilder sensation, both terrible, both brand-new.

The sensation was another surge of sickening pride. Triggered, apparently, by the sight of her Man fighting back, the confirmation that he'd come all this way to avenge, not crawl.

The thought was that she didn't understand these creatures at all.

The arm that encircled Emilia's waist came from nowhere, tightened and yanked her backward so fast that she never so much as cried out. The last thing she saw in the clearing was the Invisible Man's knife driving straight down between the shoulder blades of his queen, just as his entire head burst inside his bandages, crumbled to ash and collapsed.

And the first thing she saw when she rolled over in the dirt was a sweating, rake-thin black man with a smile on his face as ferocious as any she'd seen on the Invisible Man's. Except this smile was also scared and sad and therefore human.

"If you want to live, you've got to run. We have work to do," he said.

He didn't wait. And once she was on her feet, the urge to look back slipped off her like snakeskin.

As in, the skin of the snake that had swallowed her whole. It was nothing that had actually ever been her at all.

18

To Rebecca, leaning against the dining room table with one hand on the back of a cracked wooden chair and the other in her hair, it felt horribly like waking up. As though the last five years—the whales and cormorants, the Stockade and Jess's windmill shed, Sock Puppet and the sea mist on the sweetly rolling Strait— had been not just sleep, but self-protective coma. Now everyone's eyes had come open at once, and here was the world just as they'd left it the day the Whistler came to Halfmoon House.

She couldn't make herself join in, yet. Partly, she couldn't quite believe what was happening. That is, she couldn't believe the *efficiency* of it all. Jess had dumped all the knives out of the woodblock onto the counter, then ducked into the garage just long enough to grab a set of long-handled garden implements Rebecca had never seen before and drop them on the kitchen floor. Next, from under the pans in the back of the cabinet under the sink, Jess withdrew a stack of already cut two-by-fours. She took those straight to the nearest window with a hammer in her fist and nails in her mouth.

Meanwhile, Joel—who hadn't fled, after all, or who'd fled and come back trailing a stumbling, gaunt-faced Latina with a motionless mouth and screaming black eyes that suggested she knew exactly what all this was about— sat at the far end of the table, away from the glass sliding door to the backyard, cleaning and loading his revolver. On his face was some sort of approximation of his old smile, the first Rebecca had seen in years, like fire reflected in metal.

Kaylene, insanely, had donned the Whistler's hat and produced an aluminum bat from somewhere, and now was taking practice swings hard enough to behead the couch in the middle of the living room. Jess had glanced her way long enough to note the hat and nod approval.

Benny was at the stove monitoring the oil he'd set bubbling in all three saucepans.

For a collective last meal? Pre-apocalypse stir-fry? Last-ditch Peace Summit banquet? Had all of them forgotten just what it was that was coming?

Had there been meetings she'd somehow missed? Of the Go Down Swinging (and Also Raking and Hoeing) Club, Far Northwest Chapter?

Finally, Rebecca couldn't take standing still anymore, so she moved to the kettle to bring the Latina some tea. Benny leaned away from her as she approached. Now that she thought of it, since the second Joel had burst through the front door with the Latina and his news—

which had happened scant minutes after Rebecca had reeled away from her encounter with the woman who'd knocked at that same front door and shown her the Whistler's photograph—everyone in the Stockade had been haloing around her, surrounding but not demanding anything from or even including her. Keeping their distance.

Because I'm the only one who has actually killed somebody, she thought, and even as she thought it, she remembered it wasn't true. Jess had killed her own daughter, for God's sake.

Which might or might not have been necessary. Or right. In the same way—and with even more devastating consequences—that Rebecca's murder of Sophie might or might not have been necessary or right. At least that murder probably qualified as collateral damage. To anyone who was keeping a ledger.

Wincing at the spatters of oil leaping from the saucepans to her arm, Rebecca dropped a spoonful of jasmine pearls into Jess's Frank Robinson Day Orioles mug, added steaming water from the kettle, and took a second to watch the pearls unfold into the heat like blossoms into light. Then—avoiding Kaylene, who'd swept past to get a bread knife she seemed to think might work as some kind of bat-bayonet—she brought the mug to the table. The new woman didn't look up until Rebecca sat down.

She was younger than Rebecca had first supposed. Not even thirty, most likely. Possibly no older than Rebecca and Kaylene. Her skin stretched threadbare across her cheekbones, almost transparent despite its duskiness. Her lips looked drained not just of color but texture, worn completely smooth like runoff grooves at the edge of a record. And then there were her eyes. Those silent, screaming black eyes . . .

Understanding broke over Rebecca the way it always had, in a single burst. She hadn't experienced a flash like this in years—*God, she really* had *been asleep*—and now she only prayed this one had come in time to save them all.

In one motion, as the woman reached mechanically for the mug of tea, Rebecca seized her wrist, shoved the black sleeve of her sweater up past her elbow, and yanked her whole, bare forearm into the sunlight still spilling through the unboarded half of the sliding door.

The woman shrieked, as Rebecca had feared and expected. She tried just once to yank her arm free, stopped, and stared down at her own skin. It wasn't steaming or even reddening except where Rebecca clutched it. Not even around the puncture marks dotting the crook of the elbow, which Rebecca had *not* expected. They gaped, crusty and unscabbed, weirdly wet. Less like track marks than open mouths.

Silently, softly, the woman started to weep.

"I'm sorry," Rebecca murmured, still holding the woman's arm but gently, now. She'd been all geared up for an unmasking, a confrontation. Now she felt like she was stroking a dying cat, which was an absurd and incoherent association on all counts. Nothing about this woman was catlike, in either the cuddly or menacing sense. She wasn't dying. And she clearly wasn't burning in discomfort where the sun kissed her, either.

Not much, anyway. Not the way the monsters seemed to.

More than anything, the woman seemed embarrassed

or ashamed. She also looked less afraid than Rebecca would have been under the same circumstances. Whatever those were. *What circumstances are we all imagining we've got, here? Assuming Joel and I are even right about that woman . . . how had she even found this place? And why would she have bothered?*

"I really am sorry," she said again. "We're all just . . . What's your name?" She released the woman's arm.

Instantly, the newcomer's hand leapt to the sleeve of her shirt, but she didn't tug it down. She'd slid forward in her chair, staring down at—or *into*—the holes in her elbow. Softly, then with increasing force, she pressed her fingers into the blue veins around the holes until little bubbles of blood surfaced in those open mouths.

The sight was as mesmerizing and also just plain *wrong* as anything Rebecca had ever seen. She felt as though she were watching film of a mother bird feeding chicks, except backward. So that the mother was *extracting*.

"Stop," Rebecca snapped, grabbing for the woman's wrist again to make her.

"Emilia," the woman whispered. She was no longer crying. She pressed down harder, squeezing more blood out of herself. "My name is Emilia." She sounded like she was reminding herself.

All Rebecca knew for certain was that she wanted to yank Emilia out of her chair and fold her into an embrace. Simultaneously, she wanted to recoil as far from her as she could get. She waited for her vaunted intuition to tell her what to do, and in its absence settled for a pathetic half-measure and echoed the woman's name. Reinforced it.

"Emilia," she said, and felt more than saw Jess start to move behind her. Rebecca stood up in her path.

Jess barely even hitched her step, just altered course to flow around Rebecca again. Rebecca blocked her. The question no one seemed to be asking leapt to Rebecca's lips. She almost didn't voice it, precisely because no one else had. The possibilities it suggested seemed too terrible even for this appalling morning. But someone had to say it.

"Jess. Where's Trudi?"

At least Jess stopped moving. But she wouldn't meet Rebecca's eyes, and all she offered was a shake of her head.

"You don't know? Are you kidding? You're just leaving her and Eddie out—"

"She's fine. He's fine."

"*What?* When did—"

"We . . . got a note."

"What? From her?"

"Also, I texted. She practically texted back before I hit Send." Finally, Jess glanced up. To Rebecca's astonishment, she was almost smiling.

Reflexively, Rebecca smiled back. Almost. "Of course she did. That's how Trudi rolls. She's got Eddie? She found him?"

"She found him. I didn't ask how. I didn't ask where. I didn't even know she'd left her room."

"Well, I'm asking where. How the hell did—"

"No idea. But I told her to stay away. To keep Eddie hidden and away until we say it's okay to come back."

"What did she say to that?"

"A lot of *d*s."

Jess's smile had long since drained away. No longer meeting Rebecca's eyes, she started again toward the tackle box full of screws and nails at the edge of the counter.

"*Ds*," Rebecca murmured.

"Fuck if I know."

Harder than she meant to—and she meant to do it hard—Rebecca grabbed Jess by the shoulders and spun her around. For a second, the two of them swayed in place and clutched each other, as though clinging to the sides of a collapsing rope bridge. It really did seem as if the whole Stockade were swinging beneath them, giving way as everyone here scrambled or leapt for their lives. Except Emilia. She was still staring down at the holes in her arm as though into the abyss.

"Jess," Rebecca said, and at long last, there it was again. A flicker of her old calm and clarity. *Where have you been, Rebecca-I-used-to-be? I need you now. Come home . . .*

"Rebecca, let go. They could be here any second. We've got to—"

"What? We've got to what, Jess?" She didn't release her grip but loosened it. Turned it into an awkward caress. "What, exactly, do you think you need to do? Or can do?"

With a ferocious shiver, Jess shook off Rebecca's hands. She'd come back to herself, too, Rebecca noted. Or at least part of her had. Her gaze was her steely one, the fighting mask so familiar, now, one could almost have mistaken it for her face.

Unless one knew her better, the way Rebecca did.

"What do you *think* I'm doing? Jesus Christ, Rebecca. Why aren't you helping? Get a knife. Get a wrench. Get a fucking bobby pin and *do* something."

"I am. I'm holding up a mirror."

Just like that, Jess went still, clamped her mouth around the words she'd been about to spit and stared. It was possible, Rebecca thought, that Jess was going to punch her.

Instead, she said, "Okay."

"What do you see?"

The sound that burst out of Jess's mouth could have been a sob, a laugh, or a strangled shriek. Whatever it was, there was only one of it. For that instant, only, Rebecca thought Jess might implode, crumble to dust. But all she said was, "I see a woman born for this."

"For killing? Jess, you are so not—"

"For *grieving*. For missing. Rebecca, I miss her so much. Every second I am alive, whether I'm asleep or awake, it makes no difference. I am an organ for missing."

"With a hammer in your hand."

"I'm not the idiot who invited them in," Jess snarled. *At Natalie,* Rebecca knew. *Through grief so all-encompassing, it could only express itself as fury.* "But they're not staying this time. And they're not taking one thing more from anyone else I love. Ever."

"We don't even know it's a *they,* Jess. And we have no idea what they want."

"I'm pretty sure I know what they want," Jess snapped, so hard that her mask slipped, allowing a glimpse of the face underneath. The same one Rebecca had first seen hunched over her daughter's photograph in the perpetual gloom of the burned-out house in East Dunham, or stirring spaghetti at the stove to take up to her broken lover. Or turning in doorways to reach out, abruptly, and stroke

Rebecca's cheek. Gather one more lost girl to her because she just couldn't help it.

Stamping her foot, Jess shook her head again. "What do *you* think they want?"

You trust me, too, Rebecca thought, through no tears. They both wore their masks so well now.

"I have no idea," she said softly.

"Right. There you go."

"How would I? Or you, either. But Jess, there's one thing I do know: we can't fight them."

"We did last time."

"We had help," Rebecca murmured, and then she blinked, couldn't help it, and there Sophie was, as always, right on the undersides of her eyelids, her mouth bloody and blooming and her eyes not quite wild enough, staring up at Rebecca as Rebecca slammed the shovel down.

Jess was neither smiling nor glaring, now. Just standing there saying nothing, because there was nothing to say.

Except *I love you.* So Rebecca said that.

Jess nodded, grabbed a fistful of nails and another two-by-four, and returned to the sliding glass door. At the table, Emilia looked away from her own arm long enough to watch. Even Kaylene glanced up from the work she was doing on her bat. Sick and sad, helpless and small, Rebecca turned away toward the hall. So she was the only one who saw Sophie dance out of the shadows near Joel's bedroom door, throw her arms wide, and grin.

That grin.

"So, I was in the neighborhood," Sophie started.

Never in her life had Rebecca moved so fast, and even as she snatched out her hand and grabbed the nearest saucepan, she knew it shouldn't have been fast enough. That she was a hypocrite and a knee-jerk fighter just like Jess, after all. Also a scared little girl.

But not an orphan, anymore.

Then the oil was flying and Sophie was screaming and crumpling, her hands clawing at her face as the residents of the Stockade whirled and swarmed her.

19

*S*werving and stumbling, cursing and laughing, Aunt Sally swept through the woods, wild as a wind off her beloved, far-off Gulf. Branches, leaves, and the shadows of branches and leaves leapt from her path. She kept trying to straighten as she plunged ahead, but she couldn't get her spine around the goddamn knife Caribou had stuck in her, and she couldn't reach it, either, so she gave up trying and hurtled onward. Like a harpooned marlin, she thought, the very air foaming in a wake around her, her skin glistening against the gloom. Running not to get away—since she'd already ripped her harpooner overboard and out of his life—but just to run.

Poor, sweet 'Bou. How well she'd chosen, all those decades ago, on the night she'd somehow singled him out and elevated him out of his ordinary, servile life into living. At least, to the extent that she'd actually made that choice, because she hadn't planned to do anything other

*than feed, really. But somehow, blood, fate, perhaps even
Policy had chosen for her. Matched him to her.*

*Policy. At the beginning, that had just seemed a game
she'd dreamed up, a method for attaching numbers to
dreams, thereby randomizing decisions she saw no need to
make consciously. Eventually, to her monsters, it had become almost a religion, and even Sally herself had had fun
trying to decide whether she was more High Priestess or
Living God. At the very end, during her last years in camp,
Policy had sometimes even felt like religion to her. A system for being, if not a reason. In all her years of living and
preying, she'd never before had either.*

*If Policy had chosen Caribou for her, it had done so
superbly. He had served her for decades. He had helped
her keep their monsters safe. He had mapped out a whole
new Monster Landscape to lay over the existing maps of
the disappearing Delta, giving their evolving world form
and landmarks and names. Every now and then, for rare,
fleeting, and spectacular seconds, he had fucked her into
forgetting (though exactly what she forgot in those seconds, she could never have said. Any more than any other
living thing could, she supposed).*

*Finally, he had brought her Ju. Today, as his last gift, he'd
told her who Ju was. In so doing, he'd tripped a lever not
even Aunt Sally had imagined was there, dropped a gate
she'd long since forgotten had contained her, and set her free.*

Unleashed her.

Hello, world, *she thought, throwing her arms wide,
catching spots of sunlight on her wrists and ignoring the
sizzling sensations. Loving the sizzling sensations.* Thank
you, 'Bou. I'll never forget you.

Nor, apparently, would she jettison his taste anytime soon. No matter how many times she spat, it stuck to her gums and furred her tongue: rancid blood; fetal, half-formed skin-graft skin; bandage thread; and antiseptic.

Still. Having Caribou-residue in her mouth seemed a small price to pay in exchange for his final, magnificent offering. That last revelation, unveiled in that elegant, cultured voice he'd cultivated, or invented, because what culture had he ever known or been part of? Half closing her eyes as she rushed on, she called up his voice again. Listened to him tell her what he'd learned.

Ju is ours . . . Something brand-new in the world . . .
Brand-new in the world.

Her Ju. The truth was, Sally had known it, instinctively, right from that initial glimpse of the girl in the backseat of the Le Sabre as Caribou delivered her to camp. Certainly, she'd known by the time she settled the girl on her lap and fell into those winking, bottomless green eyes for the first time.

Yes. She'd sensed it all then. She just hadn't let herself believe or even imagine it.

Now Caribou had confirmed it. His final sacrifice, and his most profound thank-you for the bonus life she'd bestowed upon him. She hoped he'd considered it worth it as she'd sucked him through his imitation skin and into her.

She was sure he had.

Approaching the edge of the forest, beyond which daylight raged like a brushfire at the lip of a break, Sally forgot the knife, somehow drew herself all the way straight, and let out a bellow that set squirrels screaming and birds flapping and fleeing their nests all around her. The tip of the blade jabbed at the back of her throat with every lunging step, burying itself deeper in or through her spine. Like Excalibur, *she thought, denying the instinct to slow or wait and instead accelerating toward the light.* Excalibur, lodged in the Lake of Aunt Sally, to be withdrawn only by the new, true Queen of the World.

With a scream like none she'd ever uttered or caused, and with Caribou's revelation pumping down her veins, so fierce, so loud—like a goddamn heartbeat*—Aunt Sally erupted from the woods into the sun.*

Her plan was to race straight into the open and along the top of the cliff, defying the daylight, and continue racing all the way back to the abandoned barracks where she and Ju had set up camp. In her current mood, fueled by what she knew, Aunt Sally believed she could have withstood even a full-Delta summer sun, and this limp, mistwreathed thing was a pale approximation of that, about as much true sun as Caribou's burned and scabbed-over face had been the one she'd remembered. Compared to the jabbing and scraping between her shoulders and at the top of her lungs, the pain from this light barely even registered.

At least, that's how it felt for the first hundred steps. Sometime in the second hundred, though, she caught herself glancing down at her forearms, checking for bubbling, liquefaction. She found none, of course. She knew the sun's actual effects on her were sensory only, and possibly not even physical at all but entirely psychological. A warmth from back when it was possible to be warm; an array of colors from when her eyes could hold and process color, triggering memories of remembering, of clutching at moments as they thundered past. Yet that feeling of burning always proved virtually impossible to fight or ignore. Even on this mist-shrouded island, during this cloudless day that remained the color of drizzle. Even shielded and swept aloft by the marvels of this morning.

With a snarl of frustration, Aunt Sally staggered to a stop, tried to straighten again but felt the knife grind deeper into the notches in her bones. Sun spattered over her like sparks from a fire. Far ahead—too far—she saw the grassland. She'd have to get all the way there, then down the other side to reach the barracks and Ju, who didn't know yet just how miraculous she actually was.

Aunt Sally could make it if she willed it. She could do anything, after all. She was the mother of monsters, bestower of Policy, dreamgiver. Lifetaker and lifemaker.

But she'd be a shuddering, weeping, staggering wreck by the time she got there.

Except she wouldn't. The moment mattered too much, demanded the pomp and gravity only she could bestow.

Like a coronation. Because that's what it was.

Throwing back her head, Aunt Sally let out one more savage scream. Of frustration, yes. Of hunger. But most of all, of unimagined, unbounded, limitless freedom.

Then she stumbled forward again, accelerating into a trot, then a sort of ducking, loping gallop. Here I come. To say hello. To touch the face of my reward, my most exquisite gift. To introduce you to you.

By the time she reached the top of the rise and started down toward the barracks, she was flat-out running, shouting Ju's name.

20

In the cave, while Eddie splashed in the not-so-shallows at the edge of the rocks and Ju lingered in the shadows along the wall, Trudi kept reaching into her pocket and checking her phone. She didn't need to look at it to know there weren't new messages; she'd become as attuned to those vibrations as the twitching of her own muscles. The gesture was more reflexive, conversational, the equivalent of her Bellingham Harbor friend Eliana pursing her lips and blowing her forever-damp hair out of her eyes.

After the first few times, she even stopped pulling up that last text from Jess just to make sure she'd read it right. She had, she knew. And it was definitely Jess who'd sent it, because everyone else with Trudi's number actually understood how to *use* a *cell phone,* and why *not* to disable autocorrect.

*StaywhereyOu are wher e ver yo are don't come back
illsay when stay eddiehiden hide*
The fuck, Jess?

On the back of her neck, Trudi could feel Ju's gaze lingering. Meanwhile, in the not-so-shallows, Eddie kicked up spray and chattered to his hands or whatever he had in his hands. Shells and stones. Trudi knew those conversations too well and respected them too much to interrupt.

She also knew, somehow, that she wasn't supposed to text Jess back. She was supposed to stay right here—*whereyOu are*—and wait. She'd feel the vibrations signaling whatever she was meant to do next when they came.

What the actual fuck, *Jess?*

Then vibrations did come, and she fumbled the phone out of her pants so fast that she almost spilled it into the Strait.

The texter wasn't Jess, though, but Raj, doing his signature *Frog Prince* backward-text babbling, today.

Langing hoose. In hy mouse. Quinking thietly. Trere, oh Trere, is Whudi?

Trudi's laugh seemed to burst from her throat, startling her all the way back to herself. She used the phone to snap a quick pic of Eddie hunched over and murmuring to the cave water as though summoning more orcas. Reversing the camera, she framed her own anxious face, angling the phone to catch at least the shadow of the new girl—*Jew? Joo? Named, perhaps, for or by some green-eyed, Swedish owl?*—lurking just a little too far up the cave wall, weirdly still, like a spider or a stalactite with really remarkable hair. She snapped that. Then she fired both pics back to Raj with the words:

Tru Through the Looking Glass. Episode 16,338.

When she lowered the phone, she found Ju studying her again. Not just looking, but full-on examining, as if Trudi were a particularly colorful shell, an octopus that had scuttled up out of the Strait. As if Trudi were the first black girl she'd ever seen.

Or first girl, period.

God, she's really beautiful, Trudi thought, positively *heard* herself think, and realized she was probably looking at Ju the same way Ju looked at her. *Beautiful, in a twilight-in-twinflowers-on-the-hills-above-those-weirdo-barracks sort of way.*

Definitely not in a come-down-off-that-wall-and-bring-your-fairy-mouth-to-my-mouth sort of way.

Not really.

"Fuck!" Trudi burst out, shaking her head hard, stumbling before she'd even started moving. She dragged her gaze from the girl and back around to Eddie, or halfway around, anyway. She couldn't seem to get herself fully turned, but at least her feet were in motion. She half staggered, half splashed into the water, which was freezing and woke her further, still. With a pop she could almost hear and definitely felt, her eyes wrenched free of whatever had held them, and she turned her full attention to the kid.

Only then did she realize how far out on the rock shelf Eddie was. He stood almost knee-deep in water, so close to the edge of the ledge that his toes had to be dangling over the abyss where the cliff fell away into bottomless blue deep enough for orcas. Blue enough that Trudi could see his face reflected on its surface, even in cave-light, as though he were already draining into it, becoming part of it.

"Eddie, *Jesus*," she snapped, too loud. Echoes ricocheted like gunshot, and Eddie jerked and slipped, flinging a glance over his shoulder as his feet scrabbled for purchase.

Ignoring the shock of cold in her ankles, Trudi plunged forward. By the time she got close enough to seize the kid's wrist, he'd already regained his balance. He laughed as she yanked him to her.

"Ow!" he complained.

"Quiet."

"I wasn't finished."

Whatever that means, Trudi thought. But in truth, she understood, at least in essence. He hadn't finished reprimanding a crab, maybe. Telling some krill it couldn't talk to him like that, not if it wanted its screen time later.

Eliana and Raj were right, she decided as she turned and tugged Eddie back toward dry rock. It was time to get the hell out of Wonderland. Maybe she could take Eddie and Rebecca and any of the rest of her Stockade-mates who were whole enough to come along with her. Instinctively, she kept her eyes averted. That was why she didn't realize where Ju was until her reflection surfaced upside down in the water right in front of her.

For a wild, panicked second, Trudi thought the girl was *over their heads, hovering on the cave ceiling.* A gasp escaped her mouth before she could stifle it.

But Ju had simply come down off the wall, and now she

was maybe three steps away, separated from Trudi and Eddie by a barely there lapping of inches-deep inlet.

Which is what's saving us, Trudi thought nonsensically, the thought bumping repeatedly against her brainpan like one of those wind-up toy trains she'd once aimed into walls in the common room at her first orphanage, the one with beetles infesting the carpets. *She can't cross running water.* She clutched Eddie's hand, and for once, for some reason, he clutched hers back.

Ju didn't even seem to be looking at them. Not at first. She stood so still. Only her hair seemed to wave, slightly, like kelp in shallows, stirred as much by the light filtering through the cave as by current or breeze. When she did look at them, first Eddie, then Trudi, her eyes were green and full of shadows. Deep enough for orcas. Trudi could no longer keep herself from looking at that face.

Then, with a sort of mourning-dove coo, Ju stepped down into the water. Her whole body rippled, and her hair swept in front of her eyes. When it slid aside again, she was smiling.

"Cold," she said. "Sooooo cold."

"No shit," said Trudi. Suddenly, all of them were laughing, Eddie too, their voices caroming around the cavern. Dazed, or maybe dazzled, Trudi watched Ju shake, watched her gaze trail lazily all over the cave before gliding back down on her. Trudi could *feel* those eyes on her forehead, cool as a cave kiss.

She also felt a pang of something very like jealousy when Ju's gaze slid to Eddie.

"Little boy," Ju said. "Come here."

And Eddie—the fickle little shit—just up and went.

Like he *already knew her*. Stupid, trusting baby, who'd been unlucky enough to have people who loved him around him for every second of his life, and was therefore utterly unprepared to live in the world.

Shivering in the ankle-deep wet, but unable to move or imagine where she'd go if she did, Trudi watched Ju stroke Eddie's head. Her hair floated around him like jellyfish tentacles as she leaned down to whisper. There was her beautiful mouth by his ear, hovering near his throat. For no good reason, Trudi wanted to launch herself, barrel into the girl and drive her back. Hurl her down on the rocks. Get her off and away from Eddie.

So I can get on her??

What. The seriously actual. Fuck.

"I think we should go back," she said, the words spraying from her mouth like a BB-gun blast.

For answer, Ju ran a pale, long-fingered hand through Eddie's hair. The boy shuddered but didn't pull away. If anything, he wriggled closer. When Ju finally looked up, she was sporting that strange, shy smile. "I think we should go to the barracks. You know that place? Those . . . old bunk buildings, or whatever?"

"Hornby Camp!" Eddie yipped, like a little puppy.

"They remind me of home," Ju murmured.

"Me, too," Trudi heard herself say even as she wondered.

Home. As in, a room full of bunks for other girls without homes. *Which meant Ju was an orphan, too?* Was *that* what Trudi had been sensing?

"I think maybe we should stay here," she said, though she couldn't think why. Without meaning to, she smiled.

She also seemed to be swaying on her feet. Jealousy and nervousness and unexpected recognition and something else she didn't even want to think about flickered through her, yet she felt a little removed from all of it. As though none of these sensations were actually hers, or real. As though this were all just another conversation with her sock puppets. As though she'd magicked her sock puppets into walking at last.

"I think we should go to the camp," Ju said again. "But let's wait until dark. How about that?"

"Until dark," Trudi murmured. Heard herself murmur. This time, when Ju smiled, Trudi sighed, or maybe whimpered. Way down in her brain—deep, deep down where she'd buried it under even her fragmented memories of her parents, the smell of tea and towels at Amanda's worktable at the Halfmoon Lake house, the sound of bitch-queen Danni's spine snapping on the night the Sombrero Man came—something rolled over and sat up.

That smile. Ju's smile. That shiny, sweet, sparkling thing with needles in it.

She'd seen it before!

Hadn't she?

On Ju? Not on Ju. Not on the Sombrero Man, either, God knew, so why was she thinking of him?

For a split second, she had it, almost had it, almost knew.

Then Ju said, "Good," and gave the sweetest, sexiest little shrug, her hair sweeping over her face past those wet, winking eyes. "Then I can introduce you to my . . ." Her smile got even sweeter, a little confused, a little helpless, and then she gave up and flat-out giggled. "Mom."

21

A t first, while everyone else hurled themselves atop the blonde they'd driven to the floor, Kaylene froze. She literally could not think what to do. Benny and Joel and Jess and Rebecca each had a limb, plus fistfuls of hair or other body parts, and even if Kaylene wanted to help, there wasn't room. Plus, the screams felt like daggers in her ears, which was ironic given what she and Rebecca had done with their free time these last few years.

Eventually, one by one, her housemates went silent even as they went on wrestling. But the silence exposed the blonde's cat-yowl raving, which went on and on and on like feedback from a guitar plugged in and left onstage at the end of a show. If Kaylene had had her own guitar, she would have let loose just to drown out the cat-yowl, or at least give it some harmony. Make it music.

Rebecca glanced up and caught Kaylene's eye, the way

she had so many times from behind her drum kit in the eye of whatever whirlwind of sound they'd unleashed and were riding. Usually, Rebecca was smiling, those times, but she wasn't now. Her mouth had slackened into a sort of open oval, and her eyes—those quiet, see-everything eyes—were full of tears.

Because the monsters are back. Because this is one of them.

The smell of Mrs. Starkey's ice rink flooded Kaylene's nose and mouth, set her gagging. Her heart thundered so hard that she had to grab the countertop to stay upright. Rebecca saw and started to stand, but she couldn't let go of whatever she was crushing to the ground.

Memories came the way they always did.

Jack on his flying saucer on the ice, sailing through that cone of light which he'd almost seemed to carry with him into the dark. The Thing in the Hat at the other end of the rink with his arms wide open. Marlene sprint-skidding after Jack as though there were anything on earth she could do other than die alongside him.

Jack and Marlene.

Jack and the . . .

"Kaylene!" someone shouted, and Kaylene pushed off the counter, moving toward the scrum on the floor.

"Rebecca, *wait,*" Joel snarled, too late, and Kaylene saw.

Rebecca was staring down into the blonde's one open eye. She didn't look hypnotized or mesmerized or whatever it was these monsters did to people. She was just being Rebecca. Just seeing. Abruptly, she rocked back on her haunches and freed the blonde's arm.

Up the arm snaked like a powerline, like a cobra. But it

didn't shoot toward any of her attackers. It flew to the blonde's own face, the oil-flooded eye that seemed to be swelling and sinking at the same time, boiling to nothing, pooling in its own pith like a stewed tomato.

When Kaylene finally knelt, she did so behind the blonde's head. Her hand went toward the woman's cheek, which was sizzling and spatting. So many times back at the battered-women's shelter in East Dunham, Kaylene had caressed cheeks like this. Or not quite like this, those cheeks were mostly bruised, not burned. But still . . .

With a single touch, Rebecca stopped her, nudged her hand back to her side. They shared one more look. Sock Puppet, rampant. Wreaking havoc. Holding tight. Staying alive.

Then Joel bumped them both out of the way. He made sure Benny had the blonde's shoulders pinned, and Jess the legs. Standing up fast, he hurried off into the garage.

The room went startlingly quiet. The only visible movement was the blonde's relentless blinking, as though she were trying to fan her eye, cool it in time to keep it from exploding. A single drop of liquid, streaked with red, slipped from the corner of the charred socket. Even that seemed to steam, as though the woman's tears were boiling.

"Kaylene, get me a knife," Jess hissed from where she knelt on the blonde's shoulder.

Sophie, Kaylene thought, not even sure from where she'd dredged up the name. But that was this thing's name all right. It had been her name before she was a thing. When she was Jess's . . . *daughter? No. But something . . .*

"Kaylene!"

In a daze, she started to stand. Rebecca's murmur checked her.

"Hold on," she said, though not to Kaylene, and in something like her old Rebecca tone: cool, smart, and loving. Not at all the voice of a woman who threw boiling oil at other people.

Or bashed in their faces with shovels.

Wait. Hadn't that been this *thing's face?*

Jess and Rebecca were glaring at each other now. Joel returned, dropping three black felt bags with a clank at his feet. The blonde bucked, freeing her other fist just long enough to punch Benny in the face. Rabid dog snarls burst from her mouth as spittle bubbled from her lips. Eventually, somehow, the chains in the black felt bags got wound and locked tight around Sophie's arms and torso and legs. She stopped spitting, howling, even blinking. She glared up at all of them through her one unharmed eye, which was beautiful and brown, Kaylene noted. Oil droplets still shimmered on her wide cheeks.

"Now, Kaylene," Jess said. "Get me that knife." Her voice was so weighted with grief, she seemed to have to shove the words through her teeth.

"I . . . can't," Kaylene whispered.

She really couldn't. She was still gazing at Sophie's face. It almost felt as though Sophie wouldn't let her move, though she was apparently paying Kaylene no mind whatsoever.

"Jess," said Rebecca.

"Fine. Give me a hammer."

Benny got up to do just that.

There was more arguing, then. Someone said they had

bigger worries right now, and someone else mentioned not knowing how many others were out there or what the hell they wanted or whether they'd even come together. Dimly, Kaylene was aware of her own hands closing around the grip of the aluminum bat she'd been wielding earlier, and then turning to dig around in one of the kitchen drawers. She wasn't consciously aware of looking for anything, and she wasn't really listening, either—her memories wouldn't let her—when she caught sight of Rebecca again. Her friend—bandmate, fellow survivor, sister—was drawn up on her knees, now, head cocked, absolutely still, like a seabird riding a current of air. Locking in on a fish.

"Oh, 'Bec," Kaylene said, right as Rebecca plunged.

Everyone went silent, tensing for the crunch of skull on skull. But Rebecca held up inches from Sophie's face, staring straight down into that single, glaring eye. That beautiful eye.

"How are you even alive?" she hissed, and Kaylene heard the guilt there, understood the weight Rebecca had carried ever since the night she really had helped save them all.

Except for the ones she hadn't. Danni, and Jack, and Marlene, and Amanda. The only thing Kaylene could think to do was place her palm between her friend's thin, powerful, birdlike shoulder blades and leave it there, for whatever good a palm could do.

Then Joel said, "Kaylene. What did you *do?*"

He was looking, she realized, at the baseball bat in her other hand. The hand that wasn't on Rebecca. So she looked at that, too.

"Huh," she said.

Apparently, while the rest of them had wrestled over the fate of the creature who might or might not have come to kill them, she'd been festooning the bat's barrel with little stick-on googly eyes from Jess's ribbons-and-crafty-things drawer. The buttons winked in the wan, windowless light like the eyes of a thousand cave-creatures living inside the aluminum.

"I'm . . ." Kaylene murmured. "Kaylening the weaponry?"

No one laughed. Mostly, they stared. But Rebecca straightened, settling back on her haunches, and Benny and Joel let themselves sag momentarily. Even Jess released a long, slow breath. Only Sophie stayed tensed, blinking relentlessly, glaring mostly at Jess. And that was fair enough; she was the one chained to the floor, after all.

Clap her in irons, Kaylene thought, the phrase echoing in her head. In her mother's voice, just for added absurdity. Although that wasn't so absurd, come to think of it. Mother of Warm Bao had loved reading her daughter *Treasure Island* the way most of her Korean friends employed the Bible.

"Okay," said Jess. "Let's get her upstairs."

A whole host of expressions ghosted across Sophie's face like cloud-shadows in time lapse: there was fury more ferocious than any Kaylene had ever felt, a deeper and deadlier loneliness, wilder laughter.

"Right you are," Sophie finally snapped. "Don't want to continue this in front of the children." Then, horribly, she grinned. *"Mom."*

Even as Jess lunged to her feet—*for a knife? To get*

234

away?—Benny and Joel swept in, hoisting Sophie by the shoulders and ankles as she laughed. *And let them,* Kaylene knew, even before the blonde shot her a single, withering glance and, with her good eye, winked.

As though hustling away a ticking bomb, the men swept her up the steps into Rebecca's room. Jess snatched a knife off the counter and Rebecca started to object, then simply preceded Jess upstairs.

Kaylene could have followed. Brought along her freshly decorated, festive bat. Probably, she decided, she should do that. So she moved to the foot of the stairs and stood still, listening. There should have been more arguing, or else stabbing sounds. Which Agatha Christie was she remembering now? Maybe *Orient Express?* The one where they all did it?

Kaylene took a single step up. Still, she heard nothing. If everyone in Rebecca's room was arguing, they were doing it with sign language. And if they were murdering Sophie—again—they were doing it in absolute silence.

Eventually, Benny, then Joel, then Jess emerged from the room. One by one, with the barest possible acknowledgment of Kaylene, they passed her on the stairs and without a word resumed the tasks they'd been performing at the instant Sophie reappeared: mopping grease spatter off the floor and walls; setting new pans boiling; spilling more flatware out of drawers; stockpiling rusty gardening implements from the garage; affixing boards to windows. Everyone's movements seemed so terrifyingly natural that quite a while passed before Kaylene realized that Rebecca hadn't come out.

Which meant she was still in there. Up there. Alone. Her last best friend.

The croak that escaped Kaylene's lips sounded preverbal to her, barely human. A whimper and a warning and a calling out all at once, like a cat's meow. Shoving off the wall, Kaylene started upward. She got maybe two steps before Jess snapped, *"Kaylene!"* and stopped her yet again.

"Jess, hang on, I have to—"

"I need you," Jess said, and Kaylene turned.

Jess was by the back sliding door, a nail dangling from one corner of her lips like a cigarette, her shapeless sweater draping her body. The lines of light sneaking between the wooden boards streaked her face. She had a hammer in one hand, and with the other was pressing another board diagonally into place.

In a daze, Kaylene floated back downstairs past Joel and Benny. Leaning her bat against the wall, she reached out to hold the board in place. But instead of placing the nail, Jess spit it onto the floor, grabbed Kaylene's wrist, and tugged her around so they were facing each other.

"Kaylene," said Jess, ice-eyes brimming. "Thank you for teaching Rebecca how to scream."

If anything, Jess's stare right that second felt even more mesmerizing than Sophie's.

"Jess . . ."

"I mean it."

"Well . . . no problem."

Jess actually grinned for a second.

From across the room, where he was chiseling a sharper point onto some implement or other, Joel called, "Also,

236

Kaylene? Thanks for being the first one of us to remember how to play anything, period. And why we should bother."

What the fuck is this? Kaylene was thinking. *And why can't we do it more often?*

Letting her board drop, Kaylene stepped back, reached blindly for the counter, and turned just in time to see Rebecca hurry into the room. At least Rebecca didn't thank her for anything. But she did circle around, hook Kaylene's arm, and spin her into a single, mad twirl. For one moment—for the first time in the five-plus years they'd spent on this island—the Stockade felt like the Crisis Center at UNH-D. Like human curling and strawberry Twinkies and being useful in the world amid the madness of the world.

Like being in the world, period.

Abruptly, Rebecca let go and whipped her gaze around the room. "Oh, shit," she said. "Where is she?"

At first, Kaylene had no idea which *she* Rebecca meant. Neither, apparently, did her housemates, because Jess's first response was, "Uhh, remember? Think maybe five minutes back. All that brouhaha with the boiling oil and the tire chains and—"

"Emilia," said Rebecca.

Even then, it took everyone but Jess a moment to understand. Then they were all whirling, searching. The hairs on Kaylene's arms and neck snapped to attention yet again, or, rather, she became aware of them again. As far as she knew, they had never once stood down—had in fact hardened into quills and ossified—since her first glimpse of the thing in the hat stepping out of the shade of Halfmoon

Lake woods on the morning she kissed Jack. On the last day of his life.

"Here," came a quiet voice from all the way across the living room.

She was huddled in the corner, hooded in blankets with her knees to her chest and only her face and a few straggles of curly black hair visible. If Rebecca hadn't remembered, Kaylene thought, that woman could have stayed in that corner forever, or until nightfall, and then gone anywhere. Slipped out the boarded-up back, or up the stairs into Rebecca's room.

"Good," said Rebecca. "You scared us. You okay?"

The woman nodded.

"All right. You stay there."

"Planning to," said Emilia, and slowly, carefully, let the topmost red blanket slide away from her arm. In her coiled fist, she held the longest chopping knife in the house.

Given their lives, that sight reassured everyone. Joel grinned. Jess said, "Excellent. Carry on."

They went back to their business, and Kaylene turned to ask Rebecca straight out what she'd been doing locked away with Sophie, and was surprised to find her friend already across the room, headed right back upstairs. She started to call after her, thought better of it, glanced down at the countertop where she'd left her googly-eyed bat.

It wasn't there.

Goddamnit, Rebecca, she thought. *Are you taking this all on yourself? Again?*

Without a word to Jess, Benny, Emilia, or Joel, Kaylene moved to the stairs. No one said anything to her, either. The door to Rebecca's room was closed. Halfway to the landing, Kaylene stopped, held the rail, held still, and listened, while the world, as usual, tipped underneath her, threatening to drop away like a rope bridge she could never seem to get off.

Was it like this, she wondered, *for people who never met monsters? Did just being yourself and alive always feel this way, for everyone? As ephemeral as light?*

And . . . Jesus . . . did it feel that way to Sophie? What had that thing been doing for the last five years? What were Sophie and Rebecca discussing now? Assuming Rebecca hadn't already gone ahead and killed her some more?

Kaylene took three quick steps and reached the landing. She could hear murmuring in Rebecca's room, but she had to tiptoe all the way to the door and crouch at the keyhole to hear actual words.

First, Sophie's: "Yes. Right. So. How do you choose *your* meat, then?"

"It isn't the same," Rebecca said, in something very like her old, careful Crisis Center voice. But a little meaner, or maybe more afraid.

"You're right," said Sophie. "It isn't. I actually face the reality of what I'm doing."

"Oh, God, you're going to make the hunting argument? I-kill-my-own-meat-and-respect-it, so—"

"I'll tell you what I don't do. I don't do it for fun. Which, yes, put your pointy finger down, that doesn't mean I don't *have* fun sometimes. I have fun as often as possible, actually. Because honestly, otherwise, why bother? With anything?"

"I don't even know how to—"

"I also do it—"

"Do what? Say it?"

"Kill someone. Happy now? And by the way, I kill so much less than I think you think. So much less than I thought I could bear, or than I was told I'd have to. I never do it out of vengeance; I don't discriminate by color or gender identity or sexual preference; I sure as hell don't do it because I'm attracted to someone, although, I admit, that does turn out to be a fringe benefit of . . . this. Of my condition. Or maybe that's always been me, and I'm just cool like that. Because the truth is, *everyone's* kind of attractive to me, now. All the time. Even you, little cutie, sitting there so panicky-mad and sad with your hands clenched like that and your face all—"

"Please stop," Rebecca said, and Kaylene wanted to hurl herself through the door, grab Rebecca, tip Sophie out the window, and flee this place. But she stayed put, let Rebecca do her thing.

"Okay, I'll stop. It really is true, though. I am attracted to practically every single person I meet. I have no idea what that's about. Skin with sunlight in it, maybe? Eyes with fear in them? Or maybe doubt? Vulnerability? I've given up trying to analyze. I've never been the analyzing kind. I try just to enjoy."

This time, Rebecca barely managed a croak. "I don't want you to analyze. I want you to count. If I'd killed you then . . . in Halfmoon Lake woods . . . how many people would that have saved?"

There was a brief, terrible silence. As if Sophie were actually counting. But what she said was, "Don't be so hard on yourself, sweetie. You did try."

"I *wasn't* trying. Believe it or not, I really wasn't. I was killing him. *It*. The Hat Freak. You were just . . ."

"In the wrong face at the wrong time?"

Rebecca let out a single, explosive gasp, which mercifully covered Kaylene's. But not Sophie's laughter.

"My God," Rebecca hissed. "You really are . . ."

"A funny, funny gal?"

". . . a total monster."

"Right, Rebecca. I'm just so completely different from you. Actually, hold on, shut up, I'll give it to you, we are pretty different. Natalie and I were pretty different, too. Kind of like Jess and Benny are totally different. And Jess and *Natalie*, come to think of it. How about you and your long-haired bandmate with the zebras-on-drugs dresses? You and she are pretty different. *Hey*. Easy now. Put that bat back in your lap, sweetheart."

Another silence. In the midst of it, Kaylene sensed movement below her, not quite at the foot of the stairs and not exactly in the kitchen or living room, either. But she couldn't take her eyes off the door long enough to turn around and look.

Rebecca had picked out the word that shouldn't have been in that last Sophie-monologue, and now she made the leap that Kaylene should have. Her voice came out almost shy—or all the way shy—which made Kaylene want to throw open the door and hug her. But she was too busy shuddering.

"Bandmate."

"Yes. So?"

"So you've seen us play."

Astonishingly—absurdly—Sophie burst out singing, in

near-perfect Kaylene-ese: *"With your face to the dark and your fists in my hands . . ."*

Rocking backward, Kaylene had to grab for the doorframe to stay standing. She was sure she'd made too much noise even before she realized her mouth had come open, that she was apparently either about to laugh or else shout Rebecca's harmony-echo *("fists in my hands!").* Somehow, she smashed her lips together and caught her own voice in her teeth.

"Stop it," Rebecca said.

"Your wish is NO ONE's . . ."

"Stop!"

"Your wish is NO ONE's . . ."

"Please."

" *'. . . command.'* Okay, okay, stop looking like that, didn't anyone warn you your face could freeze that way?"

For a while, the only sound was Sophie laughing. Kaylene held the doorframe, held still, and came perilously close to laughing with her.

"You've seen us play," Rebecca murmured.

"I'm your number one fan."

"God help us."

"In fact, it's possible that I've seen almost every single show you little Sock Puppets have ever played. I'm your freaking groupie, except for the getting-one-or-both-of-you-in-bed part. Although, hey, come to think of it, look at us now! We're practically—"

"Stop," Rebecca snapped, sharp as a snare-hit, with an accompanying rattle of regret or something else. "Okay? Sophie, just . . . stop."

More silence, or near-silence. Silence with Sophie softly

humming. Then something changed. Kaylene didn't have to be in the room to sense it. She couldn't have said what signaled her; she just knew.

"Right," said Sophie. "Fun time's over." Bedsprings creaked, as though Sophie had sat up or rolled up on her side. Surely, she couldn't have done either with chains around her? "Look. Rebecca. You crimped-up little thunderbolt. When I need to eat, I eat. The way all living things do. I select at random, and I actually make it a point—a *rule*—not to inflict pain, if possible. I almost never inflict pain."

"Congratulations."

"The opposite, in fact. You know what? When your end comes, Mademoiselle Sock Puppet, I have a feeling it won't be anywhere near as pleasant."

When Rebecca spoke next, she was whispering. That only happened, Kaylene knew, when she was near tears. There was no way Rebecca would let herself cry in front of Sophie. Kaylene knew her too well. "My God, Sophie. You're the worst thing in the world: a monster with a sense of self-justification."

"What, like a terrorist? I have no *jihad*, little girl. Unlike my former surrogate mom down there, and unlike you, too, judging by the boiling oil you just threw in my face and the bat you're considering bludgeoning me with. Unlike cops who kill black kids—have you guys even heard about all that, shut up here on your island?—or the fuckwad rednecks I grew up with hunting gays in alleys and truck-stop bathrooms. I have no cause. I just want to live. Somehow, for some reason I really can't figure, in spite of every fucking thing life has given me . . . I want to live."

The ensuing quiet was also one Kaylene knew well. Hearing it now filled her with fleeting but furious affection; it was the sound of Rebecca, listening.

"You said it yourself," Rebecca finally said. "The Whistler told you. Remember? That's what you told me on the day we met, when I found you in Jess's attic. You told me he said that inevitably, out of necessity—to live—you and Natalie would detach from human feelings. From everything you'd ever felt. That you'd become monsters whether you wanted or meant to or not."

"Yeah," said Sophie. "But unlike you . . . and also unlike my late, lamented, stupid idiot best friend, who should still be here with me, if only so we could shriek your surprisingly not-idiot songs back in your face . . . it actually occurred to me to consider the source."

"He knew a lot more about it than you did, at the time. Or do now. He had a lot more experience, I kind of think."

"Or else he was an asshole. Born and killed and raised. And smashed flat, by you."

"With my shovel."

"While he was being devoured by me."

Jesus Christ, were they joking, *now?* It half sounded as though they might slap hands. Or would have, if Sophie's weren't chained to the bed.

Yet again, Kaylene reached for the doorknob. It was time to get in there and help Rebecca finish this. Whatever that meant. Or else ask Sophie to join the band. In her mouth, for no reason, she tasted her mother's sesame bao and Mrs. Starkey's Goose Island Night Stalkers and Benny's waffles. In her ears and on her lips, she had the song

Rebecca and Sophie had been singing. One Kaylene had written.

"*Your wish is no one's . . . your wish is NO ONE's . . . command . . .*"

"How about this, then?" Sophie said, as Kaylene turned the knob. "Can you face it, girlie? Because I face it every night. I *own* it. I am the truck you don't see coming, or the cancer that's been in you since before you were born. I'm the plane crash the statistics say you have almost no chance of being in, and those statistics don't lie. I'm lightning from a clear sky. Just one of those thousand-million things you're unlikely ever to meet. Except you're all going to meet something."

"Except you."

"*Except* me? I already met it. I'm an even rarer statistical anomaly. I got back up."

"Me, too."

"Well, yeah. I suppose that's right."

"But I didn't start killing afterward."

"Nope. You just keep eating." And then, for the first time in this whole exchange, Sophie's voice went flat. All the way dead. "And then there's this: only one person in this room has ever tried to hurt the other. And she's done it twice."

Kaylene noted the threat. In fact, she suspected she was tracking it far more clearly than Rebecca, if only because she'd heard it before. It was Kaylene, after all, who had actually had the Whistler's hands on her throat and his corpse-eyes inside her. She had her shoulder to Rebecca's door to burst into the room when she heard the sound behind her again.

That noise, downstairs. Little more than a rustle, really. Footstep on balding carpet. A quieter, heavier step than any step she knew.

Get in the room, something screamed inside her. *Don't turn around!* But she had already turned.

Just like that, it was over.

The woman down there was mostly shadow, only now detaching from the shadows around Joel's bedroom door. She would have been indistinguishable from the surrounding dark except for her eyes, which tore into Kaylene's brain and lodged like grappling hooks.

She felt—really, watched, she hardly felt a thing—her body stumble away from Rebecca's door, half fall down the stairs. She would have fallen, except those eyes wouldn't let her. They propped her up as they dragged her closer, set her burrowing through the air like one of her beloved little Dig-Dugs, helpless to do anything but march, singing, to its own cataclysm.

Like everything alive! she thought, almost dreamed as she lurched another step. The thought proved strangely comforting. *I am the byproduct of cataclysm, instantly and permanently dispersing from the second I awoke. I am living aftermath, and always have been.*

Living is aftermath.

For the sake of fighting, she fought. It really was worth fighting for, after all; Sophie had that much right, for sure. *Such good aftermath*, Kaylene thought. *Every agonizing second of it.* That was what finally set tears boiling out of her eyes, which she couldn't even blink away because the shadow-thing in the hall wouldn't let her. At one point she did get one hand to the banister. That didn't slow her progress any, but the touch of wood seemed to trigger her other senses, awaken her hearing. There was Jess's voice, over by the boarded-up patio door (which would only serve to trap them now that the monsters had gotten in). Benny's voice, too. Both of them—*oh, God*—singing. With each other. *To* each other.

"On the Good Ship Lollipop"? That's what Jess and Benny sing to each other? That's the song I go out to?

That song, and Jess's laughter. Somehow, down there— with her grandson in the woods, her first husband gone, her daughter gone, the monsters massing yet again all around her—Jess had found one more thing to make her laugh, momentarily. She'd even found someone to do that with.

A bunch of someones, actually. Including me, Kaylene thought, as her feet came off the stairs, hit flat floor. No one turned. No one saw.

The woman in the hall—woman-shaped thing with supernovas for eyes, towering without being tall, too solid somehow to *be* woman, not aftermath but the cataclysm itself—was speaking. Or at least, she was moving her black hole of a mouth, which sucked sound in rather than pushed it out. Kaylene could see words forming and understood perfectly.

Where is she? the woman was saying, soundlessly, over and over, without even breathing. The words a stream of light with nothing to break or slow or soften them. *Where is she? Whereisshewhereisshewhereisshe?*

The words filled Kaylene's mind, the part that wasn't screaming. Then other voices rose. One was her mother's, and it wasn't asking questions.

I'm coming, Kaylene, her mother said. *I'm coming. I'm coming.*

Too late, Kaylene thought, even sang. *Warm bao. Sock Puppet. Jack and the 'Lenes. Dig-Dug tunnels I dug, weapons I Kaylened, Whistler's hats I defanged and transformed, shrieks I taught whole rooms full of girls to shriek so they could all shriek together. So she and Rebecca could shriek with them. Become cataclysm. Create. Your wish is no one's . . . your wish is no one's . . .*

I have so loved being here, she thought, as the shadow-woman seized her, still mouthing those words, shouting without sound, *whereisshewhereisshewhereisshe?*

I have so loved being here, Kaylene thought again. Then she wasn't anymore.

22

Deep in the cave, Trudi crouched on a ledge and watched the darkness coming. Actually, that was wrong. The darkness wasn't doing anything. The daylight was drawing up, pulling back like curtains rising, revealing the black sky and blacker ocean.

Showtime.

How long have we been here? she wondered vaguely. She was also hungry, vaguely. That made some sense, considering that they'd been here *all fucking day.*

Don't go, day, she thought, then expelled the thought like a smoke ring and watched it hover in the air in front of her, framing the two figures at the mouth of the cave. Eddie and the green-eyed girl. Ju.

Don't go . . .

At first, when they'd headed up there, Eddie had done lots of pointing and jabbering, hopping around like a yappy little dog happy to have someone new to show things to. Ju had settled again into that weird stand-and-sway thing she did, making no move to corral Eddie. Eventually, the boy bounded away from her side and onto the rocks, scuttling after some stone or crab or shell.

At that moment, Trudi almost leapt to her feet and screamed, *Go, kid! Run!* But the second she started to move, she forgot why she wanted to. Then her eyes fixed on Ju at the edge of the light, limned like a paper cutout. Shadow puppet. Except so much more beautiful, flexible, and strange than any puppet Trudi had ever seen or made. So much closer to actually alive.

Trudi recognized the strangeness of that idea even as it filled her with pity and, even more strangely, desire. She managed to pretend for a few seconds that the desire was ill-defined, general, confusing. But it was actually fairly explicit: what she apparently wanted to do was slip inside that girl's shadow and limn her properly.

What the fuck did that even mean?

Trudi didn't know. But the desire kept her pinned to the rocks as effectively as if she'd been chained there.

Eddie was back, now. He had a crab or rock or shell in his hand, and was holding it up to the last of the light. Ju knelt, sliding her shadow over him. Their heads leaned together, and they whispered to one another. Trudi watched, mesmerized, beset by a confusing feeling. This one wasn't totally unfamiliar, at least. She'd experienced something like it at Eliana's swim meets, watching from the stands as her friend stood and chattered with her teammate-friends next to their starting blocks at the edge of the pool. Somehow, even though those kids were all people Trudi knew, their conversations seemed unimaginable at that distance.

Like the conversations of teachers in break rooms, glimpsed through frosted-glass windows but never heard, on the other side of a door in their lives, where Trudi could never go.

She would have liked to have gone, just once, to the world where pretty much everyone else seemed to live. So she could know what everyone was actually talking about.

Would have liked to? Why was she thinking that?

As if in answer, Ju's head swiveled in Trudi's direction. It didn't actually turn all the way around, just a little farther than seemed possible or comfortable. Ju looked nothing like an owl awakening, though there was definitely something quicker, more birdlike in her movements as darkness fell.

The green-eyed girl smiled.

Run, Trudi thought, to Eddie, to herself. Instead, she clambered to her feet and shuffled in Ju's direction. She felt dazed, but almost pleasantly so. She felt alive but trapped in herself, a barnacle torn loose from a perch. The tide she now rode was going to deliver her straight into Ju's smile.

Reaching the mouth of the cave, she settled on her haunches on the other side of Ju from Eddie.

So Eddie can't see, she thought. *So he won't have to see. See* what?

After a whole day in the cave, she felt exposed on the rocky cliff-side. Mist rode the sea air, unexpectedly icy. After a few seconds, Trudi realized Ju was shivering. The girl had been shivering all day, but not this hard. With a careful finger, Trudi touched the skin of Ju's arm, which looked almost as green as her eyes under the cascade of hair. It felt waxy, gossamer. Made of moonlight.

Which is really sunlight, Trudi told herself dreamily, in Raj's voice, because he was the one she'd had this conversation with. By text, like most of their conversations. She'd never actually heard him say it, yet it was his voice in her head. *It's just sunlight ricocheting off dead rock. Moonlight is as made up as moon men, bitches. As moon cheese!*

The thought proved oddly comforting. Or maybe it was just Raj's imagined voice comforting her.

Ju leaned her head onto Trudi's shoulder. Instantly, all other thoughts, imagined voices, and sensations fell from Trudi as though dragged off by the same tide that had swept her here. She held still while Ju shivered against her, felt and watched the girl's hair spilling over her own arms like lava. Except cold.

"Why are you so damn cold?" Trudi murmured.

"I just am." Ju's voice came out childlike, full of wonder. "You're not."

"I am, actually. A little."

"You get warmer than this?"

A chilly arm encircled Trudi's waist like a squid tentacle, and Ju's face nuzzled deeper into the hollow of her throat. Trudi could feel lips there, and then, finally, after a long time, a whisper of air. Even that was cold. As though in a dream—or current—Trudi felt her own arm lift, start to draw Ju even more closely against her. She didn't realize she'd been holding her own breath until she hiccoughed violently and her vision exploded with stars.

Ju laughed and wriggled closer. On her other side, Eddie yawned and laid the shells and shards he'd gathered on the rocks. His head sank toward Ju's lap.

This is it, then, Trudi thought. *Right now.* "Nnh," she

managed, the words fuzzy and thick on her lips, as though she were spitting out a gag. "Want to . . . Let's go back to Hornby Camp."

It shouldn't have been possible for Ju to get any closer without climbing inside Trudi. But somehow, she managed, and some part of her, possibly her lips, pressed right at the curve of Trudi's neck. The pulsing point. What Trudi first took for another shudder turned out to be giggling.

"Hey," Trudi said, fighting hard now, shoving words from her mouth as though dropping rocks down a fortress wall to repel invaders. "Or. Let's go to my house. The Stockade, that's what we call it. I'll introduce you to Rebecca. And Jess. And Jess's . . . guy. Benny. The world's hairiest man . . . Also best cook. Hey, Eddie . . ."

She was running out of words. And Eddie's head had finished sagging into Ju's lap. He lay there limp as a sock with no one puppeting.

"Eddie, please. Wake up."

"Up," he murmured.

"Don't go to sleep."

He was already sleeping, though. Ju's frozen hand had crawled up Trudi's back and was sliding now into the kinks of her hair. *It will disappear there,* Trudi thought, wondering if the tears now welling in her eyes were for herself or for Ju's hand. *They'll never find it.*

Then Ju really kissed her throat. Giggling.

Soft lips, damp-not-wet. Hard teeth, just touching, not biting. Cave wall. Cave kiss.

Trudi curled her fists and closed her eyes.

23

*W*hat had made Sophie stop squirming? Which sound, exactly?

Even in the midst of being chained and dragged up here, she'd tracked the other noises in the house. Her screaming had mostly been for show; her eye burned, all right, but she could see out of it. The oil had mostly tinted her vision cheap-sunglasses-red, and that was kind of nifty. Meanwhile, she'd identified and catalogued everything she heard: rattling knives, boards being nailed, oil heating, footsteps, incongruous bursts of chatter and song. Alertness to everything was a permanent state for Sophie now, a sense she could no more switch off than she could smell.

The Little Drummer Girl, Rebecca, was still prattling away on her chair next to the bed. She hadn't heard her stripy-dress friend creeping onto the hallway landing and crouching at the door. She also hadn't noticed when

Stripy-dress abruptly stopped. Rebecca was simply too busy accusing, berating, recriminating, probing. Probably, she was working herself back up to killing, or maybe, to be fair, she was still trying to understand. Even more than Natalie, this poor girl was the try-to-understand type.

Seeing Sophie squirm appeared to calm Rebecca, to give her that sense they all craved that they had any say in or control over what was coming. So Sophie squirmed against the chains. No one in this house actually knew how to use the chains, so they were already loosening.

At this new sound, however, Sophie stopped. Even the Little Drummer noticed that.

"What?" *Rebecca said.* "Look. You may not get this. I sure as hell don't. But I'm trying to . . ."

The new sound came again. This time, Sophie recognized it.

"What?" *Rebecca snapped. Apparently, she did have some sort of intuition after all. Not enough to get her to shut up and listen, but some, anyway.*

Sophie didn't really mean to smile. If she was right, there wasn't anything funny about that sound, for any of them. Smiling was simply her instinctive response to almost everything. It was just what Sophies did. No sense fighting it. "You don't hear that?"

At that, Rebecca did turn around, which bought Sophie the precious seconds she needed to listen harder, make sure.

How did she recognize that noise? By its quiet, mostly. By its very-hardly thereness. People get so used to other people coming toward them, flowing around and about

*them, their fellow drone bees in a hive they never even re-
alize they're in.*

But me, *Sophie thought. I have lain all day in rocky
fields and stirred with the snakes. I have prowled night-
time alleys with the cats, erupted into evenings with the
fireflies, surfaced in a gaggle of seagulls whose mouths
were too stuffed with fish to shriek. I have been stalked by
Whistlers and stalked them. And I know the sound of
hunting feet.*

"Uh-oh," she said. *Still smiling.*

*Was she warning? Had she meant to? Certainly, just that
word—was* uh-oh *one word or two?—proved warning
enough. The Little Drummer glanced again at the door,
then down at her hands in her lap, then at the chains on the
bed, which Sophie had started to work loose.*

"Don't," Sophie said. "Don't you dare."

*Snaking out those deceptive little hands, the Drummer
grabbed the chains right at thigh level, at the precise point
where the Whistler had once separated Sophie's legs from
the rest of her, and yanked down.*

*Even as her scars split and she started screaming again—
for real, this time—Sophie listened. She also marveled.
How did this little bitch always seem to know? Or remember?*

*Rebecca yanked again. At least she had the grace to
wince as the chains bit through Sophie's skin.*

"Stay put," *she hissed.*

*Swallowing her scream, Sophie wriggled savagely
toward upright. But that just set a thousand little skin
threads popping along the lips of her wounds. Her legs
yawned open, sucking the chain deeper. She made herself*

keep going anyway, twisting and bucking as five years'
worth of screams filled her mouth.

The bedroom door swung open.

Instantly, instinctively, Sophie dropped prone, went
dead-possum still. She had met the Whistler, and his
Mother. She had killed the Mother-fucking Whistler.

The thing in the doorway was not like the Whistler. It
was wondrous, beautiful, towering and untouchable as
the night sky. The night sky walking, winking with stars,
all of which were people—whole worlds—she'd devoured.

"Where is she?" said the Night Sky Walking. She took
no step into the room, yet permeated it completely. "Where
is she?"

The Little Drummer really was remarkable, too, in a
more earthly sense: resilient, determined, like a scram-
bling beetle with nowhere to go. Sophie watched her jerk,
writhe, try so hard not to turn all the way around. But the
chains around her were infinitely stronger than the ones
that held Sophie, and wielded by a creature who knew
what to do with them. Somehow, as her body betrayed her
and turned her all the way into that basilisk gaze, Rebecca
got her mouth open and some breath gathered. For one
moment, Sophie actually thought she might be able to
shout, to alert her housemates, for whatever good that was
going to do.

But the Night Sky stopped her just by cocking her head.

"I'll ask once more," the Night Sky said. "Where is
she?"

And Rebecca—clever little killer, or maybe she really
was confused—knitted her brow and nodded toward
Sophie. "She's right here."

If Rebecca had winked, Sophie would have saved the Night Sky the trouble. Burst from her chains and silenced the Little Drummer once and for all. But the girl looked genuinely baffled. And why not, come to think of it? Sophie had no idea what the thing in the doorway wanted, either.

Should I ask, *Sophie thought?* Excuse me, Night Sky Walking. About this she . . .

Ah, well. Too late, now. The Night Sky had already stepped back, not retreating, just drifting in its orbit, pulling everything loose on the surface of the Earth with it like the moon dragging tides. Rebecca stumbled off her chair to her feet, her fists falling open as she staggered toward the doorway. She was still fighting, or at least her mouth was still working. Poor little drummer skeleton, with drumsticks for bones.

Out the door they went onto the landing, the Drummer still fighting, the Night Sky murmuring, "Where is she? Where is she?"

The chains around Sophie's chest had simply slid down her when she sat up. But the ones around her legs dug deeper every time she twitched, slicing through scar tissue, muscle, probably some tendon. Sophie lost valuable seconds fumbling to unhook and untangle her inside-self from the metal before she could lift the chains away. Worse, she had to watch what she was doing. The sight probably would have made her gag, once, and it did make her think about the Whistler's last moments. The shrieking sort of singing he'd done as she punctured and chewed through his cranium, sucked out his brains like the meat of an oyster.

Such fun.

Once she was free, she leapt to her feet, which turned out to be a mistake. Her legs, especially the left, didn't so much buckle as slide from underneath. She had to grab her thighs and clutch them, as though clinging to a cliff edge.

Vicious little Drummer Girl.

Dead Drummer Girl, by now? Not yet, apparently, because the Night Sky was still murmuring out there on the landing. "Where is she?"

Carefully this time, pinching her wounds closed, Sophie shuffled forward. The shuffling made too much noise in the carpet. That is, it made almost none at all, but more than she usually made. Enough for Sophie to notice, which meant it was more than enough to alert the thing on the landing.

Assuming it was listening.

Reaching the door, Sophie leaned against the frame, tucking herself as deeply in shadow as she could manage. She pinched harder along the seams in her thighs. Of their own volition, her index fingertips had found their way into the gashes and started toying with the dead, cold tendons and veins in there, like cat claws kneading yarn. So stringy-squishy.

"Where is she," the Night Sky said, but not like she expected an answer, anymore. When Sophie edged forward just enough to see what was happening, she was unsurprised to find the Night Sky almost on top of Rebecca, settling over her. Claiming. Reclaiming. There was nothing gentle about the movement. It was just slow.

To maximize the dread, Sophie immediately understood. Amplify the sheer, soul-shredding terror of it.

So that's what it looks like, *Sophie thought. Is that what they see when I end them?*

She didn't want it to be. She'd imagined their ends differently.

The Night Sky was holding Rebecca's shoulders, now, and moving her beautiful, starry-eyed face toward Rebecca's throat. Or maybe her mouth.

Was that an actual feeling I just had? *Sophie wondered. She thought it must have been, though it seemed to come from far away and in blinking signal bursts. Semaphore from some other Sophie.*

Maybe the Whistling Fuckbomb had been right after all, and whether she wanted to or not, she was still gradually detaching from the Sophie she'd been.

Or maybe she still had no idea what she was supposed to feel in this specific instant. Sympathy for the girl who'd smashed her face in with a shovel and left her for dead? Kinship with the murderous, miraculous Night Sky? Relief at being alive for at least a little longer? Sorrow for never quite having lived, at least not how she and Natalie had planned? Or for never getting to live like that with Natalie?

She had no answers. She had never had answers, before the Whistler or after. So she made the same decision she always had, in both her lives:

In the absence of answers . . . how about more fun?

The snarl she unleashed was purely theatrical and completely unnecessary. She needed no psyching up, and she didn't need to announce herself; the Night Sky had to have known Sophie was there the whole time, must have heard her stumble out of bed. Possibly she assumed Sophie was . . . well, who even knew what the Night Sky thought?

But the lunge. Sophie judged that perfectly.

She caught them both dead center, waist high, at the exact instant the Night Sky's hands tightened on Rebecca's shoulders. The force of the blow did surprise the Night Sky, because when Rebecca tumbled backward straight off the landing and then elbows-over-face down the stairs, the Night Sky tumbled right along with her.

Like derailed train cars off a trestle, Sophie thought, barely stopping her own momentum by grabbing the banister, gasping as her torso continued forward, slammed into the wall, and miraculously stayed attached to her legs.

Rebecca and the Night Sky hit the ground heads first, so hard that Sophie half expected them to stick where they'd landed like axes thunked into chopping stumps. For a second, not only the two of them but everyone else down there hung motionless. Like bowling pins in midair, Sophie thought, caught in the moment right after impact.

Strike.

Then they were all flying. Rebecca and the Night Sky mashed themselves together like some brand-new, two-headed bird whose wings beat only itself. The rest of them hurled themselves into and over each other in a heap of rakes and arms and knives and teeth and screamed names and shrieks of pain.

Sophie considered staying, if only for the entertainment. She also mulled floating down the stairs and helping.

But helping whom? And to do what?

And after all, she'd helped already. She'd driven both the

Night Sky and Rebecca off their feet and leveled the playing field to the extent it could be leveled.

Also, thanks to Rebecca, her goddamn legs throbbed with pain and barely functioned. Her burned eye kept tearing up and was possibly bleeding; everything she saw through it looked haloed in red haze like figures in an Impressionist sunset painting.

The kind of painting Sophies would paint if they painted. Maybe they would someday, she thought, and grinned.

While the battle raged—while wails and screams erupted and got snuffed out, while blood spurted and sharp things whistled—she floated downstairs and through and past them all. Really floated, it seemed, barely touching feet to carpet so as not to jar her poor thighs. Like the Ferry Godmother I am, *she thought.* Or Fairy Godmother. Like a real goddamn Fairy Godmother. So real, they can't even see me.

At the front door, she paused and glanced back. It was almost beautiful, this writhing, howling haze she'd made.

Then she slipped into the dark and limped away, fast, toward the sea cave.

24

Jess was startled by the speed of her reaction. Apparently, all she'd really done these past five years was wait. Everything else—opening her shop in the mornings and lingering at the window to wait for the sun, creating the Stockade, weaving cocoons of near-normalcy around Eddie, Rebecca, Kaylene, Trudi, and even Joel, settling into a sort of playacting marriage with Benny so threaded with actual feeling that even she sometimes mistook it for real—felt dreamed, now. All this time she'd believed she was moving on, grieving, recovering. But in reality, she'd just laid herself flat in the blue rye grass like a rusted trap. She'd thought she was still Jess, but was really only springs and teeth.

Even as she swept knives into her hands and leapt at the thing swarming over Rebecca at the base of the steps, Jess marveled at her own readiness, which in truth was closer to outright enthusiasm.

In truth, she couldn't wait to fight.

And die.

Yes. That, too.

Midair, knives plunging down, she realized that she'd been leaning over this particular abyss since the moment she'd stared, for the last time, into her daughter's living eyes. The moment Natalie murmured "Mom" through her tears, by which she'd meant yes, and given Jess permission to pull the trigger.

Commanded her to, really.

The monster's arms swallowed her. They were horribly cold, slick, so much stronger than seemed possible, the constriction instantaneous even as Jess stabbed, the crack of bones audible even over the screaming around her. Somehow, with her vertebrae bulging and her shoulders popping free of their joints, Jess got at least one knife raised again, not enough to plunge, just enough to shove it deeper into one of the holes she'd made in the monster's ribs.

That was the moment Jess understood how useless this fight was.

The creature who'd come for them in Virginia and killed Sophie's Roo . . . the Whistler in the woods . . . those had been monsters, sure enough. But this thing was a rogue wave. A gale tearing back and forth across the Earth forever, sweeping away everything it touched.

As consciousness flickered, as Benny flailed uselessly into the fray to try to free Rebecca and Joel lunged in with his rake, Jess experienced one last surprising surge of feeling. Not fury, not hope—obviously—not even sadness.

No. More than anything else, she was *disappointed.* In herself. As it turned out, she'd made the coward's choice after all: she'd chosen fighting and dying. And she'd done that precisely because fighting and dying were so much easier than staying. Grieving. Loving. Functioning.

Parenting.

It took the sting of yet another knife in her back to awaken Aunt Sally to revelation. As it seized her, she almost burst out laughing, half considered holding up a hand and telling the Little Fighter on the floor and the dervish with the knives to hold up just a second, just so Sally could properly appreciate the experience. Feel the wonder.

She'd never actually been in a fight!

Was that true? How could that be true?

But it was, and she knew it. Burning the rest of her monsters alive . . . that had been a cleansing, an act of volition and participation in her own fate.

Hardly a fight, though.

If she were honest, she'd hadn't even done much killing, all things considered. Given her hungers and the length of her life and all. She'd had Caribou and her monsters to bring her edibles. Platters of flesh and beautiful bones. In the wandering days before Caribou or Mother, before her monsters . . . she'd killed then, of course, and often. But nothing she'd killed had so much as raised its voice, let alone a fist. They'd simply bowed and snapped before her like grass.

She'd been so, so many things: life-ender and then both life-giver and life-ender to her monsters; sister to Mother, who'd abandoned her in the end and died alone; lover, sometimes, though without any particular partner or any actual love; creator of a whole riverside world in the Delta where her creations hunted and danced; inventor of Policy; judge of all who came before her; avenger; God.

Victim. Yes. Hard as it was to remember, now, she had most certainly been that.

Devourer of everything.

Destroyer.

And now . . . bereft of monsters, and having murdered Caribou for the second—no, third—time, if one counted the night she'd created him . . . and with these gnat-people flying everywhere around her and wielding knives, so consumed by whatever drove them that they didn't have the sense to curl up and yield to the inevitable . . . with all the Earth and whatever meager bounties it offered spread before her . . . Aunt Sally discovered, to her amazement, that she still had sensations to discover.

The complete absence of Hunger, for one thing. In all the years she'd lived—in either of her lives—she couldn't remember ever feeling less hungry than she did right now.

And something else. Something even more primal and harder to name. She hadn't come to this house planning to do damage, certainly not to kill.

She'd come to find Ju. A totally different sort of hunting.

Was Ju the reason for the absence of Hunger, too?

For one moment, realizing that, Aunt Sally went still while the dervish-woman poked her in the back with her knife a few more times.

Ju. The one creature alive that Sally would never devour or allow to be devoured. The one creature she'd ever met who was actually worth savoring instead. Pale Ju of the

*witchy eyes. A person to savor and save. No one and noth-
ing to devour or allow to be devoured.*

Which made Aunt Sally . . . a mom?

*With a single convulsion of her arms, Aunt Sally dislo-
cated both of the dervish's shoulders and flung her aside,
flashed out a hand and caught the neck of the man with
the rake and ripped a hole in his throat.*

Her first fight!

*As she dropped down on the Little Fighter, simulta-
neously catching the flailing little hairy man in both hands
and snapping one of his arms as though harvesting corn,
she wondered if she'd be any good.*

Yet again, Rebecca thought as that horrible weight drove
her seemingly straight through the floor and the hatred
radiating off this new and even more terrible monster
flooded her nostrils and mouth. *I am reduced to watching.
Story of my life.*

Mercifully, she supposed, her head still hadn't cleared
from the plummet down the stairs. Stars whirled in her
eyes, so that the flying faces of people she lived with and
loved seemed to wink in her own firmament. Comets arc-
ing past and away. Joel hanging frozen with his rake in his
hands like a constellation in the instant before the monster hurled him across the room. Benny's white whiskers
seeming to fly off him as he tumbled backward and collapsed into himself. Benny-supernova.

From somewhere far away—on the other side of the
sky, of the cavernous thing engulfing her—Rebecca heard
a *pop,* then a scream. She couldn't make sense of either

until Jess staggered back into the periphery of her vision, one arm dead at her side. The other, which she must have yanked back into its socket somehow, raised the butcher knife. One last time, Rebecca watched Jess's face appear over the monster's back like a moon. Bright and savage moon. Jess-rise.

The knife slashed down. Rebecca forced herself into motion, did some flailing for form's sake. For Jess's sake, really, because Jess had to see the knife was doing no good, that nothing anymore could do any good, and yet she kept driving the blade up and in, up and in, her mouth twisted and eyes screwed to slits. Remote as she could be, Jess was no moon, never had been. She was a pumping piston of fury and grief, desperation and love.

My favorite person, Rebecca thought as the monster gashed her sides, as blood bubbled out of her ribs. *Person I most wished I could have been and least wanted to be.*

We are such ridiculous, tangled, strangling things.

She watched Jess's knife pump, pass uselessly through, as though Jess were stabbing water. One last time—for Jess, and also Trudi, wherever she was, and for Eddie, Amanda and Danni, Marlene and Jack, Kaylene and yes, fucking goddamnit, for herself—Rebecca fought free of her thoughts. She actually felt herself rise from her own roiling insides. *I am the Lady in the Lake,* she thought, fists rising to do who even knew what, eyes closing because what use was seeing, now? *Also Excalibur. Lady of Halfmoon Lake, with the world cascading through her.*

She opened her eyes just in time to see it happen.

Directly overhead, above Jess's stabbing arm, the newcomer appeared. Emilia. Rebecca had forgotten she was even in the house. And she couldn't even begin to imagine where Emilia had found the ax.

A song popped into Rebecca's head. More accurately, a song title, stuttered out in that crazy Internet-ghost voice, the one from Joel's favorite-ever show. The voice that had turned out to *be* ghost, the stitched-together ramblings of Jess's dead daughter. *"Be Care-Care-Careful . . . with THAT Ax . . . Eugene."*

In a concussed daze, but with her senses returning and her vision clearing, Rebecca watched Emilia's dark hair flying as she swung the ax high. She moved like she didn't need to be careful, had used an ax before. Right at the apex of the swing, Rebecca caught a glimpse of her wide-open eyes, which looked drained of color, a fainter black than they should have been, than they always must have been. Drained of Emilia, maybe. Filled, instead, with the murmurings of the monster that had come for *her.* Her Invisible Man.

Only then did Rebecca wonder whom, exactly, Emilia planned to kill.

25

That fairy godmother feeling carried Sophie all the way to the trees. Her feet barely touched grass; the film of tears and burnt eyelash through which she peered hazed the moonlight, fashioning a gossamer bubble around her. For those few moments—for maybe the first time in her entire life, or lives—Sophie felt magical: a gliding, glowing thing that winked in and out of being, grazing lips with kisses, breaking hearts. Tearing open a throat or two when she had to before vanishing again.

Then—as though her body were a magic carpet she'd been riding, but the magic had gone—gravity yanked her Earthward, and she dropped back into herself with a thud. Her left leg spasmed again along the old suture scar at the top of her thigh. She had to grab it as she tumbled over, crimping the skin like the rim of a piecrust. A wet crust at that, with all the inside Sophie-filling sloshing around and seeping through. At least it wasn't pumping, that would have been a disaster. Her foot swung too far sideways, as though fleeing her, and she had to yank as she fell, hold her leg to her leg and topple into the leaves and shadows just to stay whole.

Get back here, foot.

More pain. Lots of it, on both sides of her ripped-open wound. Pain was good, right? A sign that her nerve ends and tendons were still talking to each other, even if they were no longer touching. Again.

Goddamn Jess and Rebecca both. What was left of them. Which probably wasn't much, by now.

Was Sophie sad? Did she have any fucking reason to be sad?

Pushing to a sitting position, she dragged her leg straight and stared down into it. What fascinating insides you have, Soph, *she thought. A white pillar of bone among the rubble of muscle and tangly reddish bits, like the last standing column from a tipped-over temple. As she watched, her tendons stirred, stretched toward one another. They reminded Sophie of the figures in those paintings of Dante's hell, forever reaching out of the canvas toward the world they'd left.*

The same way I keep reaching out for Jess's trailer, *Sophie thought. Except unlike the dudes in those paintings, Sophie had never actually lived in Jess's trailer. Had only kind of been welcomed there, and the worst part was, that had felt so good, at the time. What a sniveling, stupidgrateful little girl she'd been.* Oh, how lucky I am to be given leave to visit your double-wide Paradise, Jess and Natalie. Sometimes I can even sleep over! Just as long as I understand that in the end, I belong elsewhere.

The only time she'd actually lived in Jess's house was in that creepy attic in New Hampshire in the weeks before the Whistler came, after Natalie was already dead. And the worst part was, she'd let herself feel grateful for that, too. At times, she'd almost loved that attic. Mostly, she'd loved being left alone in Jess's house, in her own room with the door closed.

Almost like a real daughter.

Whose daughter was she now? Not her dead, drugged mother's. Not Jess's. And certainly not that thing's. God help that thing's daughter.

But . . . what a thing! Not just a monster like the Whistler and his horrible Mother but something more. On her fingers—to distract herself from staring into her yawning thigh—Sophie started counting personifications of Death she'd seen in books and art: the sickle guy in that movie who sucked at chess; the gothy girl in that graphic novel who'd reminded her a little of Natalie, though Sophie would never have dared say that to Natalie; some wanker on a pale horse, unless in that one Death was the horse.

Amateurs. All of them.

But if I live long enough, *Sophie thought.* If I work hard enough at becoming . . . me . . . could I become *that*?

The thrill she felt then flashed so hard, it left phosphenes streaking in her eyes. Not once, ever, in her whole life, had Sophie had real power. Not over school, which she'd sucked at. Not over her home, because she was never sure where that was. Not over her junkie mother, or her brilliant best friend, or her best friend's mother. Not even over her own son while she'd had him, because who was she to mother anyone?

Until this exact second, she'd simply accepted all that. She'd believed it all the way down to her bones. She was Smiling Sophie, born to lose, and she always would be.

Unless she was finally becoming—had always been becoming—something else. Until tonight, she hadn't even known there were more monsters out there, more creatures like the Whistler, like her. But now that she thought about it, that was ridiculous. There had to be.

The last two times she'd met other monsters, she'd . . . well . . . Won wasn't quite the word. She'd devoured the Whistler. She'd driven the Night Sky down the stairs and given Jess and the remains of her pitiful Jess-crew a chance. Okay, not a chance exactly, that was ridiculous. But she'd gifted them a few more seconds to be themselves, and the luxury of ending their lives fighting, imagining they were still the people they'd always been.

Sophie had given them that. Not that they would thank her for it, even in the unlikely event that they got the chance.

But somehow, until tonight, Sophie had still imagined herself more like them. And that was simply another version of the same stupid, self-negating notion she'd clung to her whole life. Right now, the idea that she was like Jess or Rebecca or Natalie seemed the most ridiculous and harmful misconception of all.

Digging her fingers hard into the ground, she began dragging forward yet again through yet another woods. This time proved more painful than the last, at least physically, because she had her legs with her instead of laid out neatly in Jess's car, which meant they could let her know in a thousand different ways how much they weren't enjoying themselves.

Even so, this movement—the clutch-and-drag, the monkey-like swinging except across forest floor rather than through branches—came back so fast, and so easily. Like riding a bike, or returning to an earlier, more natural version of herself. NeanderSophie. SlothSophie, only fast. So fast. So much faster than she'd been that night with Jess in Concerto Woods, where they'd buried her best friend and her son.

George William. Little Roo.

It was his absence, she realized now, that haunted her every single waking second and most dreaming ones. Somehow, from habit or as a protective measure, she'd convinced herself it was Natalie's. How could she ever have thought that? Certainly, if their roles had been reversed—as, in some pathetic way, Sophie had always secretly believed they should have been—and Sophie had wound up in the ground holding Natalie's son, and Natalie had been left out here to roam, Natalie would never have spared her a thought. Would have thought only of Eddie.

That would only have been right. Yet Sophie had practically resurrected Natalie. Cut her voice out of mounds of cassette tape and freed it to babble forever in the ether. Convinced herself Natalie would have done the same. She'd let herself imagine, again, that people she herself assumed were smarter, classier, had better musical taste, more style, more knowledge, more soul, more humanity than she did, would have use for a Sophie. Or love.

Take Jess, for example, who had shot the same glances at Sophie since she'd been small enough to bounce, with Natalie, on a trailer pull-down bed without breaking it. Who had secretly—or not at all secretly—believed Sophie to be the corrupting element in her brooding, precious daughter's life. Where did Sophie keep getting the idea that Jess would ever be happy to see her face?

Or the Little Drummer, Rebecca, whose life Sophie had saved or at least prolonged—twice, now. As a thank-you, Rebecca had given her shovel smashes to the face, tire chains yanked through thighs. How had Sophie ever come to believe that declaring someone a friend actually made them one?

What a sucker she was.

Her right leg was still capable of movement, and was already working its monster-Sophie magic: self-stitching the wound, autocauterizing. Stat. At the edge of the woods, on the lip of the long, wide-open sea of grass she would still have to cross, Sophie managed to wedge her back against the trunk of a tree and push herself upright.

She took just a moment to survey the night. The fog looked thin, transparent, more a ripple in the air than a curtain, and the stars sparkled on the Strait like a thousand million eyes. The blue rye stems trembled in the night breeze, reminding Sophie of those little garden eels she'd seen once in an aquarium somewhere, that planted themselves in sand and waited for passing minimorsels. A lawn of mouths.

There was nothing for it, Sophie knew. She was going to have to hop or crawl out there and cross along the exposed edge of the cliffs. And there was no time to lose or waste, either, not with the Night Sky raging back at Jess's stockade, doing whatever it was the Night Sky did.

Off Sophie went.

Fast. Faster than she expected. She thought about dropping back to her haunches, scuttling like a shrew so *that less of her lay open and vulnerable to the air. But during those years of half-functioning lower limbs, she'd gotten remarkably good at hopping. So she hopped instead, hurling herself forward, and the twinkling mist fled before her. In her head, she hummed. Not a Natalie song, but a Jess one, from ages and ages ago. It wasn't even a song, really, but her personalized version of a nursery-rhyme chant. Jess had murmured this over Sophie and Natalie in that pull-down bed in her trailer when they were very young.*

Little Rabbit Sophie, hopping through the forest. Scooping up the whole world and bopping it on the head.

World . . . I gave you threeeeeeeeeeee chances . . .

She got in such a rhythm, hopping and chanting, that she almost danced right past the path that switched down the cliff face to the cave. Dropping to her hands and knees, wincing as her left leg buckled in one too many places and threatened to split again along its extra seam, she dragged herself to the edge of the rocks and peered down. Briefly, she wondered what she'd do if they'd gone. If that new walking willow of a girl or the Sock Puppeteer decided they'd had enough orcas and Sophies and just set off back for the Stockade or some other refuge of their own.

Would Sophie go after them, in that case? And if so, to do what?

Fun to think about, but irrelevant, because there was Eddie, tidepooling away, sticking his hands or face in crevices, calling or reaching out to everything living. Somehow still believing everything living would listen, if it had a choice.

And there was the Walking Willow—Ju—swaying at the mouth of the cave with the Sock Puppeteer at her feet, seemingly just sitting there. Quieter than Sophie had ever seen her.

Hilariously—bizarrely—Sophie felt herself crouch lower, actually go still for a second. As if—even one-legged—she needed any sort of plan to deal with this lot, no matter what she decided deal with meant. And yet, caution felt advisable, possibly even necessary.

But caution was not how she rolled.

Grunting in pain, she pushed to her feet, let the wind catch in her skin and fill her. She felt herself unfurling into the night, as though she'd had a secret dinosaur crest hidden between her shoulders all these years. Her first instinct was to swoop down there, grab Eddie—for whom she could imagine several uses over the next few hours or maybe years—and vanish with him. But her leg wasn't going to allow much swooping for at least another few days, yet. And anyway, she didn't need to swoop. She just needed him to look up.

He did. And the second he did, she had him.

She grinned her Cheshire cat grin, her Secret Aunt Sophie grin. Down on the rocks, Eddie shuddered, leaned in place on his sneakered feet (which were already three times the size of her little Roo's feet), eyes wide. His head seemed to stretch on its pale neck, as though it might float off his shoulders and up to her like a balloon.

An unpopped balloon-head. As opposed to her Roo's, which had burst against the piling of a pier at the edge of a whole other ocean. Because that's what her "friends" had allowed to happen. That's what the world had decided Roos and Sophies deserved, long before either of them had even been born.

Slowly, still smiling, Sophie lifted a finger to her lips, formed her lips into a kiss against it, and made a silent shushing sound. She hopped to the cliff edge, then a couple steps down the path. Even hopping, she kept so quiet, her toes barely grazing the ground. Not fairy godmother, but Ferry Godmother once more. And so she was surprised to glance sidelong and find Ju staring right back up at her.

Not swaying. Not caught. Just watching.

With those eyes, *Sophie thought. And then,* Wait! Am I caught?

And then, finally, she had it. She understood. The truth had been staring her in the face all along, from right behind those glowy green eyes, which weren't flat or expressionless and never had been.

They were screaming. All the time.

And the reason Sophie hadn't realized . . . hadn't seen . . . was because looking at Ju was a little too much like looking in a mirror.

A million questions bubbled up in Sophie's brain. None of them mattered. Raising her finger once more, Sophie gestured at the Sock Puppeteer. That one at least still looked appropriately dazed and oblivious, staring out over the Strait at nothing.

Then she pressed the finger to her lips again, made her kissing-shushing silent motion.

Slowly, as though miming her, Ju lifted her own pale finger to her lips and kiss-shushed back.

26

For a long, suspended moment after the second blow fell, the whole house seemed engulfed in a cavernous silence. It was as though Emilia's ax had cleaved not just through the skull and spinal column of the creature who'd come for them but all the way to the bottom of the world. As though she'd smashed open Pandora's box, but what had spilled out wasn't monsters or bad dreams—those were already loose, had hounded the living since the beginning of living—but the end of dreams entirely. Now everyone left on Earth was free, for the first time, to float forever in a terrible but peaceful *here*ness.

To Rebecca, it almost seemed her skin had lost its porousness, become not membrane but lid, sealing whatever constituted *her* inside. She could drift here above the wood floor of the Stockade, among windows and walls, occasionally bump the drifting, lidded bodies of her fellow survivors, as though they were all moored boats in a marina. But she could never again get topside, call out to her companions. Certainly not invite anyone else aboard, or leave.

Then Jess, of all people, burst out screaming. Scrambling out from the side of the creature's sprawling corpse—*like a foal squirming free of its mother,* Rebecca thought, then gagged—Jess lurched away, kicking. One foot caught Rebecca in the cheek and knocked her head back, and the other plunged right into the mess of the corpse's head, and it came out streaming a brownish ooze whose viscosity was more old mud than brain matter. Working her own jaw, feeling the sting of returning sensation in her fingers, Rebecca began pushing, clawing, trying to get out from underneath all this terrible weight and away from the racket.

Jess kept screaming. For a time, there weren't even words in that noise, until Jess finally managed to work her mouth into a semblance of shape, encircle the sound she was making and form it.

"Get it out!" she was shrieking. *"Get it out, get it out, GET IT OUT!"*

That seemed to trigger everyone else. Benny, badly hurt yet again, managed to roll to his left, clutching one dead-weight arm to his chest and crying out every time that arm touched floor. Bleeding scratches were etched down Joel's throat, and when he touched them, his fingers seemed to sink, as though into marshy grass. Pushing to his feet, he staggered and wound up leaning against the couch, breathing hard. Hopefully, the whistling sound he made wasn't coming through the rips in his neck.

Behind them, silhouetted against her own shadow, stood Emilia, ax half raised, staring at Rebecca through the thing she'd killed. Shudders racked her, in gusts that faded quickly and left her stone still. In her dark eyes was a glint Rebecca was almost sure hadn't been there before.

"Thank you," Rebecca mouthed, pushing herself warily, carefully, to a sitting position. The gash in her side was only a gash, apparently. Already clotting. She thought Emilia might drop the ax and keel over, or else hoist it again and slam it down on anything that got near her.

Instead, Emilia laid it gently on the floor, moved back into the corner from which she'd emerged, and wrapped herself in the blanket.

"Come on, 'Bec," grunted Joel, peeling his fingers from the scratches in his throat and touching her head as though anointing her. "Let's . . . It's the 'Bec and Joel Show again. Let's do what we do." Then he shook his head, almost tilted over again.

Hi, Dad, she thought, though she'd never have said it, not now. She didn't even mean it, really. But it had been so long. Five years. And suddenly, here Joel was. This was the Joel she'd known her whole time at Halfmoon House. She even felt a flicker of a smile through the tears she hadn't realized were already welling.

For Kaylene, of course.

Kaylene, Kaylene, Kaylene . . .

"I'm pretty sure you're not going to be doing much," she said, listening to him wheeze.

"I can do some."

"Not with that neck."

"Problem's not the neck. I think I'm concussed." Weirdly, as though he thought he was making a Joel-joke, he smiled.

"Oh. Well, that's okay, then," Rebecca murmured, and made herself smile back.

Back on her feet, Rebecca surveyed the room, the mess beneath her. When Emilia's ax had bit through skull, Rebecca had half expected beetles to fly out. Horseflies to erupt into the air. As it turned out, though, there was nothing so strange inside this creature. Just cold, dead slush.

It wasn't even spilling out, just pooling and sinking into the wood. The corpse looked too dry, somehow, papery dust rather than skin and guts. And yet—unlike the Whistler, once Sophie and Rebecca had finished with him—*this* corpse had lost none of its menace. If anything, it seemed to be spreading across the floor toward their feet. More kudzu vine than spider, but still a threat.

"Get it out," Jess said, clutching the arm she hadn't popped back into its socket to her chest.

With Joel barely able to stand, what they eventually did involved more rolling than lifting. More contact with that icy, dead skin—which was weirdly dry, like tree-stump bark—than Rebecca would have liked. And it took too long, so long that Rebecca kept glancing up mid-roll just to make sure that skull wasn't fitting itself back together. The worst part was that there *were* things moving inside it. Hair-thin strands of gray pulp that stretched free of gray pulp mass, wriggled onto the floor or under Joel's shoes, curled up, and twitched. But they did that without volition or effect. Just a few million more living cells grasping desperately at life as it left them, the way everything that ever lived couldn't help but do.

Why, Rebecca wondered, does life always feel like it's leaving?

How was it possible that she was still here? There were so many ways she should have died by now. Today's biggest threat—so far—had turned out *not* to be the monster that had come for all of them but Emilia's ax plummeting toward her head. Somehow, Emilia had stopped the blade just in time (or almost in time; there was a nick or, worse, gash still pumping blood down Rebecca's left cheek). At least now, she really could claim to know how Sophie must have felt on the day Rebecca had accidentally—no, *in*cidentally—driven a shovel through her face.

Jess had somehow stayed standing long enough to drag open the garage door. As Joel and Rebecca shoved and nudged the creature's corpse through it, Rebecca glanced back toward Emilia's corner. The woman was sitting up with her hands at her cheeks and her mouth wide open. But she wasn't crying and hadn't retreated under her blanket. So that was all right, in the same way Rebecca supposed she herself must be all right or still might be, someday, if only life—meaning death—could leave her the fuck alone just for a few years.

With a grunt, she dropped to her haunches and grabbed the corpse under the shoulders. The movement caught Joel by surprise, and he almost let go completely as Rebecca tugged the creature all the way out of the house. The body proved surprisingly light once Rebecca had its full weight on her. This woman—thing—had seemed so massive while it was alive. But the massiveness had been in her *person*, in the rage and hunger of her being. The body was already as empty as one of Eddie's shells. Dry as a bundle of newsprint.

Joel caught the corpse's feet again and helped Rebecca

tug it to the middle of the floor. Behind them, Jess flicked on the overhead light. Rebecca looked up, saw Joel bent to his work, and was suddenly overwhelmed by memories of him in his shed at Halfmoon Lake. Except there, he'd always been singing.

But even ripped open and tilting, he looked so steady, standing there. Like the Joel who kept almost becoming her dad. Working with him in this garage really wasn't so different than raking leaves at Halfmoon House, back when he'd bobbed and weaved around her, singing "Tongue-Tied Jill" and strumming his hoe while his haunted wife watched from the window, took no part, and loved that he and Rebecca loved each other.

Abruptly, without intention, Joel sat down. The way his hand cupped his throat made him look like Rodin's *Thinker,* except bloodier. And tilted. "I think I'm done," he said.

"Just stay there," said Rebecca, and went to fetch the lighter fluid.

When she'd finished coating it, she and Joel stared a little longer at the corpse. Its skin looked pitch-black and yet aglow like the surface of a lake. When Rebecca finally glanced up again, she found Joel smiling at her. Holding his throat and smiling.

"Think this will work?"

Rebecca shrugged. "She feels like leaves."

"Really old ones," Joel murmured. "Sorry I've been away a while, Rebecca. I'm sorry I left you."

"What are you even talking about?" Rebecca wanted to hug him, and also to stand right here and stare at this creature's beautiful skin until her own face surfaced inside it.

"I don't know," said Joel.

"See?" Suddenly, Rebecca didn't want to look at the corpse anymore. For one moment, she was so, so close to smiling again. A smile from a long time ago. "Same old, same old." Even she wasn't sure what that meant.

Where had the match in his fingers come from? Rebecca didn't know or care. Joel watched her as he struck it, as though waiting for words, some kind of ceremony. But there was nothing worth saying. She winced at the *whoosh* of the corpse's skin catching. *Like burning a wasps' nest*, she thought, once again expecting creatures to erupt into the air instead of smoke.

So much smoke. So fast, this woman burned. Almost as though she'd never actually been there. As if they were burning a shadow.

"I'll stay here until she's done," Joel murmured. "There's one thing I can do. You go."

Rebecca couldn't think of one good reason to protest. Turning away, she started back into the house and stopped when she heard the whispering.

"Papá?"

There was a pause. Then an explosion of Spanish, the words unfurling into the night like flags waving. *"Soy yo. Soy yo. Estoy bien. Estoy llegando a casa. Estoy . . . Dile a mamá . . ."*

Stepping back inside, Rebecca found Emilia on a phone, tears pouring down her face. She could hear buzzing and sobbing on the other end but couldn't make out words, and Emilia never really stopped talking, anyway. She'd laid her glasses on the counter, was holding the phone in both hands, and the same words kept spilling from her lips. *"Estoy bien. Soy yo. Soy yo. Estoy bien . . ."*

The swelling in her own chest caught Rebecca by surprise. For one insane second, she caught herself patting her pockets, swinging toward the stairs as though she might rush up to her room *(through the mess that had been Kaylene)* to grab her phone from the stand by the bed *(where, not fifteen minutes ago, they'd had Sophie chained)*, and punch the phone awake so she could . . . do what, exactly? Dial whom?

Her parents? Amanda? Jack and the 'Lenes?

Any 'Lene?

Kaylene . . .

Even as new tears boiled from her eyes, Joel's arms encircled her from behind. He hugged her against him, the way he hadn't since their arrival on this coast, and she almost kicked him away but didn't. She let herself stay, eyes watering at the smell of the creature burning to ash behind them. She didn't collapse against Joel, couldn't make herself do that. But she let him hold her. After a few seconds, she even hugged him back. Held on to this other person passing through her life, for as long as life would let her do that, which was never long enough.

They listened to Emilia talk to her mother and father in a language neither of them knew. Across the room, even Jess seemed to be taking a breath from prying the boards off the back sliding door—with a broom handle and one useful hand—and letting herself listen. She was bent against the counter, one injured arm tucked tight against her chest and the other reaching to pet Benny, who knelt at her feet. His breathing sounded saw-edged, harsh, but he kept doing it. For that long, rare moment, they all just stayed still. Held on.

Then Joel's knees buckled, and he almost bowled Rebecca over as he grunted in surprise and sagged against her.

"It's okay," she said, steadying herself against the door, lowering him slowly to a sitting position. His bloodied hands slid off her shoulders and steadied himself against the ground.

"Room keeps tilting," he murmured.

Rebecca felt fear—her oldest, truest friend—swooping down once more. "You're okay. You'll be okay." She hadn't meant that as an order. Unless maybe she did.

"I'm okay," said Joel.

"You sound like you're responding to a self-help tape."

"That's because you're helping, 'Bec. You're always helping."

Of their own volition, his eyes flicked up the stairs toward the landing. That body, apparently, Rebecca would have to dispose of on her own.

"You, too, Joel," she whispered, letting her tears trickle to nothing. "Okay."

Not even sure what she was going to do, Rebecca blew out a breath, got steady on her feet, and moved toward the stairs. She could feel Joel watching, and Jess, too. For some reason, she felt grateful that Emilia was still talking, talking, talking. The sound of her voice somehow provided a sort of cover, or at least comforting background hum. She'd reached the foot of the steps, was telling herself to just keep going, head up and kneel beside the body of her last, best friend and hold her hand for a while, just in case there was still any vestige of Kaylene left to say good-bye to. Start to say good-bye to, somehow.

But Jess stopped her. As Rebecca had known, from the second she'd left Joel's side, that Jess would.

"Hey, Rebecca. Do I look as tired as you?"

Rebecca didn't want to stop moving. Even more, for reasons she couldn't immediately fathom, she didn't want to turn around. She heard the garage door close as Joel somehow dragged himself back out there to monitor and eventually extinguish the corpse-fire.

But this was Jess talking. What choice was there?

She turned. Jess's eyelids had slid down over those icy-blue eyes, almost closed, almost crooked, like mispulled blinds. "You look even more tired," Rebecca finally said.

"Then I look dead."

Rebecca shook her head. "You look too tired to be dead."

Briefly, she thought one of them might smile. Try to. They just stared at each other instead until Jess's gaze drifted up the stairs. Her mouth turned down at the corners, and her throat jerked. Rebecca realized all over again how much she loved and was grateful to this woman. How much this woman had let herself love Rebecca, in spite of everything.

She was either going to say that or go over there and find the least painful way to exchange an embrace when Jess said, "Rebecca. You've got to go get Eddie."

So many things she might have expected Jess to say, and that one most of all. And yet Rebecca hadn't expected it. "What?" She glanced upstairs, saw Kaylene's flowered tights, one purple shoe dangling off her toes over the edge of the stair. "Jess, just tell Trudi to—"

"Are you kidding?" Abruptly, Jess's voice was all ice

and edge. Or exhaustion and panic. All those things Jess kept frozen deep in the center of herself. "Sophie's still out there."

"Sophie's not going to . . ." But even as she started, Rebecca shook her own head. Acknowledged her own inanity. What made her think she had any idea what Sophie might do? Sophie, whom'd they all just burned, stabbed, chained to a bed? Tried to murder. Again.

"Take the ax," Jess continued. "Do you know how to use it?"

"Not well enough," said Rebecca, watching herself move across the room, ease it away from Emilia.

"Then just . . . stay out of Sophie's way. She's hurt, I think."

Rebecca nodded. "She's pretty hurt."

"For now. Maybe this is our chance. Our last one. Get Trudi back here. Get my daughter's son. Please."

At Jess's feet, Benny stirred. "No," he said. "Jess, that's cra—"

"Okay," Rebecca heard herself say.

"And if you get a chance," Jess said. "If she really is hurt. If you find her, and you can do it . . . you have to finish this, Rebecca. For all of our sakes."

Only at the front door did Rebecca turn. Ax in one hand, knife in the other, neither of which she felt confident she could use. "You realize Sophie saved us," she said.

"She saved herself. Don't be fooled. I sure as hell never will be again, I promise you that. And I care about you, and Eddie, and Trudi, and the memory of my daughter, and everyone else in this house too much to let any of you be fooled. It's too dangerous. My daughter is dead,

Rebecca. Your friends are dead. Your foster mom is dead. None of those are ever coming back. It's enough. No more."

Her voice had risen steadily, but now, with a visible effort, Jess controlled it. Partly, she did that by jerking her dangling arm against her ribs, which wrenched a gasp from her clamped lips. But the pain worked its dark magic. Suddenly, she was Jess again. Exhausted, heartbroken, full of love. "I adored that girl, Rebecca. Even when I hated what she and my daughter got up to together, I adored her. I will treasure her memory. But that thing isn't her. And this has to stop. I will not let her do to anyone else what she has done to us. I'll take care of her myself, if you won't. I should have done it five years ago."

"I'm going to try *not* to find her," Rebecca said.

"Fine. That's what I want. I want you to come home. But Rebecca. I want you to do that with our kids."

Our. Kids.

After that, there were no more arguments to make. "Okay," she said.

"I'm coming," said Joel, staggering through the garage door with smoke from the extinguished fire billowing around him. He got two whole steps in her direction before slumping against the wall and staring at her with his head lolling and his eyes tearing.

Rebecca quieted him with a single glance. "Stay here. I've got this. Pops." Her gaze left his and floated across the room toward Emilia. *That person*, she thought, *can handle an ax*.

At least, she could when she wasn't sobbing into a phone. She was actually more whisper-singing, now, as though cooing a lullaby to a baby. Except she was the baby, newly reborn. And she was singing the song to her parents. Some sort of lilting, South American–sounding thing.

This wasn't Emilia's fight. And Emilia had been through enough.

"Well, don't just stand there," Jess said. "Get out there and bring our family home."

Rebecca settled the ax against her hip and took two steps up toward the landing for a last look at her dead best friend. From where she stood now, she could just see Kaylene's body. Not her face, which was turned down into the still-spreading pool of itself on the floorboards, but her hair spilling across the floor. One stripy-dressed arm flung wide.

Apparently, crying really was over for now. There were kids to rescue. People she loved to fight for. How astonishing, really, to find that she still had anyone left, after everyone the world had already taken. One could almost believe there always would be, if you allowed there to be.

"You know where you're going?" Jess asked when Rebecca turned.

"Trudi said 'cave,' right?"

"Yeah."

Rebecca shook her head. "The one place we never thought to look. How did we never think to look there, Jess?"

"We're not five years old."

"Or sock-puppet masters."

"Or monsters," Jess said.

"Rebecca, I still don't think you should do this by your . . ." Joel started.

But she was already gone, slamming the front door shut behind her, shutting her family safely inside.

Overhead, the sky had sucked all the mist back into itself and unleashed the moon. It glowed all over everything, glossing the grass, the leaves of the trees, the very air. Was it even midnight yet? Rebecca wondered. Was this . . . just another Saturday? Was this a Saturday night?

Just another night, yielding yet another dead loved one to tell stories about someday or every day. Another set of memories that would scream through her dreams for as long as she dreamed. Another something she'd somehow survived to share and mourn over with other survivors. The essence of living.

Even in the trees, moonlight permeated everything. It felt almost wet as Rebecca brushed through it. Owls swiveled silently in the branches above her, watching in her wake for night squirrels, moles, any little scurrying thing her passing might have jostled into the open.

Stay down, little things, she thought. *If you can.*

Hold on, Eddie.

Watch him, Trudi.

I'm coming.

27

How did *that* happen? *Sophie wondered even as it did.*

Partly, she supposed, she'd been distracted by the pain in her leg, which she'd remembered from the last go-round as searing almost beyond imagining, and which turned out to be worse. Knowing from experience that both she and the leg would survive did nothing to lessen the anguish.

Partly because of her wounded state and the distance from cliff top to cave mouth, she'd had to concentrate harder than usual to assert influence over Princess Sock Puppet down there, who'd proven a challenge to control even when they'd been face-to-face. How that girl would squirm.

Partly the Little Orphan That Could had gotten a little too good at going silent, making no sound and leaving no trace as she ghosted through everyone else's world.

Mostly, though, Sophie had let herself get mesmerized just sitting here atop this cliff, watching Ju snare Eddie. The second that girl had looked up and spotted Sophie, she'd swayed to her feet and danced away from Sock Puppet's side, gliding across those rocks bathed in moonlight, wreathed in sea spray. It was the joy in her movements—the dancing and swaying as much as the way Eddie fell into her gaze and went quiet—that drove home the revelation at last:

That girl is like me.

Ju is like me.

Rather than providing clarity, the discovery confused Sophie more. Ju was like her when? Before the Whistler? Or now?

Or both?

Whatever the cause, Sophie somehow neither saw nor heard Rebecca coming until the handle of the ax slammed straight into the small of her back, driving her half off her wounded leg and very nearly over the cliff before her face smashed into earth.

For Trudi, the moment was weirdly familiar, almost nostalgic. It reminded her of leaping up from behind banisters at Halfmoon House, right into the teeth of Amanda's scowl or Danni's taunts, and scurrying for her room.

One second, she'd been crouched on the rocks, unable to move or even think about moving, really. She'd been holding her breath, trying to render herself so small that both the green-eyed girl by her side and the Sophie thing up on the cliff might forget she was there. Relax their hold, or whatever the hell it was they were doing.

And the next—as Rebecca bludgeoned Sophie into the ground and Ju whirled to look—Trudi seemed to pop up behind her own eyes, lock back into place inside her skull and skin. Five feet away, twitching like a butterfly pinned to the air, Ju stared up at Rebecca, then over her shoulder toward Eddie, then back again. Eddie, too, had surfaced— Trudi had literally seen that happen—and now looked frantically toward Trudi.

Then Ju had him again, or else he saw her coming and ducked for cover. Certainly, he went still once more. Vanished into himself.

As Ju swept past, Trudi felt that gaze brush over her like the skirt of a fire. Sparking and dangerous, yes, but too cursory to catch her, this time. Instinctively, Trudi tensed to hurl herself at the girl, knock her over, rip out that red hair in clumps. Do *something*.

Do it now! she was screaming inside her own head. *Drive her over the edge into the sea. Even if you have to go with her.*

But she didn't move. Somehow, faster than her consciousness could track, her brain was making calculations, chattering to itself. The math didn't add up. Not yet. Sophie on her own was still way too much for Rebecca and Eddie. And even if Trudi survived the fall, somehow drowned Ju in the Strait and got free and crawled back onto land—assuming there was land to crawl onto down there—she'd never make it back up here in time.

What she did instead, as she watched Ju's arms slide

under Eddie's shoulders, was the hardest, most desperate thing she'd ever done or even considered doing.

But she did it.

Swinging the ax had almost knocked Rebecca over, which would have been disastrous even if she'd somehow managed *not* to land on the blade, which she'd used as a handle, striking Sophie with the wooden part instead.

Why had she done that?

Somehow, scrambling, she stayed on her feet, got centered, leapt sideways to stand straddle-legged next to but not quite over Sophie with the ax flipped right side up, blade end this time.

Swing! she thought as her muscles tensed all on their own. *Now, while she's down. Last chance.*

Sophie rolled over, stared up. There were tears in those wild-animal eyes. Pain tears, Rebecca understood even as she eluded Sophie's gaze. The only kind the thing beneath her could or would ever cry, now.

Swing!

"So this is you, then?" Sophie said, her meaning clear, her tone so closely approximating a human one. Half knowing, half taunting.

And maybe sad? Wild-animal sad?

Oh God, swing.

"Rebecca the ax murderer," Sophie continued. "Sophie-smasher, for the second time. Killer of the defenseless."

Don't answer, don't look, don't engage, Rebecca thought, even as she heard herself snort. "Defenseless."

"Too much?" Sophie grinned. "Overplaying it, am I?"

Grinning. The thing was actually grinning.

That helped, watching it grin while thinking about Kaylene's hair on the stair. Kaylene's striped foot with her shoe dangling off it. A *snap* sounded in Rebecca's ears. At first she didn't recognize it, didn't even realize it was a memory.

But it was. That was the sound of Danni's back breaking over the Whistler's knee in the Halfmoon Lake woods. Jack and Marlene already dead by then. Amanda about to be.

And still, Sophie kept talking. "Fine. How about this? Leaving aside the issue of whether I actually *am* defenseless— instead of just, let's see, one-legged, effectively one-eyed for the moment, beat to hell by every implement in Jess's fucking house, and seriously pissed—I'm just lying here. I'm not attacking you. I was actually running away from you. And yet you're about to kill me. Again. So. I say again: Rebecca, meet yourself. Ax murderer. Killer."

"I have no choice," Rebecca snapped. Tears boiled from her own eyes. For Kaylene, Amanda, Jack, Marlene. For Jess's daughter, Natalie, whom Rebecca had never met, and Jess, who wasn't even dead but would rather have been. For Danni, who had barely even gotten to live. For her parents, who'd had nothing to do with this, and who'd been gone twenty years now. Did she really still have tears left for them?

Propping up on her elbows, Sophie dropped the grin. "Here's the one thing today's events make definitively clear: that's you. But it isn't me."

A whirl of thoughts almost swept Rebecca off her feet and over the cliff. This one had more memories in it, thousands of them, plus lightning flashes of feeling, bursts of confusion. The ax handle seemed to thicken in her fists, gain mass, and she nearly dropped it. But she didn't. She held still until her head cleared to the extent that it ever did or would.

"Maybe so," she said. "I'm sorry."

Sophie stayed on her elbows, trying to catch Rebecca's gaze. Or maybe just looking. "Not as sorry as I'm about to be, apparently."

She really did seem sorry, or sound that way. Possibly, she had just understood what Rebecca had already realized. Had known all along: Rebecca really was going to do it.

"I'm sorry. Sophie."

Flinging the ax overhead, closing her eyes but then forcing them open, Rebecca coiled her whole body into the swing. The ax had just reached its apex when a new voice trilled up from below and stopped her.

"Hello?" it said. "Yoo-hoo."

Ax still raised and trembling, Rebecca edged one step closer to the cliff and looked.

On the ledge near the cave mouth down there, arms locked as rigidly to her sides as if she'd been chained, Trudi knelt, staring straight out over the water at nothing. Five steps to her right, a wispy, red-haired, green-eyed girl Rebecca had never seen stood right at the edge of the rocks, dangling a motionless Eddie by his elbows over empty air, the black and roiling sea below.

"Hi," the girl said. "I'm Ju."

Not for one second, as Rebecca rolled into her swing, did Sophie consider closing her eyes. The last time her own death had come flying at her face, she'd been too distracted to process or enjoy it. She'd had the Whistler's brains in her teeth and his crazy keening in her ears.

This time, she wanted to see what it looked and sounded like.

Which turned out to be the starry night sky, wind in grass, and a song surfacing pointlessly in her ears. Some old Natalie fave, nothing Sophie had really loved except when Natalie sang it. "Take Me to the River." How like herself, really, not even to hear her own music at the end.

She was mouthing words, gulping wind, swallowing the sky for a good few seconds before she realized she was scared. For real. And that the blow hadn't fallen.

A voice—not Rebecca's, not Natalie's, not her own—repeated itself on the breeze.

"Hello?"

Slowly—painfully—Sophie pushed to a sitting position. Rebecca was looking over the cliff. Her killing mask had slipped. The Little Orphan That Could and Did suddenly looked dangerously orphanish again.

Dangerous for the Little Orphan, that is.

Swiveling carefully so as not to remind Rebecca that Sophie was there, she took in the tableau: Princess Sock Puppet on her knees, looking either dazed or hypnotized; Ju with her red hair dark and rippling as a bloodstream; and Natalie's boy—Eddie—in Ju's arms, dangling motionless over the ocean.

"Hi, Ju," she called, before she was sure she had anything to say. "Maybe you should—"

"Hi, Sophie!" the girl chirped, bobbing up and down once, starting to wave before remembering she was holding

something. "*Come down!*" More than anything, she sounded like a middle-school girl welcoming guests to her first slumber party. As though Sophie were something brand-new in her life. As new as Ju was in Sophie's.

"Hmm," Sophie said, checking Rebecca, who had recovered a little. Not enough to try murdering again yet, but Sophie could definitely see thinking happening. She also took note of her own leg, which was yawning open, dangling from itself on wispy red threads. It throbbed plenty, but not in a productive, sew-stuff-together sort of way. Not yet.

"Might be better if you came up, kiddo," she called.

Rebecca stirred, looking again as though she might say or do something. But all she actually accomplished was lowering the ax. An expression composed of half a dozen expressions misted over her face: total exhaustion, bewilderment, horror, grief. Murderous rage.

And relief? Maybe? Just a little? That the decision had been taken out of her hands, at least temporarily . . .

Yep, *Sophie thought, without time or desire to analyze the thought.* We could have been friends, you and me.

Ju was coming. She had the boy in front, her hands on his shoulders so she could steer him. Princess Sock Puppet trailed listlessly behind. Again, it occurred to Sophie to wonder who was causing that, but she had too many other, more pressing concerns to pay that much mind. The procession clambered up the rocks all in a line as though doing a bunny hop. Badly, in slow motion.

Rebecca spoke, sounding submerged. "What are you thinking to do, here, Sophie?"

Sophie's smile was instantaneous, instinctive. But her shrug was for fun. "This was your plan. And apparently hers." *She nodded toward Ju.* "You guys tell me."

"Don't hurt him."

"Me? Once again, you seem unclear about who's hurt—"

"Don't let her hurt him. Or Trudi. Please, Sophie." *As though hearing herself beg was too much, Rebecca raised the ax again. Not to strike, just to hold in front of her chest.*

Sophie watched her do that. Watched those thousand feelings tumble across and then off her face, leaving her as blank as Sophie suspected she always looked, now, and almost always felt.

She didn't feel blank right this second, though. That was something.

Ju was barely twenty feet below, now, still leading Princess Sock Puppet and steering Eddie by the shoulders. Natalie's Eddie, whom Sophie had held in her arms almost as often as she'd held her own son.

Had held more than her own son, if the past few weeks counted.

"What does that girl want?" *Rebecca murmured.*

"Hmm," *Sophie said, wincing at another whiplash of pain from her leg.* "I think maybe she wants to trade."

"What? For you?"

"Amazing, some people's tastes, huh?"

"I think you're wrong. I think she wants to kill us all. With your help."

Sophie considered that, held her leg. Eventually, she nodded. "One of the two."

Ju climbed nearer, and Rebecca stepped back. The step brought her closer. One good lunge, now . . .

Just in time—or not really in time, but Sophie hadn't seized the opportunity—Rebecca seemed to realize where she was. Hopping sideways, she swung the ax out wide without quite raising it. Then she stood still, gnashing her jaws together. "Jesus Christ. It's like the fucking Pig War."

This time, laughter positively exploded from Sophie's mouth. It wasn't planned or weighted with meaning. She just laughed.

"Excuse me?"

"The . . . Trudi learned about it in school. There were English soldiers and American farmers here. Someone on one side killed one of the other side's pigs. Then they had a war about it. Or no, they didn't. I don't . . ." She trailed off, fixated on the little group approaching.

First the boy, then Ju's grinning face appeared over the lip of the rocks. Sophie smiled once at Ju, then turned her smile on Rebecca. This time, her laugh was her new, post-Whistler one. Real enough, and with her old laugh in it, and yet . . .

"In that case," she said, "who's the pig?"

The whole time, watching the redhead and Eddie and Trudi climb, Rebecca cast around inside her own head for an idea. One more trick or ploy, a last something to keep at least some of them alive. Eddie and Trudi, especially. She'd have been happy enough to sacrifice herself, if she had to. She had almost come around to the idea that she might, and that doing so might indeed do some good.

But not enough good.

She could drive her ax through Sophie's skull right now. Possibly. Or if she timed the move just right, she could fling herself at this Ju right as the girl reached the top of the cliff, driving her backward. If she were unspeakably lucky, Ju's hands would come off Eddie's shoulders before she fell.

Rebecca half believed she could accomplish one of those things, but not both. That left her with one last impossible decision to make: attack the monster she knew? Or go for the girl she didn't know at all, who might not even be a monster but was clearly coming into her formidable own, step by inexorable step.

Eddie had clambered up onto the grass now on his hands and knees. He clearly saw Rebecca, but nothing in his sweet, silvery eyes stirred. He might as well have been sleepwalking. The girl's hands had slipped from his shoulders to his waist as she tried to step up from the path using only her legs. Her eyes kept dancing back and forth between the boy, Sophie, and Rebecca, though Rebecca glanced away whenever that gaze flicked toward her, just in case.

Behind the girl, Trudi's face appeared. Unlike Eddie's, her eyes went straight to Rebecca's. The instant that happened, Rebecca understood: not only was Trudi still present in her own head, but she was much closer to control of herself than either Sophie or the new girl imagined.

That was enough. It had to be.

Faster than she'd imagined possible—faster than the conscious command to *do it*—Rebecca whirled on Sophie and flung up the ax. Even as she swung, she saw (or felt) Trudi lunge, driving the red-haired girl face-first into the rocks at the edge of the path, knocking Eddie free. He tumbled away into the grass as Rebecca's blade whistled down and caught grass, earth, the back of Sophie's left hand. The blade stuck, the force of the swing almost pitching Rebecca onto it again. She staggered toward Sophie, who'd squirmed sideways with her mouth open and snarling and her free hand snaking out, snatching Rebecca's ankle and yanking. Rebecca felt her feet go, the ground flying from her. She landed on her butt and kicked with all her might, catching Sophie flush in her wide-open mouth. Teeth exploded, and spit and blood flew. Sophie snarl-shrieked, and Rebecca threw herself sidelong, yanking the ax with her. It came out of Sophie's skin with a sucking smack as Rebecca rolled away into the grass and pushed upright.

What she saw made her shout, sob-laugh, and burst into tears.

Trudi and Eddie were sprinting free over the grass into the woods, with the wind at their backs and the night closing around them.

Gone. Free.

Shoving to her feet, bracing for the attack she knew was coming, Rebecca turned.

The girl lay where Trudi had slammed her, facedown with her hair fanning across the rocks. *Like Kaylene's across the stair,* Rebecca thought, and swung the ax uselessly at nothing before getting herself still again.

The girl was breathing but otherwise motionless.

The girl was *breathing*.

Rebecca had time to process that because, incredibly, Sophie wasn't coming for her. She wasn't even looking at

Rebecca, or at Ju either. Instead, she'd curled around her wounded hand. As Rebecca watched, Sophie whimpered, drew the hand to her face. Red frothed at the edges of her lips, poured down the sides of the hand while Sophie pressed it to her lips. It was as though she were drinking herself. Occasional shards of white—which could have been splintered teeth or bits of shattered knuckle—rode the red rivulets, glinting as they disappeared into the grass.

Don't wait! Rebecca heard herself scream once more inside her head. But she didn't lift the ax again until Sophie finally looked up. The hatred in those eyes positively glinted in the mistless moonlight. Blood foamed along the ridge of her mouth. That should have made killing her easier, was like a giant blinking neon sign in the middle of Sophie's face screaming, *Monster. Monster.*

Except it made her look more like a clown.

"You know I can't leave you be," Rebecca said. She hadn't meant to speak at all, was already edging forward.

Sophie watched her come. For a moment, Rebecca thought that really was all the monster was going to do: burn her eyes and those red clown lips into Rebecca's memory and brand her with them. So be it.

Then Sophie shrugged. "You're going to kill her, too, then? That girl?"

Rebecca made herself keep moving. If she turned, looked at Ju, even let herself think . . . and yet here was her own mouth betraying her again. "Who *is* she?"

"Search me. She just showed up. I figured she was one of yours, at first."

"Yeah, well, she isn't."

"No," Sophie said, through bubbles of her own blood. "She isn't. But I'll tell you this. She's going to need—"

"She's not going to need anything," Rebecca whispered. Made herself say it aloud. And stopped moving. One half-step and a quick, hard swing from ending this once and for all, she stopped for the last time.

"Hey. Rebecca. Isn't there some kind of three-strikes rule? Even with the death penalty? You've tried to kill me three fucking times. Don't I get to go free now?"

"Twice," said Rebecca.

"Three times. With the shovel in New Hampshire, at Jess's house a little while ago, and just now with the ax."

"I didn't mean to kill you in New Hampshire. And I wasn't the one killing you at Jess's house, either. Not . . . on purpose. So, actually, one time. This time."

"Objection, Your Honor. Technicalities."

Rebecca was no longer listening. She couldn't allow herself one instant more. Any second, that girl would stir and open those green eyes, or Sophie would strike, and then it would be too late and not just for Rebecca. There really wasn't any choice. She raised the ax.

As if sensing the moment, Sophie opened her mouth. Then she closed it again, glancing over the cliff at the light on the Strait. When she did speak, her voice had a new note in it. To Rebecca's horror, it sounded awfully close to respect. "You really *are* going to kill the girl, too."

"Jess would."

"Oh, yeah. Jess would."

Right as Rebecca swung, Sophie smiled. It was a smile Rebecca had seen only on this woman's face. Neither Kaylene nor Joel, certainly not Trudi or Amanda or Jess had ever unleashed a smile that bright. It was the grin of the girl in that picture Jess still kept in her bedside drawer, the one of Sophie and Natalie high-stepping out of waves off the South Carolina coast, fully dressed, with the world streaming off them.

So alive.

"Stop it," Rebecca hissed, as the last five years seemed to burst in her mouth and fill it with ashes. She could taste every unimaginable thing she'd done. Everyone she'd lost.

"Stop what?" Sophie said, all innocence and flashing teeth and *wattage.*

She knows, Rebecca thought. *She's doing it on purpose.*

"Living," Rebecca said.

She wouldn't have dreamed it possible that that smile could go wider, flash brighter. But it did.

"Make me," Sophie said.

28

Outside, the sun rose watery and cold, and Rebecca watched it through her bedroom window as she packed. Her hands, she noted, had long since stopped shaking. They'd stilled even before she'd gotten back to the Stockade, and they'd stayed still all the way through the tears, the seemingly endless hugs and multi-adult engulfings of Eddie and the kisses for Trudi, who'd tried to shrug off or escape every one of them but hadn't once made a break for the backyard and her windmill shed.

They'd even stayed still after Jess realized what Rebecca had done—*hadn't* done—and the argument had erupted. Not that there had really been an argument. Mostly, Jess had just screamed at her. Only at the end, when Jess abruptly crumpled against the countertop, banging her dislocated arm and crying out in pain, had Rebecca's hands betrayed her.

"Jess," she'd tried, just once, "you have to understand."

But Jess had simply leaned there, staring up at Rebecca from the bottom of a well of grief she could never climb out of. And then she'd said, "Get out."

"In the morning," Rebecca had responded, dead flat. Not because she was fighting or arguing. She just had no emotions left on which to draw. "I'm taking Trudi when I go." Then she'd gone straight up the stairs, knelt for a moment on the landing in the spot where Kaylene had died, touched the blood there—one last swoosh of color her friend had bequeathed them—stumbled to her bed and slept.

Since she'd woken, her hands had lain entirely inert except when she commanded them. That was hardly surprising, she decided. Once you'd drummed on the world enough, killed a few people with shovels or axes, what was being kicked out of one more home that wasn't ever yours?

With her duckboots—her only other pair of shoes—tucked into her single suitcase, and her jeans, work shirts, performing clothes, and toiletries laid neatly around and over them, Rebecca glanced toward the bottom drawer of the dresser. There, she'd stored all the personal items she had in this world. Drumsticks, a few photographs, some notebooks. Instead of gathering those, she moved to the window to gaze a few seconds at the evergreens glistening in the morning wet, on this clear day with neither mist nor rain. That, she thought, was a color to believe in, a gray-green salted and rain-blasted down to its gray-green essence. That was a green you could keep.

Across the grass, she spotted movement in the windmill

shed. Shading her eyes, she saw Trudi silhouetted at her window, gazing back. Rebecca held up an arm, made a motion as though checking the wristwatch she'd never owned. Trudi nodded and waved.

No sock puppet, today. Just Trudi's bare hand, waving. *We can do this*, Rebecca thought. *It's time.*

Then her door opened, and Jess came in. Half turning, Rebecca watched her pause at the edge of the bed, glancing down into the open suitcase as though into a grave. In so many ways, Rebecca had turned out to be like Jess.

Incredibly—or maybe not, given everything—Rebecca only then realized what was missing from this house. What had already been gone when she'd gotten home from the cliffs the preceding night.

"Where's Kaylene?" she asked.

"On the couch," Jess murmured, still looking down at Rebecca's things. Reaching out a hand to touch the topmost T-shirt. "Wrapped in blankets. Waiting for . . . I called her mom . . ."

Yes, Rebecca thought, crying quietly. *Just like Jess had said. I've killed. But she's buried.*

"The monster's ashes are still in the garage. Joel actually did a pretty fair job burning her. Her skin just . . ." Jess snapped her fingers. "We're going to—"

"I don't want to know about that. I don't need to know about that." She closed her eyes and held on to the window ledge for a few seconds. "Aren't the police going to be pissed? Doesn't someone need to call the fucking police?"

"They've already been here. They were here last night while you were . . ." Jess stopped, seeming to consider how to frame the end of that sentence. In the end, she just dropped acid on it. *"Out."*

"They're already done?"

"They've just started. They'll be back soon. With paramedics. We told them we'd come down to the hospital when we were good and ready, but that, of all things, they decided was just one step too far out of procedure. Believe it or not, though, they don't seem that interested in us at all this time. Or even that surprised. Apparently, *this* monster's been leaving a bit of a trail. Emilia, I think, left a trail for the cops. They've been hunting this monster for months. Maybe years. They're all excited."

"I think I'll finish being kicked out of your life before they get back, if you don't mind."

"Rebecca," Jess snapped, collapsing to a sitting position on the bed with her wounded arm pinched tight to her chest in its improvised sling. Rebecca found she could imagine the whole scene that must have unfolded while she and Trudi had been sleeping. She could just see Jess— with a dislocated arm, a sobbing stranger on the couch, a terrorized six-year-old upstairs, and two broken men for help—shepherding police, swaddling Kaylene's body, splinting and bandaging Benny and Joel, putting Eddie to bed, dragging the monster out of sight, and finally changing clothes before tending to her own injuries.

Now, here she sat, her still-dark hair loose and matted with God-knew-what on her shoulders, her gray hoodie weirdly spotless and her blue eyes washed their usual clear by the tears they always had in them but almost never unleashed. She really was a glacier with limbs. Except when she was a geyser. A force of nature. No one's mom, except for everyone's she'd ever met.

"I want you to explain it to me," Jess said, lifting that gaze right to Rebecca.

As mesmerizing as the monsters', Rebecca thought. *And almost as ferocious.*

"I . . ." Rebecca started. *Should leave,* she ordered herself. *There's no way to explain, not to this woman.* To whom Rebecca owed an attempt, at the very least, along with so many thousand other things. "There was a girl."

Exhaustion, injuries, and all, Jess startled. "What? What are you talking about?"

"I don't know. I've never seen her before. But—"

"Where is she? Rebecca, you've got to go—"

"She was . . . theirs."

"Theirs? Wh . . . oh. God. Like Sophie, you mean? Like . . ." Jess so clearly didn't want to, but her eyes slipped to the open doorway. The stairs leading down to the garage.

"I don't know," Rebecca whispered. "Yes. Maybe. Maybe not."

For a few seconds, Jess just perched on the edge of Rebecca's bed, neck elongated, head up. Mama bird in her nest, smelling the wind and watching.

Eventually, she shrugged. Shudder-shrugged. "It doesn't matter. It shouldn't have mattered. It *can't* matter."

Even as she did it, Rebecca's smile felt more like a remembered thing. An echo. "We knew you'd say that."

"*We.* You and that horror."

"Me and your daughter's best friend. Yeah."

Jess started to stand, gasping involuntarily as her arm shifted, and sank back to the bed. "I can't believe it. Rebecca, you, of all people . . . you *know* what's going to happen."

"I do?"

"To dozens of people you'll never even meet."

"I wasn't going to kill that girl, Jess. Sorry. But I also didn't want her with Trudi or Eddie. Or you. Or me. And I guess I thought . . . in a way, I wasn't even thinking, really . . ."

"You've got that right."

". . . but what I thought was that *if* that girl is theirs . . . and . . . I can't explain this, Jess, but to the extent that you trust me, or that I've ever trusted myself . . . *even if she isn't*. In that second, which is the only second I had . . . my thought was that that kid's best and only chance is with Sophie."

Even as Rebecca uttered the words, she heard how weak they sounded. Limp and lame. Wrong, too, not quite accurate. Still, there was a sour satisfaction in watching Jess's jaw actually drop.

"Chance," Jess said, after a long, long pause. "For *what*?"

This time, Rebecca's smile was immediate, helpless, at least half apology. Holding up her empty, open hands, she shook her head. "It's actually worse than you think."

She wouldn't have thought it possible. But there went Jess's jaw even lower. "What do you mean?"

"I did think all those things. Sort of. To the extent that I was thinking at all. But . . ." Again, Rebecca shook her head but harder. This time—and forever more—it wasn't just Jess's doubts raking her. "It wasn't only about the girl. In fact, if I'm being honest with either one of us, it wasn't mostly about the girl."

The silence lasted only a few seconds. But it had teeth.

Then, abruptly, Jess rapped her open palm on the bed. Not a pat. But the invitation was clear, even if she couldn't quite bring herself to utter it. Instantly, Rebecca accepted, squeezing in between Jess and the suitcase. What she wanted to do was take Jess's unslung hand. She sensed it was too soon for that.

And might be for a long time.

Jess sat beside her, staring. So Rebecca stared back, trying to communicate at least some of the love she felt, and kept going.

"She's . . . Sophie, I mean. She's . . . *thinking*."

"Thinking?"

"Learning. Processing. She's not like the guy in the hat. Or that horror who was here the night before last."

"The ones who killed your best friends. And your lover. And your best foster mother. And that other orphan—your foster sister, really—at Joel and Amanda's house. What was her name?"

"Danni," Rebecca whispered, tearing up but not looking down.

"Good. Just wanted to make sure you remembered."

"Jess, stop it," said Rebecca, not hard but strong. No trembling in her hands or voice. "It's enough."

"I'm just making sure it's clear to *you* what you're saying. I want to make sure we're both hearing it right."

"It's clear. And we are. Jess. She is not like them."

To Rebecca's surprise, Jess did take her hand, then. Not only that, she let Rebecca see her tears. Let the tears come. "I just . . . I don't want anyone else to go through this, Rebecca. Not you. Not anyone. Are you imagining that Sophie won't kill any more? Or that those deaths won't matter because you won't know about them? Because I know you, Rebecca. You're going to know. You're never going to be able to let yourself forget."

"I know. You're right." She met Jess's gaze head-on. Not in defiance. Not even in apology. But in gratitude. In love, though Jess probably wouldn't be able to see that, now. "I know that Sophie has killed. I know she will kill again. She'll do it to eat. She'll do it when she has to, which is not never and may never be. But it's close to never. That's what Sophie says, and I believe her."

"Almost never," Jess whispered.

Rebecca didn't bother nodding. Doubts stormed through her again. They would come—Jess was right—for the rest of her life. But.

"I couldn't kill the girl. I wasn't going to kill the girl, Jess. And in the end . . . *I just didn't want to.*"

"Well," said Jess, letting go of Rebecca's hand. "That is a luxury life gives to some." Even as she stood, she burst into tears. "Oh God, Rebecca, I miss her so much."

Grabbing Jess around her good wrist, Rebecca pulled her gently back down on the bed. She hadn't meant for their faces to wind up so close together. But she didn't pull back, and neither did Jess. They weren't so much staring into one another's eyes now as *pooling*. Swimming in each other. Almost becoming each other. Later, and forever afterward, in her most terrible moments, in the middle of her most haunted nights, Rebecca would cling to this memory without ever knowing exactly why.

"I'm sorry, Jess. I'm sorry I couldn't avenge her."

"Oh, fuck avenging. I don't care about avenging."

"But please try to understand. The only real reason I had to kill Sophie in that instant was that I was afraid."

"That's a good reason. A much better one than avenging my daughter."

"Not good enough." They stared some more. Pooled in one another some more. "Jess. What if . . . I mean, now we know there's more than just the ones we know out there."

"We do? So what?"

"We have to assume there are more of them. What if there are? And what if . . . Sophie finds them? Sooner or later, doesn't that seem likely? And what if by then, while she's raising that girl, she's become a Sophie who's had time to sort out what being like her *means,* or could mean. What if she's developed a way of living? The way we're all trying to? And what if she can teach that way to others?"

"That's a whole lot of what-ifs. That's a lot of maybe piled up against one absolute certainty: she's going to kill people."

This was the end, Rebecca knew. In a minute, maybe less, there'd be nothing more to say. She was still leaving, even though Jess wasn't throwing her out anymore. Jess was still staying. *This is all life is,* she thought, not analyzing the thought, trying to accept it. *This is what matters, if anything does: not vanquishing enemies, but leaving loved ones in a way that allows the possibility of returning someday. At night or after work. In the morning after a fight. Years later, after living.*

"Here's one more certainty," she finally said. "Sophie's way, when she finds it, isn't going to be our way. It isn't even going to be *like* our way. It can't be. We probably won't understand it. But what if it really is possible for us to live alongside it?"

"Us meaning the ones she and her kind don't kill, you mean?"

Rebecca hugged Jess then, gently, and kept on doing it until Jess hugged back.

Then, abruptly, they were both on their feet.

"You don't have to," Jess said.

Rebecca nodded. "I know. But it's time. Not just for me. For you, too."

"For Benny and Eddie and me to figure out how to be an actual family, you mean? A more traditional one, whatever that is."

"Yep," Rebecca said. "And it's time for me to go find or create my own. Maybe bring it back someday."

"Like daughters do," Jess whispered.

If she'd had tears left, Rebecca would have cried them. Instead, she found herself somewhere in the vicinity of smiling. "Like daughters do."

After that, she went and sat on the couch with Kaylene for a while, then returned to her room to finish packing. Benny was sleeping in the armchair, his breathing shallow and steady. Jess didn't reappear, and no one else even seemed to be moving in the house. When Rebecca finally went up and got her suitcase and came back, she found Trudi and her own single suitcase waiting by the door. In her brief and wandering life, the girl had accumulated even less stuff than Rebecca. Most of that was socks. To Rebecca's surprise, Joel was standing beside her, throat bandaged, leaning on a broom handle he'd whittled and adapted into a makeshift cane.

"Mind if I tag along?" he said. "Just to the boat?"

"You can always come, Joel."

He shook his head, then closed his eyes and held tight to the cane as if the room were spinning on him. It probably was. "'Fraid I was listening to you two from the stairs. I want to be another place you bring that family you find, someday."

"Oh, God, of course you will be."

"Yeah. But in the meantime, I should probably go back to my actual life, too. Wherever that is, and whatever it's going to be now."

Trudi had the front door open and her suitcase in her hand. She stamped a foot impatiently. "Come *on,* already," the girl said. "Let's not drag this out. I want to *go.*"

Benny stirred, lifted his head from the armchair, and waved them over for hugs. With Rebecca, he lingered, but only for a few seconds. Eddie, apparently, was still asleep in his room. Emilia was in Kaylene's room. She had a flight back home to Mississippi tomorrow morning. Rebecca found herself hoping she'd just sleep until then, and that Eddie would sleep through her going. Sleep for years. Long enough to forget all of this. Even Rebecca.

Jess had retreated to the back of the house and was staring between the nailed boards at the backyard. She barely turned around as Trudi and Joel moved for the front door. Whatever there had been to say, they'd said it, or come as close as they were able.

"Take care of her," Rebecca murmured, easing free of Benny's arms, careful not to jostle whichever bones he'd broken this time.

"Like that's a thing she lets people do," said Benny, wincing in pain.

"Do it anyway."

He smiled, a little. "I'll cook for her."

Rebecca nodded, touched his forehead right where the white hair sprang from it like spray from a broken fountain. "That's a start."

An hour later, she and Joel and Trudi were on the ferry, watching from the rail as it backed out into the Strait and turned toward the mainland. When the continent came into view, Trudi surprised Rebecca by dropping her suitcase to the deck and leaning over the water.

"Just hold tight," Rebecca murmured to her. "We're getting there."

And so they rode together, watching, never speaking, through that surprising, clear day, through clouds of seabirds skimming their wake, into the bright November morning, the world with all its monsters and wonders still in it.